# SO PIPE THE YOUNG

## JEN WATKINS

ISBN 978-1-955538-01-5 (Paperback)
ISBN 978-1-955538-00-8 (Ebook)

Cover design employs Jan Steen's "*As the Old Sing, So Pipe the Young*," 1668-70, Oil on canvas, Royal Picture Gallery Mauritshuis, The Hague

Scene separators adapted from vector image from vecteezy.com

Published by Etheridge Press, Albuquerque, NM
www.etheridgepress.com

*As the old sing, so pipe the young.*

Jan Steen
*"As the Old Sing, So Pipe the Young,"* 1668-70
Oil on canvas
Royal Picture Gallery Mauritshuis, The Hague

# ROYAL OAK

# 1

---

ON HER SIGNAL, THE FREIGHT TRANSFER WORKERS UNFASTENED THE crate. Inside lurked the four inanimate arms of a seven-foot tall surgical robot on a wheeled pedestal. The arms retracted in the crate's shadow like a spider lying in wait. The workers removed the crate, gathered the shipping materials, and retreated from the lab.

Annabelle Granger consulted her tablet while her team of white-coated technicians in clear safety glasses circled the robot. She scanned the identification tag on the pedestal to retrieve the robot's usage statistics.

"All right team, we've got the Mirai model here from St. Christus in Rhode Island. Last serviced in July. Two hundred ten surgeries performed. The hospital reports no problems. Let's dive in."

When a patient prepped for surgery, lying in his hospital bed with a needle in his arm, a disposable blue bouffant cap on his head, and his wife's clammy hand in his, considers the ways the procedure could fail, he need not fear the robot. The robot can slice, staunch, stitch, and staple perfectly, without variability, negligence, or fatigue. The robot is better than human surgeons. The robot is better than all of us.

Annabelle glanced at Tim.

People, creatures who perfected deception before lifting their knuckles from the African savannah's turf, hide their defects. Human failings are euphemistically termed "baggage." Even the oldest robots don't have baggage, maybe some technical debt, an outdated software program, a fried capacitor or two. That's it. A robot doesn't crave sugar because its ancestors went hungry. A robot would never need surgery for troublesome vestigial structures like impacted wisdom teeth or an inflamed appendix. A robot won't turn to infidelity after contemplating its own mortality. A robot is the paragon of humanity. Don't believe science fiction. Robots are manageable. It's people that pose the complications.

With her foot, Annabelle nudged her plastic stool next to the robot and stepped up. She handed Tim her tablet, a static shock jolting her where their fingers touched. While the diagnostic charts loaded onto the wall-sized screen, Annabelle put her hands on the robot and appraised it the way she would check her five-year-old for nits. She pulled a tiny screwdriver from her lab coat pocket and popped open the laser housing.

"Whoa. Would you look at that? These Mirais always do this."

Her team, all men, all tall enough to see without the benefit of the stool, crowded around her perch. She beamed a penlight at the tiny burned device.

"Check the diagnostics. Had it caught this?"

They turned to the screen where a list of priorities appeared. The burned capacitor, required by the energized cautery system to stem bleeding, was listed first, operating at sixty-seven percent efficiency.

"Eh," Annabelle said, stepping down. "Why am I even here? These things fix themselves."

The software program embodied her expertise and didn't take a salary or a lunch break. She gave one last longing look at the robot, moving her hands down the machinery before nodding in satisfaction.

"Run the calibration test suite. You know the drill. We need this kiddo out the door Thursday."

Annabelle returned to her computer in the bullpen. She had earned a desk with her back to the wall. It was a commanding position and useful for writing emails she didn't want any of her colleagues to see. Annabelle was freshly thirty-six, or the wrong side of thirty-five as her two older sisters had tittered, nine years out of graduate school with a husband and a son. She had a good job, a prestigious position leading a team of four people at one of the most advanced surgical robotics companies in the world. It had required years of expensive education in electrical engineering to get here. So why was she about to write this email?

*Because of a deep dissatisfaction with careerism?* The robots she worked with were some of the most finely articulated technologies ever engineered. Each arm, with its actuated gyroscopics, could readjust its position in space almost a thousand times a second. No tremulous human hand could compare. The engineers equipped the arms with sensitive haptic devices that helped the surgeon, who operated the robot from a shrouded console in the ER, to feel through feedback the motions of the robot.

Computer vision teams were working now in the basement of her building to upgrade the visual system for the next generation of robots. This was ostensibly to provide the human surgeons with warnings: "Danger Doctor: You are about to sever the aorta." But really, when the technology matured, the computer vision system would replace human surgeons altogether, the way the diagnostic program could replace her.

The next generation robot would function autonomously. Because it couldn't worry about that pending malpractice suit or tremor from Red Bull withdrawals, it would be a better surgeon. It would create tinier incisions, with less blood, and faster rates of healing. Technology is greedy. It spreads quickly. Braking systems in cars used to only display exclamation marks on the dashboard. Now they brake the car. It was only a matter of testing (and FDA-approval) to convert the robot's visual system from one of warning to one of execution. Human surgeons would no longer be required.

That work—designing an autonomous surgical robot—was cutting edge, research based, and exciting. It was also below her pay grade. Her work—calibration of deployed robots, or soldiers home from war as her boss liked to refer to them—was sterile, repetitive, and unstim-ulating. She likened herself to a well-paid carnival ride operator; there wasn't any genius to her rote series of actions, but lives depended on her. It was vital that her robots performed flawless operations, just as it was vital that the carnival ride operator not engage the full throttle, lest children hopped-up on cotton candy get flung through the summer night air like human cannonballs. She and her co-worker Tim called each other carnies.

Tim, he with the sly smile, was not just her co-worker, but her direct report. His sandy-brown hair, which he wore long, looked just shy of disreputable. It flipped in an oceanic curl that ended above his eyebrow. His eyes twinkled when he told a joke, which was most of the time. Annabelle had had a few disturbing dreams about Tim, disturbing because they were sexual in nature and oh so vivid. The dreams were very enjoyable. They always began with Tim admiring Annabelle's hands while she worked. He would pull her hands from an inanimate robot arm and caress them with his. His grasp was warm and made her skin feel soft. A wedding ring was never encoun-tered. In her dream, she would thrill at the inappropriate contact. He would place her hands under his sweater and down his pants. Dream Annabelle never objected, not to that, not to any of the things he did with her hands.

Annabelle couldn't control her dreams, but she could control her behavior. And yet, she didn't. Annabelle noticed that she brightened when she worked alongside Tim, that she reapplied lipstick after lunch when she would be meeting with him, that she angsted over the perfect gag gift, something significant to only them, an inside joke made manifest, for weeks before Tim's birthday. This year, she had gotten him a goldfish in a plastic bag. The twist-tie label read "To my favorite carnie." Tim named the fish Poisson after the statistical test they used to confirm their calibration results. Annabelle could see Poisson now floating in a bowl on Tim's desk with a resin mermaid with red hair just like hers keeping it company.

Summoning her boldness, she typed an email.

· · ·

*Tim,*

*Do me. In the supply closet. Please.*

*A.*

Her eyes darted around the bullpen as her cheeks grew hot. She deleted the email, aghast and exhilarated by what she had typed.

Tim was married to Sophie, a Soviet Bloc beauty with pouty lips he'd met in grad school. She worked at the biopharmaceutical lab two parking lots away in the industrial park. Annabelle thought Sophie seemed like a Bond villain in her lab coat with her improbable accent. She wondered what a woman as smart, beautiful, and exotic as Sophie saw in Tim, who was, even besotted Annabelle could see, a standard-issue suburban Midwestern male. There must be something more to Tim than what Annabelle saw at work, something sexual and primally appealing. It only intrigued her more.

Annabelle tried again.

*Tim,*

*Do you feel the way I do? Meet me for a stolen moment of pleasure. Let's see what we can create together.*

*A.*

Annabelle didn't press Send.

*Because of trouble on the home front?* She thought of her husband,

Paul, and what they had created together, their five-year-old son Heath. If there was a strain in the marriage, it started early. It started with the lawn. Newly wed and starting their careers, they bought the house that Paul wanted—a remodeled red-brick four-bedroom Tudor with an expanse of green grass on Huntington Road in the Detroit suburb of Royal Oak minutes from where they'd both grown up. The house sat across the street from the zoo. Annabelle could hear the tigers roaring in the evenings. Paul convinced her it was the perfect place to raise all the children they would have.

When they'd signed their names to the mortgage, she'd thought they'd landed the suburban guarantee—career fulfillment, happy children, and domestic tranquility. Even though Annabelle believed herself wise at the time of her marriage, she could tell now that the zephyrs of hope and naïveté had blown her to fantasy land the same as any blushing bride.

Paul, a business strategy consultant, was out of town for work most weekdays. He spent the weekend afternoons of their early marriage with his new lawnmower and electric edger keeping the expansive yard trimmed to neighborhood standards. These were the afternoons she and Paul used to spend together playing board games or at the pool.

While Paul attended to the suburban ritual of lawn care, Annabelle spent the lonely weekend afternoons online. She selected and ordered new furniture, but the furniture could never fill the house. How many sectional sofas, area rugs, and lamps did a person need? And why were lamps so expensive? Annabelle began to wonder if their blessed suburban existence was the reward for the diligent pursuit of education and careers or white-collar purgatory for people who settled for comfort and security instead of pursuing their dreams.

The house wasn't for them, but they stayed. They had lived there for seven years now. Over chardonnay in the evenings, she and Paul used to discuss their ideal futures together—meaningful, loved-filled lives spent together with a handful of children like *Little House on the Prairie*. They sat on the balcony off their master suite in the summer and in front of their gas fireplace in the winter. They spoke lazily, knowing they had all the time in the world. Summer, winter, summer, winter, the time slipped by without their notice.

She deleted her email and started again.

*Tim,*

*Have you ever thought of doing something irresponsible, like having an affair? Let me know...*

*A.*

She pressed the backspace button until all the characters were gone.

*Because they can't conceive a second child?* On their first anniversary, Paul and Annabelle agreed to start a family. Five months later, Annabelle was pregnant with Heath. She had never gone back on birth control after he was born. She breastfed him, of course. Breast-feeding while working was the hardest thing she ever did. It made her robotics internship with Dr. Watanabe while taking a full load in grad school look easy. But she did it.

For the first couple years, she and Paul figured she wasn't getting pregnant because she was breastfeeding. A year later, panic set in. But one day she burst into tears when Paul failed to notice that she had added smoked paprika to the roasted potatoes. She went to bed early cradling her tender breasts. She was pregnant again. Annabelle swelled with relief. Paul started singing in the shower, a habit of his from long ago that Annabelle had forgotten about. When had he stopped singing in the shower? Six weeks later, she miscarried.

Annabelle abandoned her usual prim posture and hunched in front of her computer screen. Her unsent email glowed before her like Hester's 'A'. When Annabelle reflected on her own behavior, she didn't like what she saw. She didn't want to be a homewrecker; mostly, she didn't want Heath growing up as some statistic of broken marriages, especially since he was already a statistic as a single child.

Annabelle tried rationalizing her feelings. She and Paul were raising a five-year-old. That could suck the thrill from any marriage. They had been married for seven years. If Marilyn was to be believed, Annabelle's confusing feelings for Tim could be attributed to the Seven-Year Itch. But she didn't like that reasoning any better. Paul was always out of town for work. If he had an itch, it was easily scratched during his many nights spent in hotels across the country. There were plenty of Marilyns. They were the buxom interns in close-fitting workwear, bored with their cubicles and interested in a man their company heralded a hero who came with a rental car and a generous travel stipend.

Whenever Annabelle felt anxious, she googled. She learned that Tim was her "work spouse," her platonic companion there to humanize the impersonal tasks of the modern workplace. She liked this term. It felt safe, better than the romance novel designations that came to her mind: fling, dalliance, liaison, tryst. Tim was her work spouse. It had never been more than that.

*Tim,*

*Is Sophie happy?*

*A.*

Annabelle checked the clock. The workday had been a complete loss in terms of getting things done. She had wasted the afternoon composing an email to Tim she couldn't send. She had to leave now if she was to make her appointment at the fertility doctor.

## 2

ANNABELLE FOUND A SEAT IN THE CROWDED WAITING ROOM. SHE'D
overheard a woman in the locker room of her gym talking about the
great Dr. Swarnavishan: "His services aren't cheap, but then the whole
reason we need a fertility doctor is because we're both thirty-three
and just now considering babies. We've been optimizing our incomes
and streamlining our expenses since our twenties. We'll be financially
independent by the time the kid's in kindergarten. The plan is to
move to Baja and live in an RV."

Optimizing and streamlining sounded like something Annabelle
should have done. Sacrificing herself for a big house and a big
paycheck—the successful path, the one she'd been pushed towards
since her kindergarten teacher designated her an accelerated reader—
was not fulfilling. What dreams would she pursue if she didn't have to
work anymore?

Annabelle stared up at the wall studiously avoiding the eyes of the
other women in crisis, those who thought single, urban, careerism
was the ticket—remember the carefree bluster of Carrie Bradshaw?—
and who now, disillusioned by the spurious, infrequent joys of a nine-
to-five, want the husband, the quarter acre, and the domestic life.

She fastened her eyes on the framed reproduction hanging on the wall in front of her. *The Arnolfini Portrait.* An interesting choice. The standing couple are holding hands like a bride and groom at the altar. The painting is well known for the hidden portrait, perhaps of the artist Jan van Eyck himself, reflected in the round convex mirror between the couple. The woman in the painting looks to be pregnant with her hand resting on a bulge in her emerald green skirts, and perhaps that is why the painting was chosen for the waiting room. But Annabelle knows the woman is not pregnant, instead merely clutching demurely at yards of sumptuous skirting.

Annabelle recalled from her Art History courses that fertility symbols abound in this painting. The couple stand next to a bed on one side and ripe fruit on the other. Above their joined hands sits the patron saint of childbirth who sprang from a dragon unharmed. The mother in this legend is the dragon. Yes, this is an interesting piece to display here.

Annabelle knew art, especially the Dutch Masters. She hadn't always been a robotics engineer. The robotics thing had been a second choice. Her first love had been painting. She was an oil painter—a portraitist—and had been since middle school. When the small liberal arts college with a brand new fine arts building accepted her application, her plan was to major in Studio Art.

Annabelle smiled remembering her artist days. Would she paint if she didn't have to work anymore? She no longer owned a single tube of paint. During her graduate robotics program, she began to funnel her creative energy into building robots. Her choice of career wasn't only a dispassionate calculation about high-salaried job prospects in an expanding field. She thought she was being more clever than her accounting, pharmacology, and pre-law peers by choosing robotics because Annabelle loved the work. Just like painting, robotics combined design and hands-on construction. The intellectual requirements were stimulating, but building the robot, breathing life into an inanimate collection of materials, was captivating.

But the workday reality fell short. Somehow, in pursuit of increased pay and status, of "climbing the ladder," Annabelle had become alienated from research and design work. There was nothing creative about her tasking, just important steps to follow each day with no surprises or hurdles, but dire consequences for failure—*I'm sorry ma'am, the engineer forgot to retune the energized tool because she was daydreaming about her co-worker and now your husband's pancreas is mush.*

But that was all theoretical. She never met any patients. She had never seen the arm perform a surgery. Her work was sterile and removed and rote. It was the kind of work—exacting and routine—that people designed robots to do so people could be free to invent, debate, heal, inspire, forgive, and laugh. Her job was all responsibility and no art.

The antiseptic lab required that she don a lab coat and change her shoes before she entered. She had learned to French braid her own hair as they required hair as long as hers to be pulled back. There were no windows in her lab and the lighting was fluorescent. To protect the lab's intellectual property, cellphones were not allowed in the building. They designed her workplace for the robots not for the people who service them.

As each flat-bellied woman in a pantsuit was called into the clinic's inner sanctum, new women came to fill the waiting room seats. Dr. Swarnavishan was doing well for himself. While she waited, Annabelle thought about how reckless her email to Tim would have been. She needed another option. Something less cliché.

Her job was boring, her husband was gone all the time, and Tim made her heart beat faster. Annabelle was self-aware enough to realize that if she didn't make a radical change, she was destined for a textbook suburban melt down. She had too much pride and had worked too hard and found too much promise in her supportive husband and wondrous son to allow herself to slide into the secretive, self-loathing mess popular with the unfulfilled middle aged.

Annabelle picked up a book fanned among others on the side table. The book featured the lifestyle of a homesteading couple. They had four kids, a horse, goats and chickens, a passel of dogs and cats. They grew the food they fed their family on an acre of land they bought cheap in a rural community.

Annabelle read about composting. She admired the names for different varieties of lettuce: Rouge D'Hiver, Gotte Jaune D'Or, and Amish Deer-Tongue. She learned an apiarist is the word for a bee keeper. She learned chickens won't lay eggs in the winter unless they have artificial light and Angora rabbits are kept for the soft fiber their fur produces. The homesteading couple kept a tidy yard with pens for the animals, sheds, fences, and rows and trellises of plants and trees. There was not a square inch of lawn to mow.

Photos in the book showed the most beautiful produce. There were baskets of tomatoes of all varieties, classic firm red ones dappled with droplets of water, zebra striped ones, ones with their mottled flesh pin tucked around their stems. There were hanging garlic bulbs, striped and webbed melons, bins of warty squashes and pumpkins. There were giant purple eggplants. Had Heath ever eaten an eggplant? And purple cauliflower. Had she ever had purple cauliflower? And there were photos of vegetables Annabelle had never welcomed into her home: celeriac, kohlrabi, fennel, salsify, and rutabagas. Annabelle's usual selections in the produce aisle seemed so banal in comparison.

Sitting there in the waiting room of the fertility clinic, Annabelle fell in love with the homesteading ideal. This was the meaningful life-style about which she and Paul used to fantasize. There was no façade about living the perfect suburban existence. No polite comparisons between cars, wine fridges, and vacations. There would be clean air and fresh, healthy food for Heath. And it was complex and important work. She had no idea the lettuce family extended beyond Bibb, Romaine, and Iceberg. She would have so much to learn again. Perhaps what they needed wasn't another child, but another life.

**3**

---

WHEN SHE GOT HOME FROM THE CLINIC, AS DYE REMAINING FROM THE infertility test flowed out of her into a pad the thickness of a diaper, Annabelle climbed the stairs to the attic. It was a small, stuffy, over-heated space with exposed pink insulation to which none in the family ventured because it contained just two things: both of her oil paintings from college. When she and Paul moved into their beautiful house, she'd stashed them here instead of hanging them for display. Was it embarrassment? Like Victorian women entering confinement in their third trimester, was it unseemly to publicly display the products of women's labor? Like for a fetus, she gave a part of herself to these paintings. They depicted something too private, a fear she shouldn't casually reveal.

Even now, she crept like a thief to the attic. It was so rare for her to be home alone. Paul had offered to pick up Heath from his after school program, figuring she would be wiped out after her appointment. Annabelle could have used this time to lay in bed and read, but instead, she was drawn to her work. She had a niche, a peculiar style. She liked to paint domestic interior scenes in the style of Vermeer. Her paintings were mathematical and precise. They had each taken her months to complete as she perched on a stool in the studio space allotted her by the school.

Annabelle's approach was to focus first on the setting, leaving her subjects as wireframe mannequins until the end. She zeroed in on elaborate tile work, the drape of a curtain, the molding around a window, and the glister from a tin ceiling. In progress, her work showed the sumptuous rooms with blank figures in them, ghosts awaiting bodies. Her models had been fellow art students in jeans and t-shirts, but she depicted them in Baroque costume: frilly white collars, yards of folded velvet, poofy hats for men and modest scarves for women.

The paintings leaned side by side against the studs under old sheets. Their silhouettes were augmented, like shoulder pads on 80's career women, by three-inch gilded frames for which her proud father had paid. Even though it had been years since she saw them, Annabelle could vividly recall her paintings. In *The Reading Room*, a gray-bearded man reads to three others at a table in front of shelves of books. *A Drink Before Sunset* was a portrait of a portly man in a floppy velvet hat seated beside a mullioned window. The sunset cast rosy hues into the cut glass.

Annabelle flipped the sheets off her paintings. Instead of cooly assessing her talent with the remove of time as she had intended, she brought her hand to her mouth in surprise. *The eyes.* She had forgotten that look.

When she began as a portraitist, she struggled to capture the like-nesses of her subjects. No matter who she drew or painted, they became sloe-eyed and expressionless. Her subjects stared, like they were drugged, out of the canvas. Her high school art teacher, Mariah, who had encouraged Annabelle's talent, thought the look to be that of aliens, like little green men in period costume.

In time, Annabelle became a proficient portraitist. She could execute a fair likeness of anyone willing to sit for her, but she preferred to derange the faces in their sloe-eyed form. This became her signature. Even though she mimicked an old style of European painting, her alien figures made the works modern. The effect wasn't obvious. One would first notice the light. Like Vermeer, she preferred her interior scenes near a sunny window. But once one studied the work, they would notice the matching look in the eyes. The hollowness of their stares disturbed the viewers. Once they spotted the eyes, they couldn't see anything else.

The paintings that she mimicked, those of the Baroque period, inspired her. She was drawn to the theme of mortality the artists coded into their work. The famous example, the one anyone who had taken an art history class knew, was in Holbein's *The Ambassadors.* It featured an anamorphic skull distorted beyond casual recognition in the foreground. But this was not the only example. Annabelle had studied the symbolism of the collection of works known as Vanitas. These paintings incorporated human skulls into still lifes featuring what would otherwise be a family-friendly tabletop arrangement of flowers, books, burning candles, and fruit. The skulls were to remind the viewer of the inevitability of death.

Annabelle liked to consider from time to time what might be on her table—what collection of artifacts she would place in an artful grouping to represent her life. She saw her diplomas, her Sennelier oil paints in their wooden box, the blusher veil from her wedding, Heath's baby booty knitted by her mom to resemble a smiling frog, and a high-torque digital servo. Then, in her mind's eye, she would add to her personal grouping a skull. Because no matter who you are, no matter what fantastic objects you possess, death shall come for you too. Think about that.

To goad on those who saw aliens in her figures, she too would encode symbols in her work. In *The Reading Room*, three long fingers with lizard-like discs on the pads curled around the ajar door. In *A Drink Before Sunset* the distinct outline of a crashed flying saucer in the field is visible through the clear portion of the cut glass pane. If Baroque masterpieces served as *memento mori*—remember that you shall die—then her work served as a reminder that you shall be replaced by alien overlords.

Paul had noticed the eyes.

They'd met in college at Annabelle's senior class art show. Paul revealed later that he and his two housemates had gone with the express purpose of meeting girls. These seniors imagined the Fine Art majors to be looser than the girls in their departments. Annabelle noticed Paul first. That smile—straight white teeth, dimples—softened from rakish by his ears that stuck out a bit. He gelled his hair upright in the front like a picket fence—a style he had not updated in the intervening years.

Paul had stepped out from the milling crowd of students, professors, and parents drinking sparkling juice and eating cubed cheese and chocolate-covered strawberries to look at her work. He leaned in to examine one of her paintings. Studying it, he cocked his head to the side like an inquisitive puppy. She knew what he was experiencing. It was the thrill of seeing some minute anachronism, a movie mistake, a glitch in the Matrix. It was the effect she wanted her work to have. She wanted to faze the viewer, get them to pull over someone else and ask, "Do you see what I see?" The goal was to surprise, to unsettle, and ultimately to delight.

Annabelle recognized this delighted senior. Paul Granger spent his time in Ilitch, the building for business classes. He sang in the campus's unsanctioned, all-male, bawdy *a cappella* group that sprang spontaneous concerts on diners in the cafeteria and serenaded unsuspecting ladies on their way across the quad to class. He was nerdy, but self-assured.

Two other singers in the group, his housemates, popped out from the crowd to retrieve him.

"Boring. Old-fashioned. Derivative," the one calling himself Steve-o said, providing an instant critique of her work in the tone of a New York gallery owner. None of them noticed her standing sentry next to her canvas.

"No, look at the eyes," Paul said, pointing out the large, black alien orbs she had given each subject. Steve-o and the other housemate, Rafe, both leaned in to look.

"Creepy. You don't need that. Come on. There must be a chick here who paints flowers that look like vaginas," Rafe said, he of the flowing locks and lusty Latin loins.

The two housemates left to go find the next Georgia O'Keeffe. They would be disappointed to find she preferred women. Paul stayed behind to read Annabelle's About the Artist laminated bio. "Annabelle Murray," he read out loud. He studied her photo next. It was a picture of her with her long red hair down squinting in the dappled sunlight beneath a blossoming tree. It was not a very professional look, but Annabelle liked it. This senior art show wasn't heralding the burgeoning careers of hotly anticipated talent in the art world. There were no connoisseurs there scouting for the next big thing, clamoring to buy art, hoping to make an unauthorized deal with an artist once the fray disbanded. Instead, this senior art show celebrated the last hoorah for creative output from future office workers, sales staff, and practitioners in the service industry. Knowing this, Annabelle selected the flattering but unprofessional photo.

Paul appraised her looks. Satisfied, he moved on to the bio. Annabelle watched the saccades of his gray eyes. "And she's an engineering major with a concentration in robotics, huh?" he said to himself before noticing Annabelle. She was standing right there. His eyes looked from her to her photo and back. Annabelle caught a moment's embarrassment flare across his cheeks before he recovered.

"Ah, the artist herself," he said. "Would you mind explaining this piece here to me?"

Standing now, in her attic, with the painting in front of her, she could remember the moment so clearly. It was unfair to Paul how they met. She could tell he was hooked on her before he guided her—with his hand on the small of her back—to her painting. He listened to her descriptions, how she painted from life models, how she got the lighting and perspective right, and why there was a hidden alien theme. As she spoke, he alternated between contemplating her work and her lips. It had been beyond flattering for her to observe his ardent interest in her work, her looks, and her intellect before he had even met her. It was like watching someone view your dating profile.

Poor Paul had sacrificed his ability to play it cool the moment she watched him read her bio. His only move was to profess his intense admiration for her and wait for her to reciprocate. She let him wait.

They spent a lot of time together in those giddy last few months before graduation. He was strong and handsome and charming and interested in what she had to say. He was smart and driven to succeed. His goals after grad school were to prove himself in the business world and to have a happy family he loved to spend time with, the kind of family he grew up in. Annabelle knew that if she had read his bio, she would have tingled with ardent interest too. But the mysterious factor that pushed his interest into love when he saw her in person—Was it pheromones? A resemblance to his mother? A waist to hip ratio indicative of fertility?—didn't happen for her. And Paul knew it. She wasn't one to feign emotions.

When Annabelle informed Paul that she had chosen to study at the Michigan Robotics program at the University of Michigan, the grad school that he was attending, he was euphoric. He interpreted it as a sign of her commitment to their relationship. In reality, the decision had been obvious. The program was excellent, and though Northwestern had offered her a more generous research assistanceship, U of M was closer to home. She could have justified the decision to attend U of M even if Paul weren't in the picture.

But Paul was in the picture. The month after he earned his Ph.D., they were married. At the reception, Annabelle's great aunt, watching her watch her new husband, patted her on the hand and said, "Clever girl. In the happiest marriages, the husband is more in love than the wife." Annabelle was appalled. She couldn't tell if what upset her was the sentiment, or that she had been found out. Poor Great Uncle Cormac.

When Annabelle accepted Paul's marriage proposal, she determined she would take his last name. She had been a co-author on a few scientific papers as Annabelle Murray. Her female colleagues warned her that changing her name would mess with her publication record, but Annabelle was adamant. She liked the name Granger. It meant farmer, which activated a safe, sturdy, competent stereotype for her. Also, Paul's undergraduate thesis on Granger causality, no relation, had enthralled her. This theory from economics held that if a particular variable X causes an outcome Y, then to predict Y one should look at the history of both X and Y. Annabelle, in the early days of her relationship, thought those Econ nerds were missing the romantic nature of this statistical concept. If Annabelle's success and happiness were Y, it used to be true that one could infer her happiness by looking at her recent events, but now that there was an X, Paul, one had to look at his recent events too. Paul's actions and choices contributed to Annabelle's future happiness and hers to his. They were intertwined. There was causality. By supporting Paul, she was investing in her own happiness. But was he investing in hers?

"Annabelle? We're home."

It was Paul, returning with Heath. Annabelle dropped the cloths over her paintings and picked down the steps quietly, closing the attic door behind her. It was time to let Paul know where he stood.

# 4

THAT EVENING, AS THEY SAT ON THEIR BED AMONGST THE CLEAN
laundry mating socks and watching *Game of Thrones*, Annabelle
proposed moving to the country to Paul.

"Paul?"

"Yes, my dear."

"I'm not happy."

Paul stopped mating.

"I don't want to go to fertility treatments. I don't want to work at
the lab anymore. I think we should move to the country. You could
keep up your consulting and I'll be a full-time mom."

Paul didn't say anything, so Annabelle continued.

"I need something different than this," she said.

"What's 'this'?" Paul asked, mimicking her sweeping hand gesture.

"Royal Oak."

That was a big admission. Royal Oak was Paul's idea of heaven. If
Dorothy clicked her heels and thought of Kansas, Paul closed his seat-
back tray table and thought of Royal Oak. The Grangers had always
lived in the suburbs of Detroit, his grandparents, his parents, his
sisters, and his brother. The Granger name was sprinkled throughout
the region. It was on Paul's father's accounting firm, on various

plaques and park benches, on bricks at the DIA and Fisher Theatre, and on an impressive monument in the Greenwood Cemetery. It was in Paul's Final Wishes that he be buried there because there's no place like home.

"This is it," Paul said. "This is the life. We're winning. We live in a nice, comfortable house on a safe street in a good school district. Our families are nearby. We both have well-respected and well-paying jobs and we are all healthy. That's all there is."

"All there is? What about flourishing? What about striving to be something more than the perfect employee? What about meaning, purpose, and passion? What about nature? Yes, our lives are safe and comfortable, but they are also trite and colorless. I'm a consumerist worker-bee drone and I don't know how to change that here." She moved her hand towards his on the bed and continued. "Let's escape. Let's move to the country. I don't even recognize myself anymore."

"No, Annabelle. That's my line. *I* don't recognize you. The country? We're living the life we've always worked for."

They sat on the bed next to each other but facing the TV. It was easier to have this conversation turned away. They could protect their hearts if they didn't look at each other. Annabelle could hide the enervation that was leading her away from her family and Paul could hide the fact that until this moment, he thought they were leading the perfect life.

Annabelle wanted to convey to her husband that only the weakest thread woven with fibers of fear and sentimentality restrained her from initiating an affair with Tim. If the thread frayed it would end her career and her marriage. She wanted to confess to Paul so he would take her request to move to the country seriously. But Annabelle glimpsed his bewildered expression and spared him. She went for conciliation over revelation. Reaching across the laundry between them, she clasped his forearm.

"It's what we wanted, remember? *Little House on the Prairie?*" she said.

He pulled his arm away to roll a pair of socks.

"Have you ever seen *Little House on the Prairie?* Death in childbirth, drowning in the pond, going bust. Those were hardscrabble, sad lives. Country living is not for you."

"Hey, Buster," Annabelle retorted, pointing a finger at his shoulder. "Don't you tell me what I can and can't do. Was I the only woman chosen for Dr. Watanabe's robotics program? Yes. Did I earn his respect and did he write me a recommendation to the lab? Yes. And did I become the youngest team leader there even after taking maternity leave? Yes, I did. Don't you start bounding my reality, mister."

"Annabelle, Annabelle, yes." Paul scooched toward her on the bed knocking over a tower of Heath's folded t-shirts. He put his hands on her shoulders and kissed her forehead. "You are a determined woman with brains, chutzpah, and fortitude. I have no doubt you could goad nature into producing a bountiful harvest for the family. But the reason you took the internship and became team leader is because you have a passion for the work. You don't have to wrench your back in a garden."

"Let's not kid ourselves, Paul. You know if they would let me build a calibrating robot to save me the tedium of my job, I would. I don't build robots, I am one. I sacrificed passion for the paycheck. And choosing to work in a garden is different from having to work in a garden."

Annabelle let a silence settle over them before trying again.

"I want to tend a garden, to eat the food I grow. I want to be valuable and what could be more valuable than that?"

"You can start a garden here."

Annabelle knew there was no way she could lead the life she wanted in Royal Oak. The place exerted a subtle but implacable pressure to conform. It started with the house—a monument to white flight and architecture-enforced elitism. Their neighbors would balk if she replaced the front lawn with raised garden beds. One was supposed to eat organic and buy local, but going full agrarian was a step too far.

"We don't enjoy the fruits of our labor. We're not even raising our own child. We pay for someone else to raise him, so I can go work to earn the money to pay someone to raise him. This world is insane. We order our groceries, bank online, and get Heath's toys by subscription, all this convenience freeing us up to do what? I'm not working on my magnum opus, are you?"

Paul furrowed his brow.

She continued, "Do you know what I do with my extra time? I research parabens and palm oil and eliminate them from our household. I determine which gas station has caused the least unrest in the Middle East. I order ethically-sourced cocoa and organic yoga wear online because I can't find them in the stores. These are not sources of accomplishment. These are empty gestures."

"You don't have to do those things," Paul said.

"Yes, I do, Paul. You have no idea. Our status here is based on my ability to signal our worth to other working mothers by demonstrating how socially conscious and environmentally aware I am."

Annabelle hated consensus on a topic that came not from facts, but from some hazy combination of custom and fashion. In Royal Oak, she felt like she was pledging for a club she didn't want to join—The Worthy. Peer-pressure should have gone out in seventh grade like Lisa Frank trapper keepers and slap bracelets, but instead it pervaded her life.

The Worthy regarded Annabelle with suspicion. When they approved of her Saab because it matched the uniformity of the white and silver cars in the pickup line at Heath's school, Annabelle plastered her hood in colorful magnetic flowers in artistic groupings. Royal Oak provoked tiny rebellions.

Imagine the classy retorts Annabelle would have for The Worthy if the Grangers moved to the country.

*I buy organic.* I grow my food.

*Our nanny speaks French.* I'm personally teaching Heath to computer program.

*I drive electric.* I don't commute.

Moving to the country would be Annabelle's biggest rebellion yet.

"I hear you. You're unhappy and that makes me unhappy. I just don't think abandoning all we've worked for is the solution you think it is," Paul said. It irked Annabelle that not even a hint of panic inflected his voice.

Annabelle had dreamt of trading in suburbia for a pastoral life long before she sat in Dr. Swarnavishan's office. The book in the waiting room only illustrated what she had been seeking ever since she was pregnant with Heath. She was the one who insisted they name their child Heath—the wide open land where she imagined her gaggle of children playing. The name would have been Meadow if she was a girl.

Children were meant to be raised on farms. Every nursery rhyme Annabelle encountered as she decorated and stocked their buttercream yellow nursery in anticipation of Heath's arrival told her so. Duck, duck, goose. Counting sheep. Eating curds and whey. Farmers in dells. Baa-ing black sheep. Cock-a-doodle-doo-ing roosters. Jack and Jill and their lack of indoor plumbing. One Mary could be asked how her garden grew and another Mary didn't have a kitten or a hamster; she had a little lamb. In fact, the more baby books she read, the more convinced Annabelle became that children should be left in charge of sheep. Little Boy Blue slept under a haystack—good luck finding one of those in the city park—while his sheep were in the meadow. And poor Little Bo-Peep lost her sheep and didn't know where to find them.

Why teach a child the sounds that farm animals make when he or she will only ever encounter one when it is dead on their plate? If they stayed in Royal Oak, Heath would be more familiar with the roar of the imprisoned tigers across the street than the cluck-cluck of a chicken, the baa-baa of a sheep, and the oink-oink of a pig. What is a child without a flock of sheep to care for?

"Children are meant to be raised on farms."

"You've got a fairy-tale view of country life," Paul said, as if he'd read her mind.

"And your view is that they're all gun-toting, Bible-thumping, uncultured hicks."

"No. That's not true. But I do think in the country our neighbors would be people who still spank their kids, who don't neuter their dogs. They'd think healthy eating means buying the low-fat box of Cheez-Its. These places are stressed out. There's addiction. A lack of social services and a depressed economy. The mill closed, or the plant, or the mine. The schools are under-funded. It's just a different mindset."

"The people who live in the country lead real lives. Meanwhile, we're surrounded by bourgie strivers."

"We are bourgie strivers."

"Yes, but we're *aware* that we are. That means we can change."

Annabelle followed Paul's eyes to the unclothed women filling the TV screen as *Game of Thrones* transitioned to a harem scene. Just when she thought she'd lost his attention, he pulled out the trump card.

"Annabelle, think about Heath. He's happy. He just started in kindergarten. He's making friends. He's growing up in a safe and privileged neighborhood. Those country kids wish they could be so lucky."

The matter rested.

5

———

THE MATTER MAY HAVE RESTED, BUT ANNABELLE COULDN'T. AFTER Paul set down his biography and switched off his bedside lamp, Annabelle sat propped against her pillows next to him in the dark rubbing dabs of lavender-scented almond oil into her cuticles. She was sulking. Between Dr. Swarnavishan and Paul, it had been established today that she was a barren harpy.

"Remember my toothache, Paul? When I was pregnant with Heath?" she asked.

Paul groaned.

Annabelle's pregnancy with Heath had been an easy one. She was a trifle nauseous in the beginning and threw up several times. But it was nothing like what happened with Paul's sister's pregnancy. Charlotte had celiac disease, and the pregnancy made her vomit all day for all three trimesters—hyperemesis gravidarum. The woman survived on Sprite and gluten-free crackers for nine months. She walked around with barf-bags tucked into her maternity pant waistbands for quick deployment. Those pants became looser as her pregnancy progressed. Her daily goal became to keep down enough calories to sustain her and her fetus. Charlotte's useless doctor joked to her that the only cure would be parenthood. Aiden is her only child.

By comparison, Annabelle had it easy. By the third trimester, no amount of yoga or partner massage eased the ache in Annabelle's back and in her feet, but all things considered, her pregnancy was a delight.

That was until week thirty-eight when she woke up with a toothache. Brushing made her wince. She went to work as usual, but by the afternoon, she swallowed the first pain medication of her pregnancy. It was a Tylenol, which her ob-gyn, Dr. Mason, told her over the phone was safe. It did nothing at all to dull the pain, which was now a persistent throb. At home that night, she researched her options. Acetaminophen, which she had taken that afternoon, could cause her baby to have asthma. There would be no more Tylenol. NSAIDs like Ibuprofen could hurt her baby's heart and lungs. She didn't need to read it to know that opioids were off the table too. With no medications that could ease her pain without jeopardizing the health of her baby, she suffered through it. Annabelle couldn't sleep that night. Her whole body was reduced to the throbbing flame in her jaw.

The next day, Paul got her an emergency late morning appointment at their dentist. The receptionist claimed dental issues and pregnancy went hand in hand, something about hormones, the acidic bile of vomit, and the often satisfied desire for sugary snacks.

Annabelle was twelve days away from her due date. Their dentist, Dr. Bob, noting her condition, was wise enough to not tilt her chair all the way flat. The weight of the baby on her internal organs had made laying on her back untenable of late. But then, the sadist shot a blast of air on the problem tooth. Annabelle jerked, lifting three inches out of the chair. Dr. Bob seemed mad that she had refused an X-ray on account of the baby. No number of lead jackets and uninformed assurances would make her feel okay about getting X-rayed.

Dr. Bob concluded that she needed a root canal. Though the lidocaine used during the procedure to numb the pain wouldn't hurt the baby, Dr. Mason via conference call determined that waiting until after Annabelle delivered was the most prudent move. Dr. Bob sent Annabelle home with a topical lidocaine solution she could rub on her gums and a warning not to eat, drink, or fall asleep until the numbness had worn off.

The lidocaine provided periods of minimal relief, but mostly, those last days of her pregnancy were a haze of pain and extreme fatigue. The daytime hours were manageable, but at night there was no escape from the fire radiating up her face. She paced the house in the dark, rubbing her stomach, and feeling like a martyr. If it weren't for her extreme caution in protecting the health of her baby, the pain would be gone. Heath didn't cut her any slack. She began labor eleven days after her tooth pain began and he was born on his due date.

Four days after leaving the hospital, Annabelle appeared once again in Dr. Bob's chair. The sound of his drill couldn't mask Heath's wails as Paul rocked him around the waiting room. Tilted as she was, the milk that dribbled from Annabelle's breasts escaped the nursing pads in her bra and ran past the neck of her maternity dress to settle in the triangle of her neck. Lying prone and embarrassed at the mercy of yet another doctor, Annabelle resolved to be done with pain for a while.

"You're a great mom," Paul finally mumbled, with a cursory pat under the covers that landed on her kneecap.

Did she really want to be pregnant again? Heath had been worth it. He was born fully articulated. He could move his limbs right down to his tiny fingers that could grasp hers. He could vocalize. He could blink. He could focus his goggling eyes on her face when she fed him. He was the most advanced technology she had ever built. If she could sacrifice something to help Heath be the happiest, healthiest, strongest human he could be, she would. But...

This could go one of two ways. Either she followed the road to redemption paved with bills from the fertility clinic and fealty to good motherhood and self-sacrifice or she rebelled.

# 6

ANNABELLE PLOPPED THE TUB OF COTTAGE CHEESE AND A SERVING spoon on the breakfast nook table in front of Heath and Paul. She pulled the defrosted bowl of mixed berries from the microwave and set that down on the table too. Paul served Heath and then himself. The Grangers held that breakfast was the most important meal of the day. Heath, her Red Haired Boy, was wearing the green donegal sweater her mom had knit for him. It was his favorite, but it no longer fit. Paul hadn't said anything to him, so Annabelle chose not take it on. There were worse things than a five-year-old with a sliver of tummy poking out above his pants.

Paul didn't seem to notice that Annabelle was glowering at him. He'd so casually dismissed her concerns last night. He could sit at the table blithely building a Jenga tower with Heath because he didn't believe she would do anything. Paul would leave for the airport in twenty minutes. He assumed time and distance would lessen her ire. He had no idea.

"Here it comes, Heath," Annabelle called, holding her finger over the blender's grind button.

Heath hated the sound of the blender and appreciated a fair warning so he could plug his ears. Annabelle had become enamored of a banana green smoothie with spirulina and ginger. Even Heath drank it down. As the blender whirled the ingredients, macerating kale fibers, rupturing blueberries, and rending the banana into a viscous pus, she thought of Paul. When had she allowed his idea of perfection to become hers?

Fifteen minutes later, the Grangers bustled out their door.

"See you Friday, buddy," Paul said, releasing Heath from a bear hug onto the driveway. He tucked his silver spinner suitcase into the back of his Jeep and waved his goodbye to Annabelle, while she loaded Heath into her Saab. That's right Paul, she thought. Best not to come too close.

Annabelle stalked into her office building that morning resolved to become the terrorist of her own life's story. It would start with an email to Tim. The abortive talk with Paul last night emboldened Annabelle. She would ask Tim to lunch. Just lunch! It was hardly an indecent proposal. If he didn't feel comfortable, the easy excuse would be to say he was having lunch with his wife, as he often did. But if he said yes, it would be a chance to see if they could talk beyond the usual workplace banter. It was an opportunity to develop their relationship into something more.

She had spent an hour that morning composing an email to Tim. She decided on a casual-and-yet-suggestive two sentences that conveyed her interest and yet offered total deniability legally and for her own ego if it was not well received.

*Tim,*

*I've something I want to tell you. Are you free for lunch?*

*A.*

.   .   .

Annabelle had closed her eyes when she clicked the Send button. She'd hit Reload on her email program for the next twenty-two minutes until Tim's reply arrived. He was busy for lunch, but could talk at two. Annabelle sent him a meeting invite for two in the lab and had spent the next three hours trying to think of a plausible pretense for this meeting to which she had not invited her three other teammates. She ended up canceling the meeting.

It was all so farcical and juvenile, but, she admitted to herself while rummaging through her purse for her car keys at the end of the day, it had been one of the most stimulating days at work she had spent in ages.

Annabelle waited under the porte cochère of her office building for the rain to abate. In any normal January, this rain would be snow, but for the past two weeks, the weather had been unseasonably warm. All but the most dirt-covered of snow had melted away, and she'd been favoring her rain jacket over her puffer coat. It was an uncomfortable reminder that Annabelle's commute, and Paul's frequent air travel, and her preference to do small frequent loads of laundry in scalding hot water, and everything about the Granger lifestyle was contributing to an uncertain climate for Heath's future. After checking the weather, Annabelle had remembered her umbrella that morning but left it in the car. There had been other things occupying her mind.

She was due to pick up Heath at his after school program. The two hours a day he spent there cost more than his full-day preschool. The program touted all kinds of modern brain-developing enrichment activities, but whenever she pulled into the cul-de-sac to pick him up, the kids were running around screaming on the playground like kids had for generations.

The rain lessened to a drizzle. She was just considering making a dash for her car when Tim popped his head out of the office building door.

"Annabelle, I'm so relieved I caught you. You didn't sign the recalibration certification for the Mirai."

"I have to pick up Heath. Paul's out of town."

"It will only take a few minutes. The Mirai is due in Rhode Island the day after tomorrow, and you know we can't ship it without your signature. We don't want any more attention from Cramer."

How could she say no to Tim? She would only be a few minutes late picking up Heath. She always picked him up thirty minutes before the program ended. He could stay until the end this time. Just this once. He wouldn't even notice because he would be having so much fun performing an obstacle course through the jungle gym involving imaginary lava pits. The other kids would time him with unflagging accuracy—"one chimpanzee, two chimpanzee." Annabelle followed Tim inside.

Fifteen chaste minutes later, Annabelle got into her car. She pulled her cellphone out of the center console to check her messages as she always did at the end of her workday due to the robotics lab's draconian cellphone-free policy. The first thing she noticed was that she had five phone messages.

That was unusual.

Perhaps it was a big day in the robocall industry. Then she noticed the text from her husband. It said: "WHERE ARE YOU???"

She flipped to her voicemail messages. One came from Paul and the rest from Heath's school. Her heart thudded as she listened to the first message: "Mrs. Granger, there has been an incident at the school. Heath is okay, but you should come right away."

She thought of the all too familiar news footage taken from helicopters hovering above schools on lockdown. The parents huddled together outside waiting to see if it was their child. Heath's school had an automated emergency texting system for parents. Heath knew to lock the classroom doors, to draw the shades, to take cover. They had practiced for this.

She dropped the car in reverse, windshield wipers waving at high speed. She zoomed through the parking lot and under the porte cochère as Tim came running once again out the door to catch her, this time making the phone sign with his thumb and pinky.

"Tell him I'm going to the school now!" she yelled at Tim out her lowered window. The Saab reached fifth gear as she burned out of the parking lot and onto the industrial park's frontage road. The next message said, "Mrs. Granger, the police have arrived. They want to speak with Heath. We are keeping him in the teacher's lounge until you get here."

She reached a line of cars waiting at the light. With two tires in the bike lane and two in the mud on the side of the road, she edged along the stopped traffic and onto the highway. She could reach the school in four minutes. The next message was a telemarketer. Annabelle fumbled to stop playback and delete it. The fourth message said, "Mrs. Granger, I have a detective here that wants to speak with you. Hello, Mrs. Granger. This is Detective Clarke. I am seeking permission to speak with your son, Heath Granger. Please call us back."

Annabelle watched an ambulance pull out from the school and drive away without its lights on. A police car followed. The final message was from Paul. He sounded panicked and angry. "Annabelle, where are you? I heard from the school. Something has happened to Heath. I'm calling you at your office."

Just like on the news, police vehicles and the cars of parents cluttered the pickup cul-de-sac. Annabelle parked in the middle of the lane and got out, slamming the door behind her. She started running through the throng toward the door of the school closest to the teacher's lounge. A woman in a camel hair trench coat stepped in front of her and took her by the shoulders. It was Stuart's mom, Donna.

"Annabelle, slow down. They're okay. Everyone is okay. Heath is safe." Annabelle wiped away the spittle that had escaped her mouth. Her eyes were blurry with tears. She tried to focus on Donna.

"But the ambulance," Annabelle said, starved of breath.

"The kids found a dead body. In the marsh." Donna gestured with her head down the slope past the edge of the playground. "Actually, it was Heath who found the dead body."

Annabelle tried to run past Donna to the school, but the woman held her grip.

"We are trying to stay calm for the kids. If we don't panic, they won't panic. That will all be ruined if you tear in there. The police are taking our information one by one and then we go home. The kids think it's fun to talk to the police officers."

As if on cue, Stuart strutted to his mom with Stuart Sr. in tow. He said, "The policeman let me touch his badge." He gave his dad a high-five. Donna released her grip with a warning glance at Annabelle. "That's wonderful, Stu. Let's go home. It's taco night," she said with the cheery mom tone amplified.

Annabelle speed walked into the school, pumping her arms with the comic efficiency of an Olympian in the sport. As soon as she whipped open the door, Miss Sara, as they were to call the program's director, ran to her with a look of relief. Miss Sara, with her hands held up palms out in the universal "calm down, I'm unarmed" gesture, cornered Annabelle. Annabelle considered hip-checking her, but with Miss Sara's formidably sized bottom, her center of gravity would be too low to make her budge. Miss Sara began the explanation.

"Mrs. Granger, Heath is perfectly fine."

And then she spotted him.

Annabelle saw Heath through the propped open door sitting in the teacher's lounge in his yellow rain jacket and alligator rain boots with the pull on handles. The adrenaline drained out of Annabelle and she began to tremble. He looked perfectly fine. With the methodical approach of a Granger, he was working through a giant cookie with M&Ms that required him to use both hands.

Miss Sara took Annabelle's hands in hers and continued. "We were launching model rockets from the sport court. A gust blew one off course. It landed in the marsh. We have a very strict rule, as does the school, that the children are not allowed to enter the marsh. We yelled to Heath, but he took off after the rocket. Miss Kara went to get him while I stayed with the other kids." Annabelle saw Miss Kara, the twenty-something grad student in early childhood education, speaking with the police officer who lets kids touch his badge.

"After ten minutes, Kara returned without him."

"Ten minutes!"

"We had both assumed he wouldn't have gone far into the marsh. The terrain is difficult. It was wet out. But she called and searched and couldn't find him. She went to get the custodian. They continued to search while I stayed with the other kids. Mrs. Granger, he never responded to their calls. They finally found him sitting quietly. When they approached, they saw he was next to a dead body."

"Whose?"

"We don't know. He was a young man. The police think he was a gang member and his body was dumped in the marsh. He'd been shot in the face."

Annabelle recoiled.

"The body was lying face down, but the back of his skull was missing. There was gore. Mrs. Granger, your son was in the marsh for thirty minutes before they found him."

Annabelle looked at Heath knocking his boots together and chewing his cookie.

"My son sat alone in a marsh next to a dead man whose head had been blown off for half an hour?"

"Yes, Mrs. Granger. I am sorry."

# ONE MONTH LATER

## 7

IT IS EASIER TO FIX A ROBOT THAN A CHILD. WHEN A ROBOT BREAKS, IT IS repaired. After a computer diagnostic program pinpoints the problem, one need only apply a specialized tool or install a replacement part. A broken robot calls for hands-on work. A broken child calls for something else; one must *heal* him. Healing, so unlike repair, is an unstructured, bewildering process. A traumatized young boy needs to hear the right words to help him put distressing events in perspective. These words and their order aren't known or agreed upon, but they are out there. The right words form an alchemical incantation capable of transforming a gruesome incident into something insignificant. The right words can heal.

Driving home that drizzling evening with Heath strapped into his high-backed booster seat, the booster seat whose proper installation had been verified at the local fire station, Annabelle didn't know the right words to say to fix him. Her schooling gave her a solid foundation for repairing complex machines, but she'd had no training for this. This was a territory more nuanced than a graduate course could convey.

Looking at her son in the rearview mirror, Annabelle had assessed whether the carnage of an exploded human head had traumatized him. Heath licked rainbow-colored chocolate residue from his fingers. What did trauma look like? If anything, Heath had looked delighted. Maybe it was the cookie and friendly police officer that had been forefront in his mind?

The incident passed through the news cycle. The headline *Royal Oak Tot Leads Police to Body* had particularly nettled Annabelle. It made her son sound like he was either a psychic or a precocious grifter. It obscured the real news: parents should now add dead bodies on the playground to their list of fears.

Paul didn't think Heath needed therapy. "We don't want him to dwell on something he probably thinks was no big deal," he had said. So Annabelle spent the weeks following what happened googling for advice on how to parent a traumatized child. Heath's behavior alarmed her. She discovered his action figures face down in a line on the floor of his closet. Mr. Rex and his assortment of non-humanoid stuffed animals remained upright. Heath had shoved Annabelle when she suggested they put the figures away together. Re-enactment and aggression were symptoms of trauma.

Heath's teachers reported that he had invented a game where a child guesses which of his hands holds a toy. If they guess wrong, they get slapped. The kids figured out that neither of Heath's hands held a toy. He was tricking kids to queue for a slap. Annabelle's cherubic child had never displayed such callousness before. And now fearless-ness too. Earlier that evening, he'd stuck his hand in the bowl while the mixer was running for a finger of frosting. Online, she confirmed this troubling behavior as yet one more symptom of trauma.

The experts recommended discussing the event. When asked, he answered questions, but Heath had always had an uncanny talent for withholding information like a spy under interrogation. Once, when asked at the dinner table why he wasn't eating his mashed potatoes, he told them he was full from lunch and couldn't eat another bite. Annabelle knew that this adult-phrased reason was a cover story.

Heath caught her adding pureed cauliflower, in a ruse to up the family's vegetable intake, to the potatoes. He gave a plausible rendition of events, but Annabelle knew what he said wasn't accurate. He wasn't a liar, she hoped, just polite.

Heath was a talented mimic able to imitate speech and actions before he knew what they meant. A year ago, a beer commercial featuring a Hawaiian surfer dude captured his imagination. Heath started wearing bathing suits in the house and instead of "Thank you" he said "Mahalo" with an accent derived from Keanu Reeves circa 1989. Heath made them laugh and laugh and he loved the attention.

Heath was his most talkative in the bathtub, so Annabelle attempted to get him talking about what happened there. The online experts advised that she use age-appropriate language and wait to see what questions he would ask. But he didn't ask questions. None at all. Annabelle didn't know if Heath understood that someone had died. They had never discussed death. They had never owned an unlucky cat or a short-lived guinea pig and Nana and Grandy and Grandpa and Grandma Granger were hale and hearty. The websites advised that she not discuss the trauma unless he brought it up, and then to have an open and honest conversation. But her child was suffering, and he was not one to start conversations. While helping him pour water over his sudsy hair, she started on neutral territory.

"Do you know why people die?"

She was ready with the parenting-approved talking points: it is not your fault; everyone will die including you, me, and dad, but not for a very long time; it is okay to feel sad. But Heath surprised her, as he always did.

While loading his car ferry bath toy he said, "I know about death, Mom. When Death touches someone it kills their body and that makes us sad, but they go to a better place, better than anywhere on the whole entire planet. It's better than Disney World and the Ice Cream Shoppe combined."

That sounded like a pretty good answer from a five-year-old. She wasn't sure where to go with it. Were they going to teach Heath about souls going to heaven? While she was raised Catholic and Paul

Methodist, neither she nor her husband were religious. She grew up
with the concept of heaven. It made her feel better to think of her
grandparents, and her miscarried baby, and that kid in her high
school who got drunk and froze to death three yards from his car as
being in heaven. She never discussed heaven with Paul. How had it
never come up? Must everything in parenting be an agonizing decision followed by a prolonged negotiation with your spouse?

Like a guest on a Sunday morning politics show, Annabelle
spouted her three talking points. When she finished, she pulled the
drain plug on the bath. She wrapped Heath in his hooded shark towel.
With an exaggerated happy show, she rubbed him dry. Since he
seemed so compliant just then, she scooped him up and rocked him
on her lap while she sat on the lid of the toilet. She held his damp
ankle and smelled his wet hair. Perhaps she hadn't nailed that conversation, but she didn't need an online parenting expert to tell her that
hugs could be therapeutic too.

# 8

---

PAUL GRANGER

Paul walked out of his hotel into the early evening sunshine of Palo Alto. The mild February air made him forget that his luggage from Michigan included a wool overcoat and shearling hat. Tonight, he was too restless to stay cooped up in his hotel room.

He'd spent the day facilitating a decision summit with C-level executives to settle whether the company would move to IPO or shoot for another round of venture funding. To Paul, the numbers were there, and the decision was obvious: IPO. But the discord ran deep. Three of the executives had founded the company, writing software from their houses to create a product they weren't sure would ever capture any market share. These three founders wanted to retain creative control of their product, to be free to take risks, and to strive for greater innovation in the space. The relentless pressure to maximize shareholder value would conflict with these goals. "We've been working all these years for something more than just a big payout and some fleeting positive press," one founder said. The newer executives were there to do what they had done with all of their previous employers—bring the company to market, cash in on their shares, move on.

The discussion had disconcerted Paul. As the afternoon wore on, the boardroom table became cluttered with the detritus of their catered lunch and multiple coffee breaks, the window shades were adjusted to account for the movement of the sun, and both sides dug in. Initially, he believed his task was to build buy-in for the IPO, but Paul had an epiphany. Either decision, venture or IPO, would, objectively speaking, support the long-term health of the company. The only threat was the ongoing rift between the executives. If they couldn't cross the divide, the company would struggle with every decision no matter how minor.

When they adjourned for the day, Paul had returned to his hotel room intending to order room service and design slides for tomorrow's summit. Then it struck him. The company's rift—the decision between two options of equal value—echoed that of his family. Should they stay, or should they go? The future was suddenly clear: if he didn't act, Annabelle would leave him.

The Sheraton's hotel room became too claustrophobic. Paul decided to walk to a restaurant for dinner. There was a Japanese place not too far away. Outside the hotel, he selected a route on his phone that would take him away from the traffic of El Camino Real. He set off through parking lots on foot.

Paul remembered the exact moment when the Great Granger Rift appeared. They were sitting on their bed watching *Game of Thrones*. Naked ladies were writhing with wanton abandon to remind HBO viewers that this is what they were paying for. Annabelle thought Paul too distracted to listen, but he heard her. He heard her expressing a deep, persistent unhappiness. What Annabelle interpreted to be a juvenile absorption in unfamiliar breasts was actually Paul trying to come to terms with the implications of what she was saying.

If he didn't act, he would lose her, maybe to an affair born out of boredom or to an ashram in India dedicated to serving the West's discontented seekers. Either way, something would change. When it came to problems—a persistent cough, a mistake in her credit report,

a disillusionment with the worldview she had heretofore held dear—
Annabelle was a seek-and-destroy missile. She embraced the continuous improvement principles she had learned from Dr. Watanabe.
Paul had learned these same principles for his Ph.D. in management
consulting. When applied to robot assembly, they worked. When
applied to human fulfillment, they had inconsistent results.

But then, out of nowhere, Heath had found a dead body, and they
had tabled the matter. Annabelle moved her discontent to the back
burner, but it still simmered there. Annabelle was a dangerous
woman. She had the deadly combination of vision and bullheadedness. Surely, there was a psychometric table out there that would peg
the intersection of these two traits as the place where all change in the
world had ever taken place.

His phone buzzed at his hip. It was likely the evening text from
Annabelle. Their three-hour time difference meant that Annabelle put
Heath to bed before Paul ate dinner. The text read: "Heath stuck his
hand in the mixing bowl. While it was running!!! All appendages still
intact."

Paul wrote back: "Thanks for holding down the fort. Headed out
for sashimi."

If it had been their inability to conceive a second child that caused
her ennui, Paul knew what to say to appease her. He was happy if they
only had Heath and they should just relax and see what happens. If it
had been career trouble, he knew what to say to that too. Annabelle
didn't have to be a robotics engineer. She could teach painting; she
could be a painter. Sure, it would stress the finances, but they could
cut back their lifestyle. It would be a good excuse to bow out of the
annual Granger family vacation to St. Barth's in February. But this
was something more general.

Annabelle had declared herself unable to lead the life she wanted
in Royal Oak. She declared the place itself, not their house, Heath's
school, her job in the industrial park or his downtown, but the entire
region stifling to her. It was the only place Paul had ever wanted to
live.

It's not that he was a sessile barnacle terrified of the wider world.

Paul knew how to hail a cab in New York City during a rainstorm, where to find the most authentic Cubano in Miami, and how to parallel park on Telegraph Hill in San Francisco. He could navigate the world's airports knowing the quietest lounge, the least busy Starbucks, and the magic words to whisper at the airline counter to get a seat upgrade. Paul was a seasoned traveler, spending almost as much of his time away from home as there, but Royal Oak was his home base. He assumed that Royal Oak was where he and Annabelle would always live, that Heath would bring his children by on weekends to go for a stroll around the block.

But Paul wasn't stupid. He knew that times had changed. He and Annabelle had become cynical about the life for which he so meticulously planned and studiously applied himself. Their liberal arts educations had trained them to see the hollowness in a life of golf foursomes and gin and tonics before dinner at six.

The trappings did not appeal to him, but other aspects of this envisioned life did. Paul craved stability, and he saw the root of stability as a strong family. His father adored his mother. They were a rock-solid couple. They had divvied the chores and responsibilities of life and each could depend on the other to perform their duties. This meant that both his father and his mother extended themselves to achieve more together than they could apart. It also meant they were utterly reliant on each other. His father didn't know where in the kitchen one could find a spoon and his mother didn't know the location of their bank.

On the surface, Annabelle grew up in a similar family. Her parents also provided a loving home and had maintained a happy marriage through the years. But her household had been intellectual and creative rather than steeped in tradition. The Murray family valued independence and following one's life's purpose, even if it took its members far away from each other or to a lifestyle untenable for the others.

When Paul reached the relative quiet of a sidewalk in a residential neighborhood, his phone buzzed again with another text from Annabelle. "Enjoy bachelorhood."

Annabelle thought Paul dodged the family drudgery by traveling most of the month. And it was true. His days while on travel vibrated to his own rhythm. He was free to conduct himself as he pleased. He worked out in the hotel gym in the mornings before he was due at the clients' office. Many nights, the clients would take him to dinner, or an executive would invite Paul over to his house to ogle his wife's new breasts, his skyline view, and whatever was parked in his garage. On nights like tonight when he was left to his own devices, he would work on his prescription for the client with PBS on in the background before going to bed.

This time of night, Paul thought while matching a street sign to his phone's direction, he devoted to analysis. Paul could analyze his family too. All he needed to do was conduct a SWOT, a tool from work, to assess his family's strengths, weaknesses, opportunities, and threats.

Strengths first. This one was easy. Paul and Annabelle were good together. When they were first married, they committed to pour their life's energies into their family and their careers, and they had done just that. If they could get past all this nonsense of late—Annabelle's unforeseen dissatisfaction and Heath's grim discovery on the playground—they would be fine. Their fundamentals were strong.

Paul moved on to Weaknesses. This required a more sober analysis. This was where the gaps in the Great Granger Rift appeared. And indeed it felt like something tectonic had shifted in their lives.

There were their careers. Paul enjoyed his job, although he had failed to attain an ineffable quality of respect that his father had earned by his age. Paul felt that he still hustled a little more than was decent for a man approaching forty. But Annabelle had had the bigger disappointment. She was a creative being, but also organized, diligent, dependable, and a solid decision-maker. It was these qualities that got her promoted to a team leader and manager rather than an engineer. It was one of the greatest disappointments for Annabelle to realize that the engineer—the designer, the builder, the inventor—was considered the lowlier position to the paper-pusher.

There was their house on Huntington Road. It was ornamental, intended for people who entertained and wanted to impress. They had only been able to produce a single occupant for the spare bedrooms and the empty rooms mocked them. It made them look like failures, or at least like over-optimists, people who counted their chickens before they hatched.

Paul loved the apartment he and Annabelle shared during graduate school in Ann Arbor. They lived off Geddes above the detached garage of a political science professor's house. The remodeled apartment was tiny, with a sloped roof that limited where Paul could walk without ducking. It featured a subway-tiled bathroom with a shower with just enough room for two. The kitchenette had too few cabinets to store even the meager aggregate of their cooking implements.

They bought a platform bed low enough to the ground to fit under the eaves. Annabelle walled it off from the rest of the space with a translucent screen she painted in India ink with a humanoid alien with a long spiky tail of which H. R. Giger would be proud. The only other furniture was a lacquered low table Annabelle bought from a robotics student graduate. They sat at this table on cushions on the floor while they both worked, while they ate, and while they watched movies on Paul's laptop.

To move around the space together, they became attuned to each other's bodies. Annabelle would drag her hand along the small of Paul's back as she stepped behind him. Paul would pin her hips to sinks and countertops so he could reach for something without fear of elbowing her. It was an intimate, cooperative way to live. It was wonderful.

In contrast, Paul was never sure where Annabelle was in their house on Huntington Road. He'd check the kitchen and not finding her there would run upstairs only to hear her laughing at a television show down in the media room.

They had not moved their platform bed, their Japanese table, or their alien-themed shoji screen from the Ann Arbor apartment. None of it was suitable for the new house. The screen went to a gallant second-year graduate student in Annabelle's program who harbored an infatuation for Annabelle. Paul took a certain pride that the kid got the screen and Paul got the girl.

There was also disappointment in their mystifying inability to produce siblings for Heath. For two people who had always attained what they set their minds to, their bodies' disobedience was unnerving. Paul loved being a father and felt blessed to have Heath, but not altogether sated. He'd had three siblings growing up. Lonely Heath was so manageable compared to Paul's bustling childhood home. The exuberant tide of youth hadn't swept Paul and Annabelle away. Instead, they ruled their household unquestioned by their single subject.

And finally, there was Heath. The dead kid on the playground had been a major setback in his otherwise idyllic childhood. Heath was working furiously to process it, to grapple with gore, death, murder, and kindergarten all at once. And perhaps Paul, in his quest to prove that Royal Oak was the perfect home for them, had diminished the importance of what had happened. He would have to do better if Heath was to recover without a scar.

Their Opportunities were wide open. They could quit their jobs and do anything else. They could homeschool Heath aboard a catamaran in the Pacific Islands, teach English in a remote village in Japan, or become devotees to Phish and follow the band from venue to venue on their summer tour. This is what Annabelle had been telling him. Or they could stay in Royal Oak. They could move to a house with fewer bedrooms. They could find Heath a child psychologist trained in PTSD. That solution stank of failure.

Now that he had thought through the Great Granger Rift, the Threat seemed obvious: divorce. Annabelle was a savvy woman. If she felt that their marriage contract no longer provided mutually beneficial synergies, then she would exit the deal. Paul winced at the thought. Grangers did not get divorced. Of course, his sister Gwen divorced her first husband. They were only married for eighteen months. Paul thought his father might have stepped in, exchanged some money to make Ethan go away. His mom took down all the family photos that included Ethan and ran them through her diamond-cut paper shredder. Six weeks later, when the leaves were on the trees, the family met a professional photographer in the park wearing outfits coordinated to only include white or navy blue for new family photos. Then they went to brunch. Ethan was never again mentioned. A life where he shared Heath with an Annabelle to whom he was no longer married was too messy to contemplate. There could be no divorce.

He should have seen this coming. Despite living within two hours of her childhood home her entire life, Annabelle was shallowly rooted. It's a wonder she even recognized Paul when he returned home at the end of the week. For her, leaving her home was no big deal. She wouldn't miss anyone. She wouldn't miss her favorite drink, Faygo's Rock & Rye over ice, or celebrating every minor occasion in their family with Sander's Bumpy Cake. She wouldn't miss the Outdoor Art Fair where she volunteered every year nor the yoga studio where she took class three times a week nor living next to the Detroit Zoo. But Paul would miss those things. He would miss everything.

Paul married the engineer Annabelle, but also the artist Annabelle. She got into her head that a country life was one free from the social pressures to consume the right way, raise children the right way, dress the right way, spend vacations in the right places, and think the right thoughts. And look out when Annabelle got an idea in her head. The best Paul could hope for was that she would include him. It was essential that she include him.

He arrived at the sushi restaurant and found a seat at the counter. He exited his phone's navigation and opened the text app. Without a moment's hesitation, Paul replied to Annabelle's last text: "Let's move to the country."

# 9

ANNABELLE WAS PUT IN CHARGE OF THE MOVE. SHE HAD STRICT BUT amorphous criteria to begin the search for her family's new home. A healthy home, she concluded, was far from cities and suburbs where air pollution and crime couldn't reach them. A healthy home was also far from major agricultural production where pesticides blew like dandelion seeds through the air and tainted the drinking water.

The east coast would be too expensive, the south too southern, the breadbasket too agricultural. And Annabelle wasn't ready to compete with the granolas on the west coast who had been prioritizing the health of their families through consumerism for three generations. Annabelle's geographical stereotyping spared a column of states in the west from Mexico to Canada. Their being spared her critical assessment was due to her ignorance of the region rather than any imagined superiority.

Paul stepped in claiming a pre-existing fascination with New Mexico, something about Billy the Kid, mining towns and trading posts, and the Santa Fe railroad. It all sounded to Annabelle like the Ken Burns documentary version of New Mexico, but she was pleased to incorporate her husband's input, however spurious.

"How do railroads equate to a happier, healthier Granger family?" Annabelle asked.

"They don't, but did you know Einstein lived in New Mexico while he was building the atomic bomb? Bill Gates and Paul Allen wrote the first language for a personal computer in a garage in Albuquerque. And Sir Richard Branson's Virgin Galactic has a terminal at the Spaceport. The state slogan is 'Everybody is somebody in New Mexico.'"

It was then that Annabelle knew for sure that PBS was responsible for Paul's sudden affinity for the state. Thank God the station hadn't been playing a show about the Iditarod when he tuned in. They would all be packing up for Alaska because of the health-inducing bond between man and sled-dog.

Annabelle wasn't sure she could tell their families they were moving to the home base of outlaws and bombmakers, but she shared Paul's positive regard of New Mexico. She knew Georgia O'Keeffe had quit the bustle of New York City for the special light found in the state. In New Mexico, O'Keeffe began painting cow skulls—her own Southwestern take on *memento mori*. When Annabelle thought of New Mexico she thought of Santa Fe, the adobe architecture, the colorful landscapes with sunsets, deserts, churches, and mountains, turquoise and silver jewelry, and painted pottery. The draw for artists was such that tiny Santa Fe was the third largest art market in the nation. While his pitch was off, Annabelle knew what Paul meant. If the New Mexican environment spurred geniuses to build nuclear bombs, dropouts to invent Microsoft, and artists to create a haven and a marketplace, think of what it might spur for the Grangers.

Paul's near-weekly travel stipulated that they should live near a good airport. No realtor website organized their search capabilities around proximity to an airport and distance from air pollution, crime, and pesticides. Annabelle used a map instead marking small towns an hour's drive away from the Sunport, Albuquerque's international airport. She was looking for a rural home, which ruled out Albuquerque, Rio Rancho, and Santa Fe. Vast tracts of what remained were filled by Indian Pueblos. But a sparsely populated region to the east of the airport caught her eye.

Annabelle, lover of researching via the Internet, found her home search enthralling. She learned about the towns in this region along the I-40 and a sliver of state road known charmingly as the Turquoise Trail. When she found the fertile valley of Box Elder with a river, a nearby former gold mining ghost town for Paul, a Walmart for her, and a darling elementary school far from any marshes for Heath, Annabelle fell in love.

There wasn't much inventory for sale in the area. She found a few subdivisions with newer construction homes that were exactly what she was trying to avoid. There were also several mobile homes for sale on sprawling acres of land with giant porches, hot tubs, chicken coops, and fire pits. Annabelle, who believed herself ready to dispense with the superficial trappings that marked social class, wasn't ready for a double-wide.

There was one home that caught her eye. The listing agent excelled at highlighting the lifestyle into which the lucky new owner would be stepping. There were pictures of the house, sure. It was built out of stuccoed adobe with a green metal roof—prototypical Southwestern architecture. But the listing featured photos of dramatic sunsets over a grassy field, snowcapped mountain peaks, a lizard sunning on a boulder, and rows and rows of beautiful vegetables thriving in a tidy garden. It was in every respect what Annabelle envisioned while flipping through the homesteading book, stubbornly infertile, in Dr. Swarnavishan's office.

The kitchen was modern, the bathrooms clean, and the bedrooms cozy and windowed. Everything was on one story. There would be no hauling laundry up and down the stairs, no heating a two-story living room, and no worry that someday, for some reason, Heath would find himself on the wrong side of the landing's railing. And there was no attic in which to hide away her paintings.

A door separated the bedrooms from the rest of the house. A door! Might she and Paul have friends over after Heath's bedtime? They could talk at normal indoor conversation levels without fear that the noise reverberated through the open concept house and into Heath's dreams. She could close the door and run a load of laundry or the dishwasher without disturbing Paul when he worked from home.

Paul loved the wall across from the kitchen lined floor-to-ceiling with sturdy bookshelves. His entire collection of books would fit. The house was much smaller and less grand than theirs on Huntington Road, but more practical. Instead of an echoing two story-entry hall, they had a built-in bench and a closet. Instead of a dining room that sat eight, they had a breakfast bar and a kitchen table. Instead of an office, a media room, and a breakfast nook, they had a spare bedroom. Annabelle could vacuum the entire house in minutes. She was mentally placing the furniture before they had even called the realtor.

Paul and Annabelle dropped Heath off for a weekend with Grandma and Grandpa Granger and flew to New Mexico. As Paul navigated the rental car toward their potential new home, Annabelle oohed and ahhed at the view. She felt it her job to cheerlead the endeavor. She remarked how by going east from the airport they left behind all the traffic heading toward the population zones. But the ride was long and tedious. It would be a major change for Paul to drive such a distance to get to the airport each week.

As they drove, Annabelle wondered if she should feel less buoyant. She was giddy with excitement over the thought of their new life and the opportunity to abandon their old one. She felt that the abandonment part should at least have a bittersweet tinge. But it did not. If she didn't feel bittersweet, should she at least feel anxious about their pending decision? They were driving out to see the only house they liked in the only town that met their arbitrary criteria. If this didn't work, what would she do? Yet Annabelle was sure she would love the house and the rural valley. She was sure she could make it work. The place matched, like the puzzle piece that fell under the table, a hole whose outlines she saw but whose details weren't yet known. This piece just had to fit.

As they exited the highway and cruised into the valley, the seclusion began. No one passed through Box Elder. If you were here, you belonged. But they stuck out in their showy black Expedition rental car. The Granger family conducted their personal travel in style because of all the upgrades, miles, and points Paul accumulated through his business travel.

The view out the windows was pastoral. They passed goats grazing among tiny trees aligned in an orchard. Where there weren't houses, snow-covered fields, or small white stuccoed churches, the land gave way to boulders and scrub pines. In the distance, white mountains intersected the cloudless blue sky. Clear, bright sunlight had replaced the bleak gray of a Michigan winter.

Annabelle found the house to be as she had pictured it. She squeezed Paul's hand as the realtor revealed each room. She bounced in her efforts to contain her enthusiasm. She lifted the blinds to soak in the warm western sunshine beating in with gusto even in February.

Back in the car, Annabelle tried to substitute her excitement with reason.

"It's a long drive for you to make each week," she said to Paul.

"Yeah, but most of my clients are in California. The flights will be shorter."

Annabelle smiled at Paul waiting for him to confirm what she thought she heard in his voice. He made her wait.

"There's only one problem."

"What's that?" Annabelle asked.

"All the spicy Southwestern food is going to give me indigestion."

## 10

ANNABELLE'S BOSS, THE LUGUBRIOUS DR. CRAMER WITH THE LONG spider fingers, was devastated when she put in her notice. He asked what he could do to get her to stay. Annabelle told him what had become her party line: "I am sorry to be leaving this vibrant company. I will miss the amazing work we do here, but my family is moving away for the health of our son." She replaced the words "company" and "work" as the situation demanded, "yoga class" and "poses" for example. Heath was a convenient excuse. Traumatized little boys need not move to the country; he wasn't a pale-faced consumptive looking to spend his last days working on his spiritual purity. But no one questions a mother.

Heath accepted the news that they would be moving with his typical equanimity. His grandparents were a different story. Paul and Annabelle told her parents first. Neither of them were receptive to the news that the Granger family was decamping for the west.

"What your dad and I are trying to say is that you're going to be all alone out there. Paul will be away for work and you won't know anyone. You won't have any backup," her mom said.

Annabelle resented the idea that she couldn't handle Granger family operations on her own. She had only ever called upon her parents as "backup" a few times. She couldn't understand their extreme unhappiness over this move. Even though Paul and Annabelle lived only forty-five minutes away, the Grangers didn't spend as much time with Nana and Grandy, as they'd taught Heath to call them, as they could have. The Murrays weren't the kind for Sunday dinners. When it was extended-family time, they spent it with Paul's parents.

Paul's father, Ross, was a corporate tax attorney. He left his firm in his early thirties to start his own and never looked back. They moved multiple times during Paul's youth to bigger houses on the same street. His mom, Judy, raised the kids and was a sustaining member of the Junior League of Birmingham, Michigan. No car trip with the Grangers passed without Judy pointing out a park she and the ladies of Junior League had landscaped, or a school where they had volunteered, or a building where they had hosted a healthy cooking class. She was proud of her contributions to her community.

Annabelle met the Grangers and all three of Paul's siblings, plus the eldest's first husband (who she never saw again) at a backyard party held at Ross and Judy's house the summer she and Paul graduated from college. Paul's parents welcomed her. She intrigued them. Paul, a confirmed nerd, had never brought a girl home to meet the family. His two sisters sandwiched him both in terms of birth order and seating arrangements at the dining table on the patio. They tag-teamed to tease him good-naturedly throughout. It is a mode of interaction with him they have never outgrown. The youngest Granger, Paul's brother Lucas, spoke only a few words to Annabelle that first dinner. He spent his time hopping along the stepping stones in the garden talking on his phone. He was still in high school at the time and Paul's lady friend didn't hold his curiosity the way she did for the others.

At that first dinner, the tight-knit Granger family overwhelmed Annabelle. They all knew everything about each other and they already knew everything about her: that she and Paul met at a college art show, that she painted aliens, and she built robots. They knew her dad was a college mathematics professor and her mom a middle school teacher. Paul must have been sending emails or making furtive phone calls about her to them. It was unnerving. Her introduction to the family was like a police interrogation. She hadn't stressed about this first meeting. She believed that Paul made his decisions independent of the assessments of his family, in the same way that she did. But at this dinner, she felt like she was being watched, like there was a real possibility that they would find her wanting and send her off into the summer evening without Paul.

Of course, the Grangers weren't police matching evidence to a crime, but family members matching her personality traits to those of the young man they all loved. Over this dinner and others that seemed to occur at random, but every month, the Grangers decided that she passed. They welcomed her into the family fold. His sisters, Gwen and Charlotte, had been especially defensive of Paul, viewing him as some kind of innocent lamb out amongst the college she-wolves. He had obviously not been including the details of his drunken exploits in his missives home. But once they held their Granger-only family meeting that concluded that she was good for him, Gwen and Charlotte had embraced her like a sister. They added her to the group texts, email chains, photo drops, and Facebook posts that composed their active family story-telling.

The only time she felt excluded was the dinner where Paul told his family that he and Annabelle were getting married. Judy, who had perhaps had too many white wine sangrias, worried aloud about her grandchildren having red hair or "carrot-tops" as she called their hypothetical babies. It leaked out that evening that Judy held some notion that gingers were mercurial nymph people who could not be relied upon or invited to mix in proper company. Annabelle had encountered weird hair-color-based prejudices before, but it surprised her coming from Judy, and it hurt. Annabelle felt a zing of pride when the nurse placed newborn Heath on her chest in the hospital and she noted his matted, copper-colored hair. He took after the Murray side of the family: fair skin, freckled, dimpled, occasionally dangerous. She contented herself knowing that Heath's red hair, which Annabelle knew was a recessive trait, meant there was a ginger hiding somewhere in the Granger's grain silo.

Annabelle both loved and mistrusted the closeness of the Granger family. The mistrust meant she was ready when something strange happened to Paul when he turned thirty-five last year. He became sour and poisoned by his new age. It had taken a long time for Annabelle to figure out what had changed for him, even now she wasn't sure if she was just over-analyzing what was a simple fear of death. Perhaps, like the Old Masters, she should have left a skull on his desk to help him contemplate his own mortality. Instead, she was ripping him away from the influence of his parents by transplanting a Michigan boy to New Mexico.

This was not something they discussed, but Annabelle believed Paul felt disappointed in himself because he was not matching the timeline set by his father. By the time Ross was thirty-five he had three kids and one in the oven. He had quit his lucrative job at the accountancy firm and started his own and it had proven a wild success. By comparison, Annabelle believed that Paul found his life inadequate. When Paul told her in college that his dreams were career success and a happy family, she thought those were goals she could get behind. But she hadn't considered what he would be like if his dreams didn't materialize as envisioned. Annabelle tried not to be hurt by the knowledge that Paul's life disappointed him, and by extension she and Heath did too.

They told Grandpa and Grandma Granger of their plans to move to New Mexico over dinner at their house. They usually met at Judy and Ross's big house in Birmingham, but Annabelle convinced Paul that they should break the news on their home turf. Over baba ganoush and falafel that Annabelle picked up, Paul let them know that they were moving. There was dead silence and then Ross laughed. Judy took Heath's hands and started saying passive aggressive things like, "Oh, Heath, isn't that just great. You will have to make all new friends. I sure hope there is a zoo across the street from your new house," until Ross told her to stop. Paul showed realty pictures of the new house on their iPad. Judy and Ross made the appropriate noises, but she could tell what they were thinking: *Why would you give up a beautiful red-brick house in Royal Oak for a mud hut in a desert?* They wouldn't have understood if she tried to articulate that they were escaping the red-brick house, and Granger family dinners, and twinkly eyed Tim, and dead bodies in the after school program.

They wouldn't have understood if she told them she no longer wanted to play in the snoot competition. She was willing to accept the loss. They were never winning. Not even their perfect house on Huntington Road was suitable. It was, in terms of its postmark, in Royal Oak even though most of the homes on the street had addresses in the swankier neighborhood of Huntington Woods. They lived adjacent to, but not in the right neighborhood. Annabelle secretly delighted to see the faces of Heath's school chums' parents when they deduced that she lived not in The Woods but in Royal Oak. The sneer that shimmered across their agreeable visages would disappear in an instant, something detectable only by those being condescended to and the CIA. But their manner would always change, for now they felt superior. The moms would think, sure she has youthful elegant hands, but she's from over *there*. The dads would think, even if she can rewire her house while I have to call an electrician to change a lightbulb, at least the electrician will go to Huntington Woods. It was this frivolous pettifogging that left Annabelle amused. Huntington Road continued to Royal Oak. Because of the vagaries of the postal system, next-door neighbors divided by nothing more than a hedge existed in different neighborhoods, and it was on this flimsy basis that certain people discriminated. It was a sorry way to assess one's self-worth.

Annabelle knew that even the estimable Ross Granger felt a niggle of doubt over his first-rate Birmingham address when nearby Bloomfield Hills became the place to reside for those who had done well for themselves. There was no winning this game. You had to live somewhere. The only way to escape it was to live where people were proud of their neighborhood for a reason that had nothing to do with net worth.

While Paul assured them he would keep his same job and Heath would get to have a stay-at-home mom, Annabelle put Heath to bed.

When she returned, they were still talking at the table. Annabelle paused on the stairs to hear what they were saying. She couldn't make out any words, but she could imagine it went something like this: *Why don't you drop off your wild, red-headed wife to live out her fantasies in New Mexico and you and Heath stay here?*

Judy and Ross hadn't been gone more than ten minutes when the Granger clan's communication network came online. "You're moving to New Mexico?!" Gwen found the house realty listing online and began commenting on every photo. They were glowing, positive comments and Annabelle appreciated her support. But she could tell by all the dings coming in to Paul's phone that his siblings were communicating with him privately. She figured they were being less politic in those messages. It didn't matter. She and Paul had already paid for the house. She'd given work her notice. They were moving.

## 11

THE GRANGERS SAID GOODBYE TO THEIR HOUSE ON HUNTINGTON ROAD and drove away in the early morning of the last Friday in April. From Chicago, they joined the path of historic Route 66. They would follow it across the Midwest all the way to Albuquerque. The moving van would meet them in Box Elder on Sunday. They had stacked it with a fraction of the furniture Annabelle had purchased over those lonely weekends in the beginning of the marriage when she was sure that filling her spectacular new home with seating vignettes and attractive storage solutions from Pottery Barn was important. They sold all the superfluous sofas, slipper chairs, area rugs, and lamps off their lawn on their last weekend. What didn't sell, they drove to the Goodwill. Another carload of the detritus from their early years of marriage went straight to the dump. None of this felt sad.

Paul's Jeep, ferried by a car service, would meet them in Box Elder on Sunday. Annabelle had insisted they drive to their new home together in one car as a family. It was a practical demand and a symbolic one. It meant she and Paul could take turns driving the nineteen hours it would take to get there. And it symbolized that they were traveling into their new lives as a cohesive family unit.

They spent the night at a hotel in Branson, Missouri. It was the mid-way point. After exhausting every car game she and Paul had ever learned, they spent the last few hours listening to Judy Blume's *Fudge-A-Mania* series. It ended just in time. Annabelle couldn't take another moment of storyline revolving around girls with cooties.

Saturday morning, they went to Silver Dollar City, Branson's frontier themed amusement park. Annabelle had planned their trek across the country to include a fun break. Paul and Annabelle had been hyping the amusement park in the days leading up to their departure. It felt like something tangible with which they could excite Heath instead of endless goodbyes to the only house he had ever known, his school friends, and his grandparents. It also was their reward for his good behavior in the car for the nine hours it took to get there.

Annabelle was looking forward to Silver Dollar City too. She loved rollercoasters. She loved that there were lucky engineers out there whose job it was to construct structures that move people through space in ways that disturbed their equilibrioception. It was steel harmonizing with biology, not to terrorize and rattle as some thought, but to thrill. To thrill was to elicit one of the most elusive facets of joy and these engineers could summon it with the right combination of G-force and weightlessness, drops and inversions. Rollercoasters were an unsung contribution of engineers to humanity. Even if Heath had cried, kicked, screamed, and whined for the entire twelve-hour drive, they would have gone to Silver Dollar City for Annabelle.

They stood ready at the gate when the park opened at ten. Heath, they discovered, was a wild man. The rides excited him. He got that from his mom. After rushing through each ride in the Kiddie section, they could tell he was looking for a bigger rush. He and Paul, who was not a thrill-seeker, waited while Annabelle rode the spinning coaster. She felt a little guilty seeing them from the rollercoaster platform. Paul held her coat and purse while Heath bounded in energetic circles around him. Annabelle loved the dread followed by the euphoria as the machine hurtled her through the designer's composition of plunges, arcs, and dips. The ride did not disappoint.

Paul and Annabelle discussed over lunch if Heath was ready for a rollercoaster while he played arcade games. They decided to try the wooden coaster with him. Paul sat next to him and Annabelle rode in the car behind. Heath had just reached the minimum height requirement, which made Annabelle a little nervous. When the lap bar came down, she asked Paul if it secured Heath, but he didn't hear her over the ride sounds. As the cars ratcheted up the first and highest incline, Annabelle questioned their parenting. Heath was the youngest kid on this ride and it was climbing to a startling height. As the cars reached the apex, at the moment before gravity took over, Annabelle felt as much fear as she ever had on a rollercoaster. She leaned forward and held onto Heath's shoulder. She hoped he felt it was a reassuring hand, but she intended to press him down in the car if the lap bar failed to do so.

As they dropped, Paul made staged gleeful whooping noises and smiled at Heath. Annabelle couldn't tell from Paul's face if Heath was panicking. They rolled up another incline with a steep dip into a tight curve. Annabelle clutched Heath's shoulder. Her eyelashes fluttered in the wind and her teeth chattered in time with the rumble of the cars. The ride seemed endless. Finally, the brakes caught the cars, and they lurched to a stop aligned with the exit platform.

When they climbed out, Paul gave Heath a high-five. Heath looked to Annabelle no worse for wear. And he skipped ahead of them as they went for ice cream before leaving the park. Paul told her that Heath's face had been a mask of terror the entire ride until the moment they stopped. Then the rush hit him.

Annabelle strapped herself into the driver's seat and fiddled with the GPS while Paul secured Heath in his seat. She would start the ten-hour overnight drive to their new home and Paul would take over in the wee morning hours. Paul and Heath fell asleep, lulled by the road and the heat of the spring sunshine through the windows. Annabelle glanced at Heath in the rearview mirror. She felt very proud of her family and their bravery today. They had all boldly faced down fear. And now they were traveling West into the unknown as surely as if they were in a Conestoga wagon.

As Annabelle merged onto I-44 and wiggled to a comfortable long distance driving position (when were driverless cars going to take this tedium off her plate?), Paul spoke. Evidently, he had not been dozing, but contemplating the enormous change upon which they were embarking.

"I know you think embracing the domestic arts will give you a creative outlet," Paul said, his head still propped by his merino sweater against the passenger window. "But I know you. You need intellectual stimulation. You need to work. I give you four weeks before you're crawling up the walls."

# WEEK ONE

## 12

ANNABELLE HAD SPENT THE WEE MORNING HOURS IN THE PASSENGER seat, her head nodding and continually jerking her awake. After a diner breakfast, where she discovered a crust of drool on her chin—Why hadn't Paul said anything?—, and a run through Walmart for groceries, Annabelle was eager to brush her teeth and put in her contact lenses. But the Grangers existed in a transition state, exiled from their old home and not yet arrived at their new one.

Mid-morning, Paul turned off the main road into the Box Elder valley. Annabelle sat up in her seat, eager to hype their new surroundings to her family. First impressions matter and she wanted to instill the magic of country life from the first moment. "Look, Heath. Sheep!" She pointed out her window at a few woolly animals munching lazily in their well-trampled pen alongside the road. The sheep were unperturbed by the passing of their car.

She scanned the homes lining the road looking for features that might interest him. There were more fences than she remembered from their home shopping visit. These fences were not the wrought iron sentries that walled off golf communities or the low stone walls of the older mansions on Lake Shore Drive back in Michigan. These were rustic, utilitarian fences—intermittent green stakes threaded

with barbed wire and metal grids stapled to wooden posts with
tubular steel gates at the driveways.

Mud from a passing pickup truck sprayed the windshield. The
driver had lifted two fingers from the steering wheel in greeting. It
was their first welcome to Box Elder. "See how friendly they are?"
Annabelle commented to Paul.

When she saw the green metal roof of their new house, Annabelle
steeled herself with a deep yoga breath. She was preparing to take her
new home by force. Maud would be waiting for them. Annabelle
didn't know what breed Maud was, maybe a Great Pyrenees?

When Annabelle and Paul first visited the property, fresh from the
airport and full of excitement, they had arrived in their rental car
before the realtor. Maud, whose thick white fur made her look even
larger than she was, stood on the top step of the porch, shelling them
with ferocious barks. Cowed by her defense tactics, she and Paul had
remained in their car. The realtor himself seemed rather terrified of
Maud, but he put on a good face and sidled past her with them in tow.
They reached a detente, and the dog resumed her place on an old
couch cushion under an eave.

The Grangers had never owned a pet. Annabelle felt proud of her
confidence in her husband that they had moved straight to the baby-
making phase of their relationship without an intervening will-he-
take-care-of-a-dog phase. But every country kid needs a dog as a side-
kick, especially since medical science would not be providing Heath
with a sibling. They agreed to take Maud—who'd lived at the house,
outdoors, her entire life—as part of the real estate deal. Maud was
flea-bitten and deaf as a stone. She was also intimidating. Annabelle
had been researching dog ownership. She knew that the ancient beast
needed training to transform her into a family dog.

Maud was waiting for them on the porch when they pulled into
the gravel driveway of their new adobe home. She remained at the top
step neither barking nor wagging her tail.

"Stay in the car," she told Paul and Heath. Should Annabelle be
mauled, she wanted Paul to drive away before Heath could witness
her carotid artery spray their front door. As the parents of a trauma-

tized child, it was their responsibility to protect Heath from viewing any more violence to human bodies.

Annabelle approached the porch steps radiating calm, assertive energy certain that César the Dog Whisperer would approve of her technique. The dog didn't move. Annabelle conquered the bottom stair and stopped. She was eye level with the dog.

"Hi, Maud. You good girl. What a pretty dog you are," Annabelle intoned in a low voice.

Annabelle seized another stair.

"We're here to be your new family."

She held the key to the house in her hand and showed it to Maud so the dog wouldn't think she carried a weapon. Annabelle was aware of how ridiculously accessible her throat was. The pale white skin must beckon from her dark jewel-neck shirt, like Mina's did for Dracula. As Annabelle lifted her leg to take the next stair, the dog moved. Not a lunge, but a retreat.

Maud allowed Annabelle on the porch and watched dispassionately as she unlocked the front door. Annabelle looked at Paul and Heath through the windshield. They were deep in conversation and seemed to have entirely missed Annabelle's harrowing mission and ultimate success.

As she crossed the threshold, Annabelle wondered if César's technique would work on Paul and Heath. If she radiated calm, assertive energy as the movers, arriving now, conveyed their furniture and cardboard boxes into the unfamiliar house would they become convinced that all this work and change was the start of a beautiful life together?

The first chore once the movers unloaded the boxes and the moving van drove off was to assemble their beds. The evening was fast approaching, and it was vital that they all have a safe, familiar place to lay their heads tonight. Annabelle was a big believer in sleep. No one can be their most creative, loving, curious, and compassionate selves if they are not well rested. She was with Arianna Huffington on this one. Missing sleep deprives people of their intellect, their scintillating personalities, and their decision-making skills.

Annabelle ensured that her family operated at their full capacity by sticking to bedtime routines that were scientifically proven to improve sleep. There was no screen time an hour before bed. The blue light prevented melatonin production. All light prevented melatonin production, so their bedrooms in Royal Oak featured blackout shades. At the end of every day, her family members turned back the covers of a made bed.

They began in Heath's room. He had a corner bedroom facing the dirt road. The bathroom separated his room from their room by only a few steps. It would be quiet, but close, a huge improvement from the house on Huntington Road where a long landing with railings over-looking the living room and entry hall below separated Heath's bedroom from theirs. When as an infant Heath added independent locomotion to his repertoire of behaviors, Annabelle had had to satisfy her fear that Heath could slip through the balusters by pressing his soft little skull against them. Now that he was five, Heath could handle the landing responsibly, but Annabelle still felt better having his bedroom close by.

Heath's four-poster Ikea bed featured a frame above to support a canopy tent. When Heath moved to this big boy bed almost three years ago, sea creatures had been his fleeting infatuation, so Annabelle had painted an underwater scene for him on the headboard. She'd had no art supplies remaining from her painting days, so she'd gone to the artist's store for the first time in years. On a dark blue background, she had painted a giant squid, a frilled shark, and a pufferfish. But the star attraction was the anglerfish, those bloated deep sea monsters with the light hanging from their heads in front of their gaping maws. Annabelle had drilled a hole through the headboard and stuck a tiny LED bulb where the anglerfish's light should be. She had attached a switch to the bed, so Heath could be in control of turning on or off this nightlight.

"Here you go, buddy. Try turning the metal circle with the screwdriver," Paul said. He had tied a canvas tool belt around Heath's waist and loaded it with Allen wrenches. The bed was easy enough to reassemble. All it took was to push the screws into the holes and then lock them in place with the spin of the "metal circles." But Paul, with his supernatural font of patience, was allowing Heath to do that part. It took an incredible effort for Heath to summon the hand-eye coordination to fit the screwdriver into the indentation and turn, but allowing Heath to help was an important part of his feeling ownership over the move and his new room.

Annabelle cast an eye out the window. Soon the distant mountains would block the rays of the early evening sun. What a contrast to the flat Midwestern horizon. Annabelle was anxious to get settled before the dark approached. She wanted her belongings to surround her before the foreignness of their environment closed in.

While Paul and Heath locked the screws, Annabelle hustled. She opened the box with Heath's bedding and pulled the fitted sheet onto the single mattress as it bowed against the wall. She stopped when she heard Heath ask Paul, "Dad, what if you leave and don't come back?"

Here, at last, were the moving jitters for which the parenting website had prepared her. Annabelle took a moment to radiate calm, assertive energy, but her husband answered first. He and Heath seemed to pick up a conversation that had begun out of her hearing.

"I'll come back. It'll be just like in Royal Oak. I go away for work, but then I always come home to you and your mom. Turn this last screw, buddy."

Empty platitudes. Misdirection. That's why they pay Paul the big bucks, Annabelle thought. Heath concentrated on the screw.

With the bed finally reassembled and the mattress in place, Annabelle smoothed the fishy comforter across the sheets, Heath assembled his stuffed animals around his pillow, and Paul hung the blue silk that served as the bed tent.

"What a cool room you have, Heath. Good job assembling that bed. Do you want to help with Mommy and Daddy's?" Paul asked, executing one of their extended high-five maneuvers.

Divorce lawyers had designed their bed, but Paul and Annabelle got it screwed together with a minimum of swearing and only one scratch on the wall. They hefted their mattress into place and made the bed together. Annabelle couldn't remember the last time they had made the bed together. It was so much easier to pull on the fitted sheet with someone on the other side. They added the flat sheet, a blanket, and the comforter with perfect coordination. Feeling the rush of assembly line efficiency, Annabelle picked up a pillow, shoved it in a case, and tossed it across the bed to Paul for placement. They had five more pillows to go. With the last one bagged and tossed, Annabelle swept up Heath and handed him to Paul, who tucked him in amongst the pillows. They both climbed onto the bed next to him and took a moment to cuddle their son.

---

## 13

PAUL VOLUNTEERED TO MAKE DINNER WITH HEATH WHILE ANNABELLE unpacked the kitchenware. Thank goodness they had been clever enough to stop at the Walmart that morning to get cleaning supplies, paper products, and groceries before heading to the house. There would be no swinging by the store or ordering in now that they lived thirty minutes from the nearest town.

Heath, still wearing the tool belt like a kilt, and Paul stirred a sizzling frozen meal in the skillet while Annabelle looked for the bowls. She had found the plates, glasses, and silverware, and put them away in the most ergonomically sensible locations, but the box with the bowls was eluding her.

She was rummaging through a box when she overheard Heath say, "Why'd Mom make us move here?"

With diverting fanfare, Annabelle pulled from the box the family Kamishibai board.

"Hey guys, look what I found. Where should it go?" she asked, pulling out the corkboard with the red and green cards. "I think this is the perfect place," she said, leaning the board against the wall on the kitchen counter next to the breakfast bar. "Heath, I bet you can get to it by sitting on the kitchen stool, right?" Heath abandoned Paul at the stove and showed that he could climb up on the counter to get to the board. "Perfect."

The Kamishibai board was the foundational tool of Granger household administration. She learned about Kamishibai and many other Japanese management techniques from her robotics instructor, Dr. Watanabe. He used to work for Toyota. At Toyota, they used the visual card system to ensure quality control, safety, and cleanliness in the workplace. Annabelle implemented a family Kamishibai board when Heath turned four to encourage responsibility and contribution to the household.

Annabelle split the board into three sections—one for the morning hours before school and work, one for the after-work hours, and one for bedtime. Heath's morning responsibilities were getting dressed, teeth brushing, and bed making. After school he did his schoolwork, set out his clothes for tomorrow, and packed his backpack with what he would need the next day. His pre-bedtime tasks were to brush his teeth and clean up his toys. When he completed a task, he switched the color of the card on the board from red to green. Annabelle and Paul had daily tasks as well for laundry, yard work, meal planning, and home maintenance. The family reviewed the board every evening to make sure they were on track.

Annabelle, unsure where else to look for guidance, ran her household with many concepts pilfered from the Japanese. The Grangers do not wear shoes in their house. That rule kept the floors clean and made playing board games, rough-housing, and eating snacks with Heath on the rug more comfortable. Heath was being introduced to Japan's Studio Ghibli cartoons in addition to the Disney canon that Annabelle grew up with. She figured the plucky girls who served as Ghibli's main characters in most of those movies would undo any princess narratives he internalized from the Disney cartoons.

More significantly, Annabelle embraced the Kaizen productivity philosophy—a commitment to continuous change for the better. The intended application is in large corporations like Toyota, but Annabelle felt it applied to the family as well. The Kaizen philosophy obliged them to seek ways to simplify and automate the processes they used to run the family. For instance, when loading the dish-washer, they placed matching utensils next to each other in the bins for ease of returning them to their drawer.

They met regularly as a family to evaluate how they were doing and make consensus-based decisions on how to improve the house-hold. The Kamishibai board helped. It wasn't as onerous as it sounds. The Kaizen productivity philosophy was more a mind-set than a collection of rules and meetings. The goal was to handle the tedium of life with efficiency, so there was time for the activities that allowed them to thrive as individuals and as a family. The primary tenet was to not fear abandoning a practice just because it had always been done. It was that tenet that allowed Annabelle to quit her job and got the Granger's out of the suburbs.

After dinner, Annabelle let Paul get Heath ready for bed while she did the dishes. She knew the Kamishibai board had been a diversion, not the end of the conversation. Heath was likely asking Paul his question again—Why did Mom make us move here?—, and Annabelle didn't want to hear Paul's answer. *Because she was at work when you found a dead body, Heath. Because she can't make a little brother or sister for you, Heath. Because Mommy is crazy, Heath.*

Annabelle found the switch for the porch lights and opened the front door. Maud lay on her couch cushion surveying the evening with regal bearing. Her front paws dangled off the cushion. They'd forgotten to buy dog food for Maud and none of the leftovers from dinner—zucchini lentil pasta with corn, carrots, and asparagus—were suitable. Annabelle told Maud she'd be right back. She returned a few minutes later with a plate of Heath's Dino Nuggets and set it down next to the dog. Maud consumed the nuggets in three gulps and licked the plate until it fell off the porch.

"My goodness, you were hungry," Annabelle said. "I've never been in charge of a dog. I will do better."

She tapped the top of Maud's head, but retracted her hand before Maud could lick her. Annabelle was sure the dog harbored an undiag-nosed contagious infestation.

When Annabelle stepped off the porch to retrieve the plate, she noticed the strangeness of her new environment. The light from the porch did nothing to illuminate the ground where she stepped. At the house on Huntington Road, Annabelle could operate out her side door where they kept the trash and recycling in the pitch black. Here, in the twilight, Annabelle had the sudden fear she might step on a snake. She knew from her online research that New Mexico had seven types of venomous rattlesnake. But stepping on any snake, even a non-threatening one, would be a dreadful experience.

She reached into the sharp twigs of the pruned bushes that ran along the porch feeling for the plate. Could there be a raccoon or possum that lived under the porch, something with sharp teeth and long claws? She patted the ground feeling for the plate. She was on high alert, listening to any rustling that might signify her encroachment on a creature's lair. Instead, she heard whispering.

She stopped her search to listen. The whispering stopped too. She thrust her hand into a bush and found the plate suspended in the twigs. Standing, she listened again, but no longer heard any whispers. Annabelle refused to be the horror movie damsel who quavers, "Hello." Instead, she dismissed the noises and marched back into the safety of her new house.

# 14

ANNABELLE JOINED PAUL AND HEATH FOR STORY TIME. HE CHOSE HIS two favorite books and nestled into bed. He switched on his angler-fish nightlight. Under the blue silk canopy, everything looked as it had in Royal Oak. Paul snuggled and read to Heath while Annabelle listened. She knelt on the carpet and stroked Heath's ankle through the covers. They had lost two hours in the time change from Royal Oak to Box Elder and spent all of last night hurtling down the highway at seventy-five miles an hour, so it shouldn't have surprised either parent when Heath nodded off before *Shark vs. Train* had ended.

As they filed out, Paul slipped a finger into Annabelle's waistband and whispered into her hair, "I'm ready for bed too." She pressed her back into his chest. He wrapped his arms around her and they swayed together toward their new bedroom.

"Mrs. Granger, I don't believe I've ever had the pleasure of doing it with you in New Mexico," he whispered.

She turned to face him, still pressing her weight into him. "Yes, you have. On our honeymoon remember?" He arched an eyebrow. "The Four Corners?"

"Ah yes, The Four Corners, of which New Mexico is one. How could I forget?"

For their honeymoon-slash-grad-school-graduation reward, Paul and Annabelle had rented a campervan in Las Vegas. They spent two weeks driving around the Southwest. The photos of the trip featured them in front of the most stunning vistas in America—the Grand Canyon, Bryce Canyon, Zion, Arches, and Moab. It was rocks and sky, rocks and sky.

Annabelle was not a camper. She did not care for sleeping anywhere but in a bed. And she dreaded the tribulations surrounding hygiene and bathroom usage. Paul planned the trip to minimize her discomfort. They stayed many of the nights of their honeymoon at proper camp sites with bathroom facilities where she could have a poop and a shower, as Paul indiscreetly phrased it. And Annabelle found she enjoyed sleeping in the pop top of the camper van—their love nest.

She had agreed to the camping trip because she'd guessed—correctly it turns out—that the experience was ripe for misadventure. They would be out of their element, facing the elements. Anything could happen, and she wanted to find out, prove to herself, that she and Paul could handle the rocky roads of life literally and metaphorically.

They worked together well, Annabelle hopping out of the passenger seat to ensure the van fit under the roofs of fast food drive-throughs and to guide Paul with cryptic hand signals out of tight parking places and past hazardous ledges with precipitous drops in remote wilderness. They asked each other how they were allowed to do this. Who thought it was a good idea to allow two inexperienced outdoors people to drive an enormous unfamiliar van through desolate, dangerous terrain? Shouldn't there be an insurance waiver or some roadside signage warning them they were getting in over their heads?

Her favorite part wasn't the helicopter tour over Tower Butte in the Grand Canyon—although that was terrifying and breathtaking—

nor the wine tasting in Moab, nor the hike to North Window at sunrise. Annabelle's favorite part—the misadventure for which she had hoped—occurred when they pulled up behind another rented campervan stuck in deep sand on a narrow portion of the road between two rock walls. The one-way two-track road had been rocks and sand and potholes for twenty minutes up til then with ponderosa pine forest amid craggy boulders on either side. There was no way for Paul and Annabelle to drive around the stuck vehicle, and even with three people pushing—Paul, Annabelle, and the husband of the woman in the van's driver's seat—, they couldn't get the van free. Reversing back down the rutted road was a recipe for two stuck vans, so, with no cellphone service, they made the best plan they could think of. Paul and the other fellow smeared on sunscreen and each wore two liters of water on their backs as they walked out to the main road for help. It was the beginning scene of a horror movie. *Let's split up.*

Annabelle stayed with—what was her name? Jessica? At first, they sat leaning against the stuck van, which the couple had dubbed The Mango, talking in the shade. But Annabelle was restless. She studied the situation. The front tires of The Mango were clear of the sand. Both back tires were mired. But the sand existed only in a small pocket. If they could get the van forward only twelve inches, it would be free. She and Jessica tried to shovel away as much sand from in front of the tires as they could. Then they laid sticks and bramble down in front of the tires to give them some traction. Jessica drove The Mango while Annabelle pushed. It didn't work at all. The tires were sunk too deep. Hot and sweaty and frustrated, they tried packing dirt from the forest floor with water around the tires. This too was unsuccessful.

Annabelle thought of a better plan. She and Jessica assembled the jacks from each van and with arduous pumps lifted the back end of The Mango. With the tires hanging in the air, they were free to pile rocks and tree limbs across the sandy morass. They set The Mango down and Jessica tried driving free again. It worked! Annabelle hadn't needed to push at all. She got in her van, which she now thought of as

The Peach, and drove in a low gear at a steady pace between the rocks. She passed the sand trap without issue.

The best part of the trip was she and Jessica honking and pulling alongside their desert-dazed lovers in their rescued vans. The looks on the men's faces were of unabashed relief. They were dizzy with heat exhaustion. Almost all of their water was gone, and they hadn't seen a single other vehicle. They were beginning to believe they had made a dreadful error leaving the vans. The Mango and The Peach met at a bar up the road where the couples clinked glasses and the boys celebrated their women like the heroes they were.

During their interminable drives between parks and campsites, Paul and Annabelle had been teasing each other about making love at The Four Corners. It was a cliché, but also a dare. As they ticked closer—it was easy to forget when planning a road trip how many hours would be spent on the road—they each continued to bring it up, challenging the other to back down. When they were twenty miles from the Utah-Colorado state line, they made a practical plan. It required some skillful maneuvering, of both the navigational and romantic kind, but they did it. Three times they pulled over and made love in The Peach's nest that day (they had already ticked Utah off their list more than once) as they rolled clockwise through the states. It was a dare accepted, a commitment honored, and it was fun.

Paul must have been remembering their honeymoon too because he picked up Annabelle and maneuvered her sideways through their bedroom door like a bride across the threshold. He tossed her on the bed and closed the shades while unbuttoning his pants. It was the only multitasking the man could do. Annabelle pulled her t-shirt over her head and rocked out of her sweatpants. She kneeled on the bed, pulling Paul to her. She enjoyed being taller than him in this position, kissing down on him. He lifted his henley off and let his Dockers slide down his hips.

Paul had a very nice body. He was fastidious about his appearance. He was always well groomed. Even today, moving day, he had shaved his face smooth. His casual clothes were a cut above too. He didn't own pants with an elastic waistband nor t-shirts with logos or cheeky sayings.

He hadn't always been a model of sartorial splendor. In college, he dressed in the approved male uniform of the time: cargo shorts, checked button-down with short-sleeves, and hoodie. It all changed when he started consulting. Paul said he needed to instill confidence in the people who hired his consulting firm. The fastest way to do this was through attire, manners, and demeanor. After that, he let his work do the talking, he assured her. Little did these clients know that the man who wore cufflinks across the boardroom table from them farted under the covers when he first woke up in the morning, without fail. He was Annabelle's olfactory alarm clock.

Annabelle flipped her hair, coquettish yes, but she was trying to cover the patch of white hair that had appeared along her usual part line and about which she had recently become self-conscious. Paul noticed not and rolled down her underwear while smattering kisses along her décolletage, which Annabelle noted, was fetchingly displayed in her workhorse plunge microfiber t-shirt bra. He climbed on the bed and pushed her back toward the pillows while she pulled down his four-way stretch boxer-briefs with her feet. These were maneuvers practiced many times before, sexy only because of their familiarity. Her bra was a front loader. He unclipped it with a snap of his fingers. Annabelle pressed her arms to her side so her breasts wouldn't hide in her armpits, a trick they learned after breastfeeding Heath.

Then it was time for Paul's moves. He knew just what to do, in the same bed, on the same sheets, in a different room. After a flutter of kisses along her stomach, making her suck in her breath, his fingers traced the magic runes. Somehow he had more fingers than a hand should have. With his other hand, he pinched out sympathy tattoos on her left nipple. Just at the right moment—somehow he always knew— he invited rightie into the action. He suckled and flicked his tongue on her right nipple. At this point he always whispered something to her, like it was the only time she listened to him: "I'm so excited for our life here, Annabelle." She curled her toes until her foot cramped. It had been a while. "All right," he said, proud of her orgasm. Annabelle felt like one of his clients sometimes—analyzed, diagnosed. Unlike his clients, though, Paul stuck around to administer the solution for what ailed her himself.

Then it was his turn. She rolled on top of him and clipped her feet around the tops of his knees like she was getting ready to ride the mechanical bull at a San Antonio dive bar. But it was never like that. Just a precise combination of long, slow strokes during which he looked at her face and fondled her breasts followed by a series of quick hip circles—learned as Omnis at a hula dance class long ago—during which he squeezed his eyes shut and grasped her hips. *Aloha aku, aloha mai*, she thought. Give love, get love.

Paul nestled on his side next to Annabelle. Her neck rested against his extended arm as she gazed at the unfamiliar ceiling. His big hand lay across her stomach. The weight of his hand as he relaxed and fell asleep crushed her organs. Her bladder told her it was time to go to the bathroom even though she had just gone. There was a riot of activity taking place in her stomach under her husband's palm. Microbes were digesting her dinner, breaking it down into vitamin and mineral components, using what they can and shunting the rest down the line. Paul's head rested against hers. His breathing filled her ear with humidity and blew her hair across her neck in a way that itched and tickled.

Sleeping next to her husband, while comforting, wasn't comfortable. Typically, he was gone four nights of the week. It was those nights, when she was the only responsible person in the house with a five-year-old down the hall, that she slept most soundly. When Paul slept beside her, the covers maintained a tension over her body brushing her as they vaulted up to the peak of his shoulder. There was always a gap of cold air entering this space between them. Annabelle sometimes karate chopped the tent away, but the covers pulled unevenly. It was her side that contributed to the new valley. His side stayed in place, as if still tucked in.

When he entered a period of sleep where he breathed deeply, the covers would pull and release ever so gently across her nightgown with the rise and fall of his chest. He occupied more than half the bed, which might have been his right as the larger person, but still. It left Annabelle with only a subset of her preferred sleeping positions without getting a knee in her back or his clammy feet against hers. And God forbid, if he wanted to spoon. He would drift off tickling the hairs on the back of her neck with his loving whispers while her collarbones bowed under the weight of his flaccid bicep. She didn't know how women whose husbands were home every night did it.

She placed her hand tenderly over his on her abdomen for just a moment before lifting it off of her and escaping. Annabelle pulled on her nightgown. She switched on her bedside lamp, but nothing happened. Paul must not have plugged it in. She followed the cord down to look under the bed. Nope, he'd plugged it in. She peered through the top of the lampshade. No bulb. Classic.

"I'm going to go find the lightbulbs," she whispered to Paul. He was sound asleep.

When she got her bedside lamp working, she switched off all the other lights in the house. She checked that the back door and then the front door were locked. Thinking of the whispers, she peered out the window of the front door into the dusk. She didn't want to open the door and disturb Maud outside on her cushion.

She returned to bed. It was her habit to read before falling asleep and with the strange environment, she needed the routine. She congratulated herself on her cleverness storing her current book in her bedside table drawer before the move so she would be sure to find it when she needed it. But she read only two pages before the words started to blur. She checked her cellphone. It was only eight, well, ten where they came from. She looked at the little alarm bell icon and swiped to turn it off. Tomorrow was Monday, and she did not need to be anywhere. For the first time since completing graduate school, Annabelle was unemployed.

She drifted off to sleep cataloging the bark of distant dogs, the hum of the refrigerator, and the familiar purl of her husband's breathing.

## 15

SOMEONE WAS TRYING TO GET INTO THE HOUSE.

Annabelle's ever-vigilant internal nighttime monitor, the one that activated when the nurse first placed newborn Heath in her arms, jerked her awake. She lay still waiting to hear what had wakened her, afraid even to breathe.

It was the whispering again, close by.

Through the shades of her bedroom window, she saw the glow of flashlights. People were creeping on her porch.

"Paul, wake up. Someone's here. Wake up. Listen."

Annabelle swelled with relief when Paul reached full consciousness, apprehended the danger, and then rose from bed. She was less relieved when she heard him open the front door. The whispering stopped and silence ensued. Had hoodlums disabled Paul so quickly? Annabelle was frozen in place with the covers clutched to her chest.

"What are you kids doing?" she heard Paul say.

Kids? Annabelle found her glasses and tiptoed to meet Paul at the door. As she approached, a girl's voice asked, "Can your son come play with us?" Annabelle peeked under Paul's arm as he held the door ajar. Five kids stood before them.

Her heart burst with excitement. There were kids in the neighborhood and they wanted to play with Heath. This was more than she could have hoped for. She had always dreamed of a childhood for Heath filled with impromptu kickball and street hockey games, bike rides, and secret forts in the woods. She wanted for him the rough and tumble outdoor adventures filled with camaraderie, loyalty, and the moments that cause one to mature and find their courage and heart. It is through the friendship of a good group of neighborhood kids and the support of a loving family that one turns into a fine young man.

Paul said, "He can't come out and play. It's late. He's asleep. You all should be home too."

"He can play tomorrow," Annabelle assured them. Paul shot her a look.

"Go on. Get home," he said.

The smallest kid shouted into the doorway. "Come. Out. And. Plaaaaay."

"No. Shh. Come back tomorrow," Annabelle said, taking the door from Paul and closing it before they could wake Heath. She wanted his first night's sleep in the new house to be undisturbed.

"Oh, Paul. Isn't it wonderful? He will have friends." She took a seat at the breakfast bar.

"I don't know about those kids." Paul began opening cabinets in the kitchen.

"What do you mean you don't know about them? They're kids. They showed up a little late, but it's only 8:30. Maybe they keep late bedtimes here."

"Where are the glasses?" Paul asked. Annabelle pointed. "Those kids were doing something to the dog when I opened the door." He filled his water glass.

"To Maud? Is she okay?"

"She's fine. She seemed happy to have the attention. They were in a circle around her chanting or something with the flashlights held up under their chins to make their mouths look bloody and their faces spooky."

"Chanting? You think we have moved into the meeting place of the local child coven?"

Paul drank all his water. "It's so dry here," he said, wiping his mouth with a kitchen towel.

"I think the kids startled you. They were saying hi to Maud. Glad that she still lives here. And they did the flashlight thing because they are kids and that's what they do."

They walked back to their bedroom in the dark. Paul flipped the deadbolt as he passed the front door.

"Are we going to let Heath be friends with anyone who shows up at the door?" he asked.

"Not if they are thirty years old with a lollipop and promises of a model airplane and a koala bear in the trunk of his car."

"You know what I mean. Those kids will get to be Heath's friends just because they showed up?"

"Honey, if Heath makes friends with them, that's great news. We want him to make friends and get drawn out of his shell. He needs to escape the specter of being the kid who found the dead body."

"I know. But when we sent him to preschool, we knew who his friends would be."

"No, we didn't. We never expected him to get in. We didn't know anyone. Remember how nervous we were? I think you tried three different ties when we dropped him off for his first day."

"We didn't know individuals, but we knew what they would be like."

"Why, Dr. Granger. Are you being a snob right now?"

"I guess I am." Paul pulled up the covers and turned his back to her. "But I don't mind being a snob if it's what's best for Heath."

Annabelle leaned upright against her pillows.

"How could being a snob ever be what is right for Heath?" The question was rhetorical. Dr. Granger, the snob, was already asleep.

## 16

THE NEXT DAY, MONDAY, ANNABELLE AND PAUL HUSTLED TO FINISH unpacking. Thanks to Annabelle's superior boxing and labeling skills, the movers had done a fair approximation of getting the boxes to the rooms where they needed to go. Annabelle hung up Heath's clothes, but she let him handle his own toys. It was a protracted exercise as he unboxed, rediscovered, and played with each toy.

When Heath's prattling stopped, Paul ducked in on him to find Heath asleep on the carpet surrounded by toys. He and Annabelle both snapped pictures on their phones and sent them out with messages about their moving day to family and friends.

Annabelle's former neighbor and dear friend Di wrote back immediately.

"If you hear a banjo, start paddling faster," it read followed by a still from *Deliverance* of Ned Beatty looking terrified.

This was classic, unfiltered Di. When Annabelle told her the Grangers were decamping for New Mexico she used their shared love of horror movies to try to convince Annabelle that city people who move to the country never get what they bargained for. It was touching at the time, but now that they'd moved couldn't Di have just offered her well wishes like everyone else?

Annabelle grabbed her purse and called half-heartedly to Paul, "I'm taking Maud to the vet." He was engrossed in shelving his books. She would not be missed.

When Annabelle had charmed her way into a same-day appointment for Maud at the local vet, she had not imagined transporting her there to be a herculean task. Annabelle inferred from Maud's behavior that the dog had never ridden in a car before, perhaps had never been in an enclosed space at all.

After opening the back of her husband's cherry red Jeep (Maud wasn't going in her Saab) and patting the bumper and swinging her arms at Maud to indicate to the deaf dog that she wanted her in the car, Annabelle had struck on bribery. She proffered bacon left over from the Granger's extravagant first breakfast. She tossed Maud a piece—which was caught out of the air and swallowed in one action—and showed Maud the rest in her hand. With ostentatious gestures, she set the bacon in the back of the SUV and waited for Maud to jump in. Maud did not approach the vehicle. Annabelle sighed, puffing her bangs off her forehead. This was harder than breastfeeding.

Annabelle resorted to dognapping. She tossed a trashy pillowcase over the dog's head and heaved her up. From snout to tail, the animal was long, but weighed almost nothing. Maud didn't fight, but swung her head from side to side with the pillowcase hanging over her eyes like a disabled Hoth Walker.

While navigating to the vet's office, Annabelle concluded after a monologue with herself that turning Maud, shabby beast that she may be, into the family's pet was worthwhile. Families with dogs had children with healthier gut bacteria. The dogs tracked dirt and with it microbes that improved children's health. Heath had been a C-section delivery, so he missed receiving important vaginal bacteria on his entry into the world. Fresh garden vegetables full of nutrients and daily immersion in the bacteria-teeming natural environment would be the antidotes to her family's previously sterile existence. Annabelle would use research and care to build the Granger's ideal life in the country. It would start with improving Maud.

Her phone rang. It was a local 505 area code. Annabelle pulled over to answer.

"Mrs. Granger? This is Dr. Chavez at Box Elder Veterinary Clinic. You've moved into Pat and Melinda Martinez's place and you've adopted Maud?"

"Yes," Annabelle said, wondering how she knew.

"I see we have an appointment to see Maud today and I want to save you the trip and Maud the anxiety of the car ride."

"Ok." Annabelle glanced at Maud panting and pacing in fear in the way back and felt too guilty to tell the vet they were already on their way.

"Maud has heart worm. It's the reason for her emaciation and labored breathing. The treatment is a drug full of arsenic. The trick is to administer a dose that will kill the worms, but not the dog. In Maud's case, the constriction of blood by the worms has been going on for so long that they have damaged her organs. Given her age and the advanced stage of the disease, I don't think Maud would respond well to the arsenic treatment."

"So we don't do anything?"

"It's up to you, but sometimes the treatment is worse than the disease. I'll transfer you back to reception and they'll take your info and update Maud's patient card."

After the call, Annabelle googled heart worm. She read that the disgusting malady was transmitted through mosquito bites and entails what it sounds like, worms eating through the heart. Annabelle saw an autopsy picture she wished she could clear from her mind. The good news was that the odious disease was not transmissible to humans.

This diagnosis changed everything. Annabelle no longer felt like the benevolent rescuer of a geriatric mutt who would otherwise be condemned to the gas chamber on her first day at the humane society. She wasn't going to be able to cure Maud with money and science. She would preside over Maud's decline the same way the Martinez's had.

Annabelle reprogrammed her GPS for the country supply store. She may not be able to cure Maud, but she could pamper her.

When she pulled in to the parking lot, she cracked the windows and told Maud she would be right back.

The doors to the store pushed open in the middle like a saloon. Inside the store smelled like Quaker Oats and leather.

"What can I help you with?" the clerk behind the counter asked. She was the only customer.

"Dog food?"

"Puppy or adult?"

"Adult."

"Twenty-five pound bag or fifty?"

"Fifty?"

The clerk keyed it into the register.

"What else?"

Annabelle realized that the clerk's questions encompassed their full range of dog food choices. She'd been expecting to weigh the benefits of a variety of brands, consult the nutrition labels, evaluate the shininess of the modeling dog's coat, and ultimately choose the most expensive brand.

"A collar?"

The clerk pointed to a wall with collars clipped to a wire rack. There were pink collars and ones with bones printed on them, but the only one large enough for Maud was plain black nylon. Annabelle brought it to the clerk.

He rang it up.

"Wait, and this." Annabelle grabbed a twenty-three dollar dinosaur-squeaker toy. The clerk arched his eyebrow.

Annabelle handed him her credit card.

"ID please."

Annabelle produced it.

"Michigan? You're a long way from home."

"We just moved here."

The clerk nodded and handed her the receipt. She felt his disapproval.

"Drive around the side and I'll load the dog food."

Annabelle returned to the Jeep which now smelled like old dog.

Paul would not be pleased about that. She backed up to a loading area following the hand gestures of a teenager wearing leather gloves. He popped open the tailgate.

"Stop!" Annabelle shrieked, startling the kid.

Annabelle hopped out.

"Wait," she said.

The kid held up both hands.

Annabelle climbed into the backseat and clipped Maud's new collar around her neck. She wrapped her fist around the collar, holding Maud tight.

"OK, now," she said.

The kid opened the tailgate leaning away from Maud.

"Is she mean?" he asked.

"No, I just don't want her to run off. I'll never be able to get her back. She's deaf and I'm her new owner and I've never owned a dog before."

The kid nodded. The clerk appeared with a plain white wax paper sack slung over his shoulder. He placed it in the back next to Maud. It read "Adult Dog Food 50 lbs" in black Helvetica. So much for pampering.

"You have a good day," he said, closing the tailgate with care to avoid clipping Maud.

As Annabelle transferred from the backseat to the driver seat he heard the kid ask the clerk, "What's with her?"

Annabelle drove away, her cheeks burning. Did she seem so foreign?

On their drive home, as her blood-sugar dropped, the enormity of the change hit Annabelle. She couldn't let on. The move was her idea; she would be the one to make this new lifestyle a success.

When Maud and Annabelle returned, Paul and Heath were whispering together under a blanket on the porch swing. They stopped talking when she climbed the steps. She couldn't bring herself to report on Maud's health.

*Dad, why isn't Mom helping the dog?* she imagined Heath asking.

Annabelle anticipated another talk with Heath about death, this time of pets instead of murdered humans, soon.

Heath needed to make friends before he bonded with an ailing and incurable dog. The five kids from the porch last night hadn't returned. Annabelle felt angry with how Paul had handled them. If only he'd been more welcoming, they would have come to play with Heath. But, as was so frequently the case, there was no time and no point in being angry with Paul because he would leave for work before the sun rose tomorrow morning. With him gone, she could run the show as she pleased, no consultation with Dr. Granger required.

Paul had worked for the same consulting firm since he got his doctorate in Management and Organizations. It was a job where one kept their hands clean. It was based on presentations in darkened boardrooms, claps on the back, and emails that struck the right tone of confidence and camaraderie. It was called strategic management. Paul likened it to being a diagnostician like House on TV. A business has symptoms that indicate it is ailing. Paul has to figure out what is wrong and solve the problem, return the company to health.

Paul was aware of the stigma attached to business consulting gigs —getting paid big money to helicopter in and proclaim that everyone was doing it wrong and then disappearing. It was a profession rife with jokes. Question: How many consultants does it take to change a lightbulb? Answer: What's your budget? But if lawyers could handle all the ribbing, so could Paul.

He had distinguished himself in his career. Some months before their move to Box Elder, his bosses had promoted Paul to a senior consultant. Because of his increased salary, Annabelle was free to be a stay-at-home mom. Like Paul, she would distinguish herself in her career as Heath's mother. She would be the one to guide his development, not daycare workers, classmates, or teachers. Her.

That night, Paul set his alarm for four-thirty a.m. It was an hour drive to the Albuquerque airport and he had a seven o'clock flight. This is what his life would be like from now on.

He kissed her forehead the next morning as she lay in bed telling her he'd see her Friday afternoon. Half-asleep, Annabelle muttered some valedictory reply. She wasn't even sure which city he was off to much less which company was paying exorbitantly for the next two days of Paul's consideration. With him gone, she and Heath would build the structure for their new lives.

When she heard Paul's Jeep drive off for the airport, Annabelle listened to the hums and shudders of her strange new home. She recalled her mom's concern that she would be all alone out here with no backup. But what nonsense. She was frequently parenting alone; the only difference was that now she was doing it in New Mexico.

## 17

DAN QUINTANA

I've known Pat Martinez my entire life. We walked to school together as boys. To earn money for the high school prom, we made a business rounding the neighbors' cows up to take them to the BLM land for grazing in the spring. And we attended each other's weddings and those of our children. Pat and Melinda Martinez were my dear friends and good neighbors.

A few years ago, Melinda started forgetting things. I suppose her illness was very hard on Pat, hard for him to handle on his own. I didn't realize how hard until one night when I couldn't sleep; under a gibbous moon out my window, I saw what looked like a ghost in the field. Once I overcame my surprise, I saw that it was Melinda in her white nightgown out wandering barefoot and confused. Her hands were frozen and her feet were cut and bleeding. I called Pat, but there was no answer. So I guided Melinda to my truck, and we headed back to their house.

It is just the way of the roads in Box Elder that I can walk to Pat and Melinda's house faster than I can drive. On the way, I saw the

square familiar headlights of Pat's Buick LeSabre ahead. We rolled
next to each other his window already down. He'd guessed my cargo.
Pat had been out driving looking for her, unsure what to do.

What I'm saying is that it came as no surprise when Pat told me
they were moving away to a retirement community in Rio Rancho
where he could get some help with Melinda, but that didn't make the
news any easier. Neither of us had ever lived anywhere else, except
during our years in the army, and neither had our parents. We were,
both of us, connected to the land and the community. The thought of
him leaving, even though I understood and sympathized with the
reason, felt like a betrayal. It made me feel alone in my own neighborhood.

My wife, Delfina, is a realtor, but Pat listed his house with a real
slick guy from town. Pat needed to get a good deal on the house to
afford Melinda's care. The realtor did a great job with the advertise-
ments too because the house had not been listed two months before
Delfina heard through her realty sources that it had sold to a young
professional couple from Michigan with no connection to Box Elder,
or even to New Mexico. Delfina knew that Pat had gotten his full
asking price.

*"El piensa que nomás sus naranjas valen,"* Delfina and I sniggered
when the shiny station wagon of foreign make pulled in to the old
Martinez driveway. *He thinks only his oranges are worth something.* It
was a joke, a kind of inverse of "There goes the neighborhood." We
didn't mean it. They looked like earnest folks. I noticed the wife out in
the garden and it seemed like they were accepting the Martinez's old
dog as their own. Pat would be glad to see that. Maud must be going
on seventeen years. The Martinez's weren't even grandparents when
they got her. I will be sure to tell them the next time we talk. Melinda,
if there is any Melinda left, would be heartened to hear her garden is
being cared for.

Not many outsiders move here. When the kids go away to school,
they might come back with a husband or wife from far off, if they
come back at all, but most everyone who lives here was born here. It's
not that we're hostile to outsiders, not at all. We're not usually given

the opportunity to show our welcoming side because there isn't much draw to come to Box Elder.

Once farming your own plot stopped being an attractive lifestyle which happened in my generation and for my older brothers, having a farm property with land to maintain began to seem onerous, not like a kind of wealth. Those in my generation dealt with it by moving away like my siblings—all but my sister who lives with her husband across the river—or by getting other jobs and working their land on the side.

That's what I did. I live in the house in which I grew up, although it has changed a lot since then. I became an electrician, worked when I wanted to, harder when I was raising my daughter, and less strenuously now. In between work, I tended the field growing chiles some years, alfalfa others. When I knew we'd have plenty of water, I grew the three sisters: corn, beans, and squash. It is a trio from traditional farming techniques taught to me by my father. The sisters thrive together. The corn stalks hold up the beans. The beans fix nitrogen in the soil for the greedy corn. And the broad squash leaves shade the soil conserving water for all.

Farming is hard work, no doubt, even with my Kubota, but working the field pushes me outside instead of indoors watching baseball and John Wayne movies. It keeps me in touch with the land, makes me patient and observant. Some years there is devastation—drought, insects, or hail—and there is always great beauty. Both make me grateful. Both are out of my control. Those long evenings in the summer—what do they call it? The eventide?—I sit smoking my pipe overlooking my crops as the soil cools and the bats come out to feed. Those nights I feel sorry for the people inside staring at their phones, missing the day transitioning to night.

My wife works too, selling houses in the new construction developments off the highway. Those are an eighth of an acre lots in planned designs with streetlights and sidewalks along the asphalted roads. The new construction houses appeal to young couples like the one that bought Pat's place. I understand the appeal. They are easier to maintain and don't have the quirks of the old houses in the valley. In fact, my daughter lived with her husband, Trey, in the development just west of town, the one called Mountain Vista. It was a nice house, big. It smelled like new carpets and had a two-car garage.

Dinah and Trey lived there until it wasn't a new house anymore. When Trey finished his certifications and got the job as a Journeyman Lineman and would be gone for a few weeks at a time, Dinah wanted to move back to Box Elder so we could help with our granddaughter. Even though they were making more money, they moved into a trailer on the Baranowski's property and Delfina sold their house in Mountain Vista. I had thought one day they would inherit my house and Trey would run the Kubota to turn the field each spring and fall and Dinah would teach my granddaughter how to keep chickens.

It is hard for me to talk about them.

Instead, I spend my time thinking about the days of my youth. Maybe it is my stage of life. I can recall every moment of my childhood here. I remember running around with Pat and our other friends, playing in the bosque along the river, listening to the portable radio in my father's workshop, stealing the largest squash from the neighbors, and doing my chores for Abuelita to earn money to get a Coke in a glass bottle at the gas station.

Many things have changed for me here. We're much richer now. We own more things and our old homes have been renovated and updated. I can remember when electricity came to the valley. Now I have an electronic solar-powered farm gate at the end of my drive and I can stream baseball games on my iPad. I worry about something else that has come to Box Elder along with all the progress, though—not a technology, but a mindset, the thing that poisoned my daughter, something insidious. It's taking our children from us.

It was hard for me to see a new family in Pat and Melinda's house. They don't leave the porch light on the way Pat used to and the unfamiliar cars in the driveway unnerve me. I miss Pat every day. But I was glad too that the young family moved here. We need new life in Box Elder.

There was a time when families split their lots to accommodate houses for their children. They divided a house on twelve acres to four houses on three acres each. And those lots would be split once again for the next generation. The housing mitosis makes the jumbled nest of addresses here so different from the pre-planned order of places like Mountain Vista.

We used to worry about where our children's children would fit. But we don't have that problem anymore. Most of our children moved away and don't plan to come back. Now, the old timers hope to sell their homes to outsiders like Pat did. It was good that Pat could sell and good that young, professional people would want to spend their time in the garden. It gave me hope for our future.

Why am I being so morose? My wife warns me of this. Things are not at all as bleak as I have described it. There is a renaissance in farming that has brought renewed interest in the larger parcels of irrigable land. These farmers operate as small businesses rather than growing to feed their families. They can get organic status quickly as the traditional farmers never wanted to pay for fertilizers or pesticides, so the land is free of toxins. The newer restaurants in Santa Fe are hungry for organic locally grown produce. Trucks rumble down the main road picking up produce for delivery most every day of the week in the summer.

We are growing varieties of crops that have never before been sown here: rhubarb, kale, collards, and mushrooms. A young couple from Albuquerque owns a small plot down the road that used to only be chiles. Now they grow cut flowers for sale to the hotels and markets. A sign at the end of their driveway advertises sunflowers, hellebores, hydrangea, aster, and larkspur. In the summer, their field is a riot of colors. I have noticed more bees and hummingbirds since they started up.

The Greens, an old Box Elder family that has been here almost as long as mine, get more money per sheep than ever before now that they label them as humanely raised. She sells her spicy harissa lamb sausages and lambswool baby clothes at the farmer's market at the Rail Yards. Although, I don't know what they will do now that their daughter was taken from them.

I've heard there is a community-supported agriculture program starting up with support from New Mexico State. If you get listed with them, people buy a subscription for the food you produce. They pay up front so you don't miss a season because of tractor repairs or a line of fence taken out in a gully-washer. The university even sends some of their ag students out to work for free. The kids are happy to do it because they get credit toward their educations. If you miss out on the ag students, you might catch the hippie buses that roll through. They are full of teenagers who call themselves woofers. We used to call them campesinos. They will work in the fields for room and board. Oatmeal and some grill-outs and an extension cord to their van suit them just fine.

Without a doubt, a young couple can lead a good life here. What it lacks in jazzy nightlife and cellphone service, it makes up for in opportunities to see the fruits of your labor and to sleep soundly with exhausted muscles from your efforts. In Box Elder, we mark the change of seasons, the transition of day to night, and the shifts in the weather. We have a deep and constant commitment to the land. That commitment is both draining and rewarding. We do not differ from the stalks of corn in the field; we work to grow, we hope to thrive, and we take our sustenance from the sun and the soil.

## 18

WHEN ANNABELLE GOT UP THAT MORNING, SHE WAS DETERMINED TO set the tone for the Granger family's new start. They would lead wholesome lives with lots of fresh food and outdoor time. They would reconnect with nature and learn about the natural world. Heath would be delighted that his mom now stayed home to spend time with him.

For Heath's breakfast, she would make pancakes from scratch. She was gathering the ingredients when he arrived in the kitchen in jeans and a Thomas the Tank Engine long-sleeve shirt declaring he was ready to go to school. This surprised Annabelle. They had been discussing the move for a month. Annabelle had read *The Berenstain Bears' Moving Day* to him. Heath said goodbye to his kindergarten friends, and he knew that he wouldn't be starting school here in Box Elder until the fall.

She believed the term was "Monday morning quarterbacking." It means it is easy to look like an expert when you have full knowledge of what will happen. But that is not how parenting works, nor most of the decisions we have to make in life. We make the best decision we can and then course correct when new information becomes available. Another applicable punchy adage would be "Hindsight is 20/20."

It was clear now that it had been a mistake to start Heath in kindergarten.

He'd began kindergarten at the "big school" as he called it a few days after turning five. He was the youngest kid in his class. But his age wasn't the problem. If they hadn't enrolled him in kindergarten, then he couldn't have been traumatized by what happened at the school.

She and Paul had discussed holding him back for another year instead of sending him to the big school. It would be Preschool Plus. But his preschool teachers said he was ready for kindergarten and the school said he was ready, and Heath himself said he was ready. So they sent him to kindergarten. If only an angelic Monday morning quarterback had warned them by blowing the whistle or dropping the red flag or holding up the yellow card or whatever they do.

Their decision seemed to be a good one. Heath was always excited to go to school in the mornings. He enjoyed his worksheets. His penmanship improved. Recess became his favorite subject. His class shared the afternoon recess with first graders. The older, cool girls found Heath irresistible. Annabelle understood the appeal. To kids his own age, he might look like a retiring wallflower, but the older girls saw bravado and mystery in his aloofness. His dimples likely helped too. The girls carried him around the playground like a king on a litter, Heath's teachers reported. And Heath confirmed on the car rides home that recess with the big girls was the highlight of his day. This was before what happened.

Paul had wanted to enroll Heath in his new school in Box Elder right away. Heath had only one month remaining to finish kindergarten. But her online searches about child trauma morphed into searches about the right age to start kindergarten. She was blaming herself. If Heath hadn't started at that school, then he wouldn't have communed in a marsh with a murdered teen and she wouldn't have a creepy, glassy-eyed, three-and-a-half-foot automaton who had started bed-wetting again.

Annabelle read about redshirting, waiting a year to send your child to kindergarten. The practice made your child emotionally, cognitively, and physically at the top of their class. The research was in. High schoolers who'd been redshirted for kindergarten were satisfied with the decision their parents had made. What more could a mother ask for?

So when Paul pushed to start Heath in school in Box Elder, Annabelle uttered the magic words: "After what happened, he needs a break." And Paul had relented. She tried not to play the after-what-happened card too frequently. She didn't like manipulating Paul. Their relationship was supposed to be built on mutual respect. But with the new house in the new town and Paul constantly away for work, she couldn't stand to send Heath away all day. They needed to bond, to do all the things she missed when he was at daycare and she worked through checklists at the robotics lab—a job considerably less significant than raising a human.

While Heath climbed up on the counter to update the Kamishibai board for his morning chores, Annabelle rubbed his back and broke the news again.

"You aren't going to school today, sweetie. You will start school with all the kids in the fall at the beginning of the school year."

"Dad went to work today. I want to go to school."

"I'm so glad to hear that you want to go to school and you will in the fall. Today we're both staying home. Would you like to make pancakes with me?" Annabelle raised her eyebrows.

Heath submitted to having an apron folded and wrapped around his little body and he stood on his kitchen stool to help her add the pancake ingredients from the recipe on her phone into the glass bowl. He was silent, and Annabelle knew he was furiously computing the implications of this move from Michigan in his head.

The pancake batter was easy to prepare, barely more difficult to make from scratch than from a premix. But they didn't have any syrup, so they both slathered on butter to help the pancakes slide down their throats.

After breakfast, Annabelle made a fanfare of adding a new chore to the Kamishibai board for Heath: feeding Maud. They went to the entry closet with a tin cup. Annabelle showed Heath how to scoop out a cupful of kibble from the giant bag and then they stepped outside.

The blinding Western sun had led Annabelle to believe from the warmth of her house that the day was balmy, but they were met with a biting cold. It was the last day of April in New Mexico, and spring had not yet sprung. They were without their jackets, so Annabelle hustled Heath over to Maud's new food bowl on the porch. Maud uncurled from her cushion and met them at the bowl.

Heath dumped the food into the bowl, but dropped the cup in too. As he reached to retrieve it, Maud shoved her muzzle into the food and chomped down. Horrified, Annabelle grabbed Heath's arm and pulled him away. She studied his hand while rocking him on the porch swing.

"She didn't bite me," he said. He wiggled free from her arms and went inside. Annabelle retrieved the cup and shook a warning finger at Maud who was gumming with glee through the kibble.

"Sweetie, Maud is an old dog," Annabelle said to Heath when they both were inside. "She can't tell your hand from the dog food. I think feeding Maud is a better chore for me to do."

Annabelle had just delivered to her son his second disappointment of the day. He looked withdrawn and resentful. Annabelle wondered why she didn't have a son who engaged in dramatic tearful tantrums fixable with five minutes alone and then a cuddle. Instead, she had a brooder. He was already so inscrutable, she feared what his teenage years had in store for her.

"I know. Let's bake a loaf of bread." This had been one of Annabelle's fantasies about quitting work and moving to the country. She could serve hot fresh bread to her family.

"You can't bake bread. It comes from the grocery store," Heath said.

Aha. This would be a teachable moment. She wrapped Heath in the apron again and set him on his kitchen stool. She pulled out her bread machine. Paul had given it to her as an anniversary present some years ago. She had prepared a few loaves just to see if she enjoyed it, but it never caught on. She and Heath measured and dumped in the ingredients. Even with Heath's help, the whole event took only ten minutes. Heath watched the machine knead the bread through the window for a minute before growing bored. It would be three and a half hours until the bread was ready.

They spent the rest of the morning as they usually spent quiet weekends, playing Candy Land, reading books, and building with blocks. Heath put himself down for a nap. He had dispensed with napping at three, but the move must have tuckered him out. Or the boredom, the isolation, the quiet.

Annabelle took a photo of him to post to her friends and family back in Royal Oak, but as she stepped through the Instagram uploader, she cropped Heath out of the photo. Instead, her post featured his sea monster headboard with the blue silk canopy. It was an impressive example of #DIYhomedecor and showed that she wanted to #makehomematter.

Without Heath to occupy her, the day ticked by. Annabelle was sifting through a box of her and Paul's memorabilia—his baseball cards and coin collection and her vintage Nancy Drew hardcovers with the yellow spines—when she heard her phone ping. The notification alerted her to twenty-nine likes and seven new followers on Instagram. She scrolled through the comments under the photo of Heath's bed, many from admiring strangers. "Your son is lucky to have such a talented mother," one comment read. Annabelle spent the next hour arranging and photographing indoor vignettes to highlight her new #adobelife for Instagram.

Heath awakened minutes before the bread machine alarm blared alerting Annabelle and anyone within a one-mile radius that it had finished baking her bread. She pulled the pan out of the machine and showed the loaf to Heath. He looked unimpressed, but Annabelle thought it looked perfect. It had risen evenly and was a warm golden brown. It smelled delicious. "Do you want some?" she asked. Heath shrugged.

Instead of cutting the loaf with a knife, she ripped off a chunk, allowing a cloud of steam to escape. This got Heath's attention. They each tried a bite. It was good, but one can't just eat a piece of bread dry, even fresh bread. She slathered the chunk with butter and let it melt. They were halfway through the stick already. After they ate, getting grease and crumbs everywhere, Annabelle considered the remaining loaf. She remembered why the bread machine had not caught on for them years ago; consuming an entire loaf of bread with no preservatives before it turns rock hard is a meal-planning challenge.

Annabelle was about to suggest that Heath get out his coloring books when there was a knock on the door. Maud had not bothered with a bark to forewarn them. Time to meet the neighbors, Annabelle thought, fluffing her hair and scraping a crescent of dough out from under her nail.

## 19

IT WAS THE FIVE CHILDREN FROM THEIR FIRST NIGHT. THEY STOOD IN A
tight group at the door. The tallest child, a full foot taller than the
others, was a girl with round cheeks and dark eyes. She wore a pink
beanie that covered her hair, all but feathery bangs that hung to her
eyes. She was much older than the others, but still a little girl, her
chest flat and her tummy round.

"Can your kid come play with us or is he still sleeping?" she asked.

"Come. Out. And. Plaaaaay," reprised the smallest boy, a mischievous gleam in his eyes. He had spiky black hair and a jean jacket
slipped off his shoulders. Annabelle could imagine his mother
constantly warning him to button it up.

The other three kids looked Heath's age. One boy had blonde
wispy hair and an elf nose. The other two—a boy and a girl—must
have been twins. She was taller than him but they had matching
round black eyes and worried expressions. He wore a baseball hat
backwards and she had a bow barrette sliding out of her hair.
Annabelle thought they seemed like perfectly normal neighborhood
kids. They didn't look at all like the dog torturing thugs Paul was
certain he saw the first night.

Annabelle cast an eye to Heath. She wanted to follow his lead, but if she did, he would turn away the kids and Heath would spend his afternoon and all the days until school began in the fall in a brooding silence. She made a quick decision.

"We'll be right out. Wait for us." She closed the door against the chilly wind. "Come on, Heath. Get your jacket on. We're going to meet the neighborhood kids."

Annabelle didn't want to be the creepy new lady who disappeared with the neighborhood's children inside her house, so they would meet outside. She spread the remaining butter over her loaf of bread and zipped Heath into his jacket. She sat on the floor of the porch and offered the kids bread. They gathered in a circle around the plate and took turns pulling hunks off with their grubby hands. Heath sat next to Annabelle leaning on her leg. Maud approached with her arthritic shuffle and breathed over Annabelle's shoulder, trying to determine if she wanted any of the food that was on offer.

"This is Maud. She's friendly," Annabelle told them, unsure if this was true.

"We know Maud," said the elder girl.

"Right. This is Heath," Annabelle said, elbowing him. "Why don't you introduce yourself?"

Heath had been observing the kids. He was neither wary nor excited. Annabelle and Paul had discussed with him on their drive to New Mexico how he could introduce himself.

"You say, 'Hi, I'm Heath. I'm from Michigan. We moved here to have a healthier family. I'm in kindergarten,'" Paul advised.

"No, he can't say that," Annabelle had snapped at him. "He won't be in kindergarten until fall."

Paul had sighed.

Long car rides always made Annabelle combative. It wasn't the kindergarten part—and the intimation that Paul disapproved of Annabelle's redshirting principle—that had irritated her. It was the reason for the move. *We moved here to have a healthier family.* What a stupid thing to say and behind Paul's stupid words Annabelle felt an ounce of derision. In his words she heard her know-it-all husband, who assessed, diagnosed, and improved in his sleep, teasing her: *You're not as rational and self-controlled as you let on, babe.* After Heath's incident, Paul had been so easy to convince to move. He'd suggested it. Was he going along as a joke, a test? *Let's see how you get out of this one.* Did he think her neurotic episode would end and they would return to Royal Oak in six months with some good stories to tell over cocktails?

His life wasn't much disturbed by moving. He still worked for the same company, still traveled each week to visit his clients. She was the one who quit her job, who would spend her days at home. She was the one who had to make this work.

"I'm Heath. I found a dead person in the marsh at my school," Heath told the kids.

Annabelle gaped at her son. "Why don't you tell them about Silver Dollar City? Remember the Fire Spotter?"

"We're going to go play at the river," the elder girl said, taking Heath's hand. Heath looked delighted.

They were already tumbling down the porch stairs when Annabelle said, "Where's the river?"

"It's close. It's where we always play," the girl said, tightening her grip on Heath.

"No. I want Heath to stay in the yard where I can see him. He's only five."

"I just turned five," said the mischievous littlest boy. He turned a proud grin toward her displaying his pearly white baby teeth.

"He's too young for school, but those three are in kindergarten. We go to the river when they get out of school." Annabelle understood that this elder girl thought of herself as the shepherd for this little flock of lambs.

Annabelle should have wondered why there were kids out and about on a Tuesday afternoon. She had forgotten that the kindergarten here was half day. If she had put Heath in school when they arrived in Box Elder, he would have been in the class with the twins and the elfin blonde boy. They would already be friends. Annabelle told herself to relegate the review and worry over that parenting choice until later. The task at hand was to get the kids to accept Heath.

"Why don't you all play in the yard here?" Annabelle suggested. She needed them to stay with Heath and not run off leaving him behind because he had the only uncool mom in the neighborhood that thought an unsupervised five-year-old at the river seemed like a recipe for disaster. The elder girl shrugged.

"What are your names?" Annabelle asked. "I'm Mrs. Granger," she said, choking on the title to which she had never grown accustomed.

"You have nice hair, Ms. Granger," the elder girl said, stepping close to Annabelle to finger a lock of her hair. "I'm Harley. Do you think I'd look good with red hair?"

"Yes, I think so," Annabelle said, gently gathering her hair away from Harley's greasy fingers.

Harley addressed her flock: "Come on."

They followed her to the edge of the property and down into the sandy ditch that edged their driveway—an arroyo the realtor had called it. Here the cottonwoods and elm trees, the only species that looked like proper trees to a Michigander, grew tall and gnarled. Heath and Annabelle watched them go from the porch steps. The kids popped up on the other side of the arroyo and Harley pulled a rope out from a weed-choked barbed wire fence. It had a plastic disc knotted in the bottom. Harley grabbed the rope and swung out across the arroyo to the other side. She lifted the swing high above her head and released, propelling it back to the next kid on the other side of the arroyo. Heath looked delighted. It's true they weren't in the yard, but they were close enough that she could supervise.

"Go play," she told Heath.

## 20

WHILE THE KIDS PLAYED WITH THE ROPE SWING, ANNABELLE WORKED ON her vegetable patch. She had been fantasizing about it since they put in an offer on the house. The previous owners had cultivated a good-sized garden and a mini-orchard with mature plum and apricot trees. They equipped both with a drip irrigation system to ensure easy watering.

The garden surrounded the back patio. The realtor, inferring Annabelle's interest, had pointed out various highlights of the plot— the asparagus patch, the trellis for peas, the blueberry canes. To Annabelle, it had all just looked like a mess in the February snow and cold. But she had confidence in herself to learn what needed to be done. She figured if she could transform servos, cables, gears, and bearings into articulated robots, she could turn seeds in a garden patch into food.

Although the garden looked better than it had during the home showing in February, dead leaves, desiccated vines, and ash from the wood stove covered the ground. But plants were growing already. It needed tending. Annabelle went to the shed and gathered her gloves and hand tools. With a glance back at the kids rocketing themselves over the sandy expanse, she disappeared around the side of the house.

She set to her task. Just like work at the robotics lab, the undertaking was kinesthetic. It required her hands and that she was aware of her body around the delicate subjects. But unlike the lab, the work was dirty and imprecise. On her hands and knees, she dragged leaves from the bed using her gloved fingers like a rake. She heaped them on the patio. Underneath, the earth was dark and moist.

She uncovered pill bugs and gave them the opportunity to roll away before scratching again at the soil with her hand fork. Annabelle was a protector of life. Although she ate meat, she felt she struck a good balance between ahimsa and the modern world. Perhaps her tires ran over ant mounds, but she didn't kill with malice aforethought. It was her habit to transfer spiders out of her home in a cup sealed with a piece of mail and to dodge marooned worms on rain-soaked sidewalks. Of course, she squashed mosquitos, but they were vectors for disease.

The blustery day made her nose run and the wet earth and leaves turned her fingers to ice cubes, but she was sweating under her jacket. Unlike at the robotics lab, Annabelle was unsure how to proceed. She wasn't sure of her goal for the day in the garden or how she would know when she had accomplished it. When she uncovered a sprinkler head, she repositioned it. Perhaps that was unnecessary. Perhaps a passing dog-walker watching her work would snigger at her ineptitude and wasted effort, but this was Annabelle's garden now and by touching everything she asserted her ownership.

Annabelle couldn't distinguish the dry twigs of a dead plant from one hibernating for winter. She didn't pull any from the ground. There were plenty of greens too. She didn't recognize their leaf shapes. Feeling bold, when she first encountered a plant, she tasted a piece. In this way, she found a very bitter variety of lettuce, green onions, and mint. It felt wholesome and somehow daring to tend her garden in this way. She was out of her element and enjoying that sensation. The house on Huntington Road had come with mature landscaping. All Annabelle had ever done was rake out the garden beds, trim the bushes, and admire her handiwork when the crocuses, forsythia, and tiger lilies took their turns blooming.

Annabelle knew, squatting dirty and sweaty and cramped in the exposed earth, that she was getting in touch with an ancient human practice. Cultivating the soil to produce food should be a sacred ritual. Agricultural production is one of the most fundamental human gifts. It separates us from the rest of the animals. It lured the hunter-gatherers from the forests, allowing them to stay put and civilize. As Annabelle communed with her garden, she prayed it would grant her the ability to stay put and civilize too.

She collected a heap of moldering leaves in her arms and carried them behind the shed, scattering bits of debris as she went. Her cloth gardening gloves proved insufficient to the task. Her fingers were stuck with thorns from a pernicious mini-tumbleweed that caught in the corner of the garden and perhaps with the spines of a cactus she'd not noticed. Behind the shed, she dropped her load. Poof! A composting heap. Gardening was easy.

Annabelle pulled off her gloves and examined her hands. They were red and there was a tiny speck of blood, but nothing she could see accounted for the sting, like many tiny paper cuts. When she pulled the gloves back on, the pain of cloth on her skin let her know that her hands were riddled with tiny invisible spines or splinters.

Not to be deterred, she scooped up another heap of leaves. While transporting them behind the shed, she looked for Heath and the kids. The swing hung motionless from its tree branch. It was the archetypal symbol of a missing child and for a moment a panic seized her. But one can't kidnap six children without some screaming. Annabelle listened over the ambient sounds of the gusty day. She heard the kids talking in the arroyo. She tiptoed closer, intending to make sure everyone was okay without disturbing them. Harley was directing them to collect rocks. It all sounded copacetic. But then Harley asked, "Was he dead when you found him?" Annabelle froze.

"I think so," Heath said.

"Who was he?"

"I don't know. My mom said he was a bad guy. I didn't see his face. He was lying on his tummy."

Annabelle wanted to keep listening, but she couldn't hold on to the mass of leaves forever, and she didn't want to interrupt the conversation when she dropped them. Harley seemed to do a better job of talk therapy than she or Paul had accomplished in months. Annabelle backed away. As long as Heath could process what happened with someone, Annabelle didn't care with whom. All that mattered was that he didn't keep it bottled up. And if seeing a dead guy gave him some kind of cachet with these kids, Annabelle was glad that some good could come of the whole awful situation.

Returning to the garden, Annabelle was impressed with what she saw. The ground looked raw, but tidy. There were herbs and vegetables growing and beautiful white buds on her apricot trees. It was all very promising. Annabelle used her new outdoor broom to sweep the remaining leaf litter from the patio. Soon the weather would warm up and they would roast homegrown veggies on the grill out here and tell stories until the stars came out. She took some photos for Instagram appending #spring, #flowerpower, and #naturelover.

When she rounded the corner, the kids were once again flinging themselves across the arroyo on the swing. Now a team of three swung a weighted plastic grocery bag too. She admired their concentration as they timed the arc to intercept the swing. They were learning the principles of pendulums, force, and motion. Kids were unparalleled learning machines and free play like this activated their minds. They would likely discover all six simple machines before the day was done. Annabelle admired their engineering too. They had tossed a line over a lower branch and attached the grocery bag. Their building materials were harvested locally, improvised from what they found caught in the brush. They added rocks to give the bag weight and steady its motion. These kids were inventors.

Then she watched Heath accept the rope swing from the littlest child. Heath placed the disc behind his legs and held the rope. Instead of flinging himself, he looked nervous. "Go, Heath. Don't be a baby," Harley called. Heath jumped from the side of the arroyo and swung out just as the three kids, Heath's new classmates if Paul had had his way, heaved the grocery bag toward him. Instead of leaning back on the swing, Heath held his body tight to the rope. That was the only thing that prevented the rock-weighted bag from slamming into his head.

"Dammit," she heard the twin boy say through the kids' groans of disappointment at having missed their target.

"No! Stop that! This isn't safe," Annabelle called, running over to them. With his feet back on the ground, Heath released the swing, dizzy with relief. She pulled his head into her hip and stroked his hair. Now that Annabelle was closer she saw that the line they had used was a rusted length of barbed wire and the plastic bag was ripping under the weight of the rocks. An image flashed for Annabelle of the rocks slamming into Heath's little body and the tetanus-infested barbed wire slicing across his face and eye as he fell from the swing.

"He could have been hurt," she rebuked, spittle flying.

"Come on, guys. Let's go to the river," Harley said.

Heath pulled away to follow them, but Annabelle held his shoulder.

"The River Sticks!" the little one cheered in a monster voice as they skipped and tripped and jogged down the arroyo.

# 21

That evening Annabelle and Heath soaked their hands in bowls of Epsom salt and hot water while they sat on the couch watching *The Sandlot*. Annabelle's delicate hands had become ravaged by the afternoon spent in the garden. The alkalinity of the soil had withered the skin. Her cuticles were frayed and some nails ragged.

Annabelle's hands were her best feature and her greatest vanity. They were slim with long, elegant fingers. The skin was smooth and pale and unfreckled and her nails were rounded and naturally pink with white tips.

As a self-absorbed teenager, she had practiced several poses that displayed her hands to their best effect. When thinking, she curled her fingers under her chin with her pointer extending up to her temple. When sitting, she hung one elbow over the back of the chair, allowing her wrist to cantilever her fingers in delicate arches next to her breast. When she gesticulated, her index finger extended straight while the rest maintained their natural bend. The poses began as self-conscious choices, but had become her habitual postures.

Annabelle's makeup routine was minimal. She waved her mascara brush a few times over her clear lashes and she swiped her lips with a perfect pink lipstick from CoverGirl, a shade she had been wearing since high school. She sometimes wondered if she should upgrade her beauty routine to something more sophisticated, or at least to makeup that couldn't be purchased at the grocery store in the same aisle as the toothpaste. But it never happened. The only thing she cared to primp were her hands. A few evenings a week, she worked on her nails, buffing them, massaging the cuticles with almond oil, and occasionally painting them.

But the damage to her hands today extended beyond the cosmetic. She was stung by a phantom pain whenever her palms came in contact with fabric. Through a quick search on the Internet, Annabelle learned that the local cactus, chollas, had fine, tenacious spines that burrowed and stung. The spines weren't dangerous as long as one didn't make the natural mistake of trying to pull them out with one's teeth. If the sharp invisible spines made it down the throat, that was when issues could arise. Annabelle hoped that soaking her hands would help to soften and loosen the spines from her skin.

Heath's soft, chubby hands had fallen victim to the ancient plastic rope of the swing. That was why his were soaking. Both mother and son were pooped from their afternoon spent outside. The warm water and quiet evening were soothing.

Annabelle had chosen the movie. She remembered loving the antics of a pack of boys with their summers free. The high-stakes were, delightfully, a baseball trapped in a yard with a terrifying dog and a team of snobby uniformed little leaguers. But the subtext was that friendship, daring, and play were what living was all about.

That lesson appealed to Annabelle. She had always imagined for Heath a childhood full of boisterous camaraderie and child-sized adventures. The vision was a world, as programmed as a video game, that escalated its challenges to meet and expand his capabilities, leading him from boyhood to manhood. These were the adventures that could only happen when boys were free to spend their summers in a sandlot instead of enrolled in summer academies and enrichment programs. She did not want Heath to suffer the sterilized boredom of existence before he had to.

It was an endearing movie; however, there were some aspects that

Annabelle had not recalled. There was more swearing than she would have liked her five-year-old to hear, inventive as it was. Some gross little boy humor amused Heath in a way she didn't care for. And some scenes did not age well. The ultimate insult for boys was that you throw a ball like a girl. That was not a message she wanted her son to internalize, although Harley could surely demonstrate that throwing like a girl was a compliment. If she ever came back for Heath.

Annabelle realized that the kids who came today were not used to or appreciative of parental vigilance. She had never met children so independent. They weren't insolent exactly, just free to do as they pleased. If the heedful mom at Heath's house bummed them out, they were free to leave. She couldn't call their parents. She didn't know their last names, their parents' names, where they lived, or any phone numbers.

Annabelle teased strands of plastic rope with tweezers from her son's hands while he learned such charming terms as "crap face," "scab eater," and "fart smeller." She hoped he forgot them all before Paul returned home on Friday.

Once Heath was asleep, Annabelle pulled out her book. She was reading about gardening. Paul said if her book was a gardening book, then *War and Peace* was a beach read and Dante's *Inferno* was self-help. It was true. The book didn't offer any suggestions for stopping slug infestations or praise the virtues of no till methods. Instead, it presented a novel perspective, at least to Annabelle, on plants and their nutritional value.

Plants, the author argued, don't want to be eaten any more than a cow wants to be turned into a hamburger. Through the natural selection arms race, plants developed an array of armors and noxious substances intended to repel would-be eaters. The plants we eat are full of poison. It is only through mitohormesis—the principle that toxicity in small doses is beneficial—that we survive a salad.

All those phytonutrients that Annabelle had envisioned feeding her son from their garden to give him strong bones, good vision, and a healthy cardiovascular system were stressors for his little body. The author argued that these stressors challenge the body's cells, which produces a revved up response. It is this response that produces the healthy outcome we associate with consuming fruits and vegetables.

The theory went even further by promoting the concept of xeno-hormesis—plants that are stressed, from pests, drought, or cold, for example, produce noxious compounds that confer stress resistance to the people who consume them. The healthiest plants to eat aren't the coddled greenhouse beauties from Miracle-Gro commercials, but the rugged battle-hardened veggies from a war-torn garden patch. And the reason those vegetables are healthiest is that they are best equipped to damage one's body, thus producing a vigorous response from one's otherwise cosseted couch-potato cells. She had heard the adage: "The difference between a poison and a medicine is the dose." She wasn't sure how universally it applied.

Annabelle thought the book profound. Its worldview was radically different from the symbiotic kumbaya she had envisioned. Had all the smiling, anthropomorphized vegetables in Heath's picture books soft-ened her brain? The carrots weren't absorbing the nutrients from the soil and the sun's radiance to provide nutritious sustenance for her family. And she, as the gardener, wasn't there to provide a stress-free environment for her vegetables.

She had thought the skills of gardening to be something akin to the skills of parenting. Vegetables grow in nurseries. We sow them in environments where they will thrive. We tend to and nurture them. The analogy had seemed clear. The book would change the way she interpreted gardening. Did it also change the way she interpreted parenting?

Annabelle turned off her light. She would need her sleep if she was going to convince Heath tomorrow of how wonderful their new life together was going to be.

## 22

HEATH AWAITED HIS FIVE NEW FRIENDS AT NOON THE NEXT DAY. LUNCH came and went and the children never arrived. Heath was despondent.

Annabelle tried her best to cheer and distract him. She believed it was her watchful parenting that kept the kids away and she feared that Heath thought the same thing. Perhaps out of guilt, she baked him chocolate drop cookies. He accepted the warm cookie, but it did nothing for his mood.

While cleaning up from lunch, she made a plan. An online map search of Box Elder revealed the skinny blue ribbon that represented the river. It was less than a half mile away. Annabelle pulled Heath's alligator rain boots onto his feet and zipped up his jacket. They would see what this river was all about. And maybe they would find the kids, and Heath could play with them while she supervised.

They walked out the driveway to the county road. There were no sidewalks in this neighborhood and this nullified everything Annabelle had taught Heath about road safety. She decided the best course of action was to always hold hands and she would walk on the side closest to traffic.

Not that there was any traffic. Box Elder was a sleepy valley. Nary a jogger, dog-walker, Jehovah's Witness, nor delivery person had passed their house since they'd moved in. Her map search revealed few businesses—just a well drilling company, a hair salon run out of a home, and a taco stand.

There wasn't a gym she could join, which was fine with her. Her former yoga class's newest student was a six-foot tall woman who made self-deprecating remarks about her statuesque body through-out. *It is only in this class I realize how wrinkly my knees have become. I can only guess what sea creature I look like when the top of my head touches the mat.* Others joined in or reassured her, but the woman made Annabelle roll her eyes so hard she fell out of her tree pose.

Annabelle had envisioned the people of Box Elder being interested in her family. She thought she'd be pouring mugs of coffee at the breakfast bar for neighbors who dropped by eager to check out the city-slickers. She and Paul would be invited to social events because they were new blood. She had miscalculated. To meet people, she would have to arrive unannounced on porches like the kids had. First, she would have to figure out the etiquette and logistics of walking through the farm gates that sealed driveways off from the road.

Just then, a bulldog with engorged breasts growled from a yard and ran at Annabelle and Heath. The split-rail fence would do nothing to stop her. Annabelle yanked Heath up to her hip and rushed past with her head down. The dog ran along beside them barking.

Remembering what she had recently learned about dogs, Annabelle avoided eye contact and tried to look calm when all she could envision was the dog sinking its teeth into Heath's calf as it bounced against her backside. She marched until the barking stopped and didn't set Heath back down until she confirmed the dog wasn't following them. Annabelle readjusted Heath's hat and looked into his face. He did not seem perturbed by their near-mauling. They continued.

When she heard a car coming, they stepped to the side to wait until it passed. The driver waved. There may not have been a welcome wagon or a casserole or any visitors except the kids, but the drivers slowing when they passed and waving was a good sign.

They made steady progress. Heath was a poky walker and the rain boots aggravated his sluggish gait. They had almost reached the dirt road that would dead end into the river when Annabelle turned to see Maud lumbering after them.

Maud hadn't thought to leave the property in the month that the house stood empty. A single upended bag of dog food and a five-gallon bucket positioned under the gutter had sustained her. But now she wanted to go walkabout.

They waited for Maud to catch up. Annabelle didn't have a leash. Even at home they didn't have a leash for her. Annabelle had forgotten the possibility that the old dog would want to go for a walk. Now Annabelle froze with indecision. Should they return home with Maud?

Annabelle knew nothing about the dog—if she was friendly to strangers or knew how to not get hit by cars. She didn't want to lose Maud or get a ticket for having an unleashed unlicensed dog. And she wasn't sure if Maud's hollowed-out arthritic hips would carry her to the river and back.

That's it. They had to return home.

"Let's go back. We'll get to the river another day," Annabelle said.

She tugged at Heath's hand. He refused to budge. He yanked his hand from hers and crossed his arms.

"Let's go, Heath," Annabelle said, adopting her stern parenting voice.

"No."

"It's not safe for Maud. I don't have a leash for her. Come on. Come, Maud."

Neither of them budged.

"Maud was born here," Heath said.

Annabelle contemplated how ridiculous they must look to anyone watching out their windows. She was arguing with a five-year-old and a dog about turning around after a four-minute walk. Annabelle relented. She took Heath's hand and they ambled with Maud in the lead toward the river. Once they turned onto the dead-end dirt road, Annabelle relaxed. Maud wheezed and hobbled down the road. She seemed committed to remaining with them. Was their new family dog exhibiting loyalty already?

They entered a copse of trees at the end of the road. A path with rutted two-tracks continued where the road left off. Annabelle cocked her head in surprise as they approached the riverbank; there was no water in the river.

The dry ground comprised sand and some scattered smooth stones. The riverbed was broad with more trees on the far bank. An island of a sort split the middle with tangles of shrubs and grasses and marooned tree trunks and a rusted out car.

Annabelle stepped into the riverbed and lifted Heath down. Maud found a gentle slope to follow. Next to the island, the sand turned mucky and a stream of water dribbled past. It was only three feet wide and when Maud stepped in to get a drink, the water didn't reach past her ankles.

When the kids said they played at the river, Annabelle was imagining something quite different. She thought it would be a rushing river speckled with boulders. Something with trout in it. Something in which Brad Pitt could fly fish. The trickle of water before her was no more than would flow through a gutter in a spring rain. This water was cleaner though, clear in fact. Given that there were no parks or jungle gyms in Box Elder, except for the one surrounded by the elementary school building, the river seemed like a reasonable place for kids to want to play.

Heath threw rocks in the water and used sticks to pull leaf blockades to the side. He dug paths to reroute the water to fill the deep depressions left by his boots in the sucking mud. He heaved large stones into the river to direct more flow to his footprints.

While Heath worked on his civil engineering skills, Annabelle kept an eye out for the other kids. She thought she heard them whispering from the trees as they had that first night in Box Elder. But no, it was just the psithurism of the cottonwood leaves. It was a shimmering cha-cha-cha sound to which she was yet to grow accustomed.

Annabelle took out her phone to photograph the decomposing skeleton of a single leaf pressed into the mud. She then snapped a landscape shot while straddling the river showing the budding trees and snow-capped mountains. She would find the best hashtags and upload the photos to Instagram later.

Heath found a straight bark-free branch. At first, he attempted to ford the river by laying the branch across and using it as a tight-rope. It was too unstable for him to get past the first step. Next, he tried sticking one end in the river and pole vaulting to the other side. It worked. Annabelle cheered and his success surprised even Heath.

His return vault was a disaster. He slipped and went bum first into the stream. Annabelle pulled him up. The shock of the icy cold water, snowmelt from the distant mountain range, left Heath gasping and tearful. He held onto Annabelle's shoulder as she dumped out each boot in turn. She couldn't do anything to ameliorate his soggy pants and socks.

"Let's go home," she said, taking his hand.

That was the magic signal for Maud. She almost skipped toward home. Had this unbridled beast who could have stayed at home or left at any time come along as a guard dog? From what did she think she was guarding them?

Maud found the sloping bank and headed up the dirt road at a canter. Annabelle and Heath ran behind. Annabelle hoped to get him home and into a bath before Heath's shivers turned into something worse, but she was running out of breath. She told herself it was the high altitude at which they now lived that belied her fitness, not the lack of attendance at a gym for the past week.

At the road, Maud crossed and went straight through a sand-bottomed thicket between two fences instead of following the county road to their driveway. "Maud!" Annabelle called. Maud was deaf. There was no getting her attention. Annabelle and Heath looked both ways and crossed the street after her.

"We can't lose her," Annabelle told Heath, explaining her rational-ization for trespassing and pushing through the thicket. Once they were through, Annabelle recognized their location. This was the arroyo that ran along their driveway. It was an eroded sandy path about five feet wide with root-snarled sides just over Heath's head.

Trees and shrubs grew on the banks taking advantage of the water that occasionally flowed through.

Annabelle and Heath followed the arroyo home. This was the route the kids had taken when they left. It cut off a good portion of the walk and let them avoid the aggressive mama bulldog. Annabelle pushed Heath's soggy bottom up the side of the arroyo and onto their driveway.

Maud waited for them at the top of the porch steps. Everyone was home safe and sound. Annabelle appraised Maud. She was so different from the dopey labs, couch-hogging Bichons, and shivering chihuahuas of her friends back home. She was autonomous and proud even in her old age. Maud was quickly earning her keep.

## 23

---

THE NEXT AFTERNOON, WHILE ANNABELLE COMPOSED PHOTOS OF HER latest baking project for Instagram—a banana crunch cake with coconut cream drizzle whose recipe she found through Pinterest—and Heath played with his blocks, they heard shouting outside. Heath ran to the window and then opened the front door. Annabelle joined him there.

The kids were back. They were swinging across the arroyo. What a relief; Heath's uncool mom hadn't chased them away permanently. She waved and called to them, "Heath's coming to play," while Heath got his jacket and shoes.

"Good Morning, Ms. Granger," they recited back like pupils in an old-fashioned school. She ignored the fact that morning had ended thirty minutes before.

Heath ran past her and across the yard without a kiss goodbye.

Annabelle bundled up and headed for the shed. According to her home harvest book, it was time to sow seeds indoors for transplanting to her garden when the soil warmed. The previous owners who, the realtor told her, were moving to a condo in a retirement community, had left the shed full of tools and supplies. She had seen a cardboard

box full of dust-covered Burpee seed packs when she put away her
garden tools the other day. She planned to investigate her options.

A single cobweb-crusted bulb hanging just inside the door did
nothing to dispel the spooky, dark corners of the shed. It smelled like
rotting wood and damp earth. Annabelle was sure she heard the
scamper of mouse feet when she swung open the door.

She thought of hantavirus. Her pre-move investigation into the
dangers of her intended new home told her that inhaling the dust
where infected rodents have urinated or defecated caused a fatal lung
disease in humans. It was prevalent in New Mexico. She would figure
out how to clean the shed and seal it against rodent invasion, but for
now she took a big gulp of air, dashed in to retrieve the box of seeds,
and ran back out to the sunlight.

After inspection, Annabelle concluded that the box was merely
dust-covered not feces-laced. She flipped through the packets. Based
on the guidance of her gardening book, she selected cucumber,
zucchini, and sweet corn. She envisioned pickling cucumbers, baking
zucchini bread, and munching an ear of buttered corn hot off the grill
while she made breath-hold dashes into the shed for empty black
plastic seed trays, soil, and a trowel.

Before beginning her planting, she surveilled the kids in the
arroyo. They were now swinging two at a time. One kid stood on the
disc while another clung with hands and feet hanging below. This
seemed dangerous to Annabelle but acceptably so. There might be
tears, but no trips to the emergency room or life changing injuries. It
was nothing like the sadistic gauntlet they were running two days
before.

She followed Heath's red head as he swung across the arroyo with
Harley. She studied the way he bounced, his extravagant hand
gestures, and his concentration holding onto the swing. He looked
happy. He looked like a normal kid.

Planting the seeds was tedious. They were too small and unwieldy
to select from the packet and push down into the soil while wearing
her cotton gloves. She abandoned the gloves for increased dexterity,
but the soil wedged under her fingernails. She studied her dirt-

covered hands transferring seed to tray and wondered if the task would not be better accomplished by a robotic arm. Something that would not grow tired or bored. But, Annabelle reminded herself, there was no money in household gardening for robots to get involved and besides the point was to spend the time doing it herself, to gain the health benefits, both physical and spiritual, of connecting with the earth and with cultivating living things. That was worth a little dirt under her nails.

Annabelle allowed herself a moment to consider what she would be doing at work right now. She'd be in the lab, making jokes with her team next to a robot straight out of a visionary's dream. Annabelle let a tingle of the confidence she felt in her lab coat when she ran through the checklist, recalibrating a piece of technology so advanced most people didn't believe it existed, run through her. Annabelle knew if she worked as hard as she had worked to become a robotics engineer that she could feel that same confidence as a mom, as a homemaker, and as a gardener.

The task was finished. She had filled four trays with seeds. She carried them inside one by one. The best place she could find to set them was on her dresser in front of the window overlooking the porch. She cleared her family photos off the top, sliding them in a pile into her underwear drawer. It was strange to see the containers of dirt in her bedroom, a space she tried to keep as clean and free from projects as possible. But here the seedlings could be warmed by the sun without getting any direct rays. It would have to do.

Annabelle ducked into the bathroom. Dirt smudged her cheek and the clips holding her hair had loosened, allowing strands to hang down. She washed her hands watching the black water slosh in the basin. She had come a long way from her sterile robotics lab.

"Do you guys want some lunch?" Annabelle called to the six kids from the porch steps.

The kids held a conference.

"Okay," one yelled back.

Annabelle prepared three boxes of macaroni and cheese and washed a bunch of grapes. She pulled seven plates down from the cupboard and seven forks from the drawer. Annabelle considered what it would be like to have a huge family—hand-me-downs, raucous Christmas mornings, constant companions for Heath, and having to buy the eighteen-egg carton at the supermarket. She divvied the food on the plates, giving herself a few tongs of pre-made bagged salad instead of the grapes, and called the kids inside.

Recognizing the storybook nature of seven people, when she handed each child their plate, she gave them a dwarf name from *Snow White*.

"Here you are, Doc," she told Harley.

"Bashful."

"Take a fork, Sleepy."

She got to "Dopey" before realizing these names were not very complimentary, but she continued because the kids were finding this hilarious. The dining table only sat four, so they ate in a circle on the rug. The hilarity continued through the meal. They teased the angelic-looking boy with long blonde eyelashes that Annabelle had ineptly designated Dopey. She tried to rename them all based on Santa's reindeer, but they weren't having it.

They ate with their fingers sending elbows of pasta and escaped grapes across the carpet. As one unit, they set down their plates, said, "Thank you, Ms. Granger," and headed for the door, Heath with them.

"Heath, wait," Annabelle said.

Heath turned around dejected. He knew he was supposed to take his plate to the sink, but that is not why she had stopped him.

"Are you having fun?" she asked, giving him a thumbs up.

As an answer, Heath ran to her and hugged her legs. Before she could tear up, he was back outside.

The twin boy, the one she had dubbed Sneezy, popped his head inside as Annabelle crawled on the rug to collect the plates and forks.

"Why was the macaroni and cheese white?" he asked her.

"Oh, that's just what color the cheese is."

"You're not trying to poison us?"

"No. Why would I poison you?"

"Okay," he yelled over his shoulder, already returning to the rope swing.

The kids were odd. Maybe even troublemakers. They ran wild. Annabelle saw the looks that passed between them during lunch, like they were hiding something. Like Annabelle was the fuddy-duddy not in on the joke.

She remembered the games of her childhood. One of her best girl-friends had a treehouse. It was in the woods next to the putting green on Hole Eleven. They used to shout into the backswing of the golfers and then hide on the floor of the treehouse. Her friend's mom would bring Kool-Aid and Fruit Roll-Ups. So much sugar, Annabelle thought. Was there even any fruit in those roll-ups? They would lower a bucket from the treehouse for the snacks and haul them up. During those days, parents were food dispensers and temporary obstacles, not hall monitors. Perhaps kids felt the same way here.

After lunch, Annabelle went to her garden with her home harvest book and her phone. Using these, she identified kale and the tops of carrots and radishes. The food growing in the earth felt like a blessed bounty left to her from the home's previous owners, like a welcome basket.

There hadn't been any rain since they arrived. The soil had been dark and moist when she removed the leaves the other day and now it was hard and dry.

She flipped open the control panel for the drip system drilled into the stucco of her house. She turned it on and navigated the interface to learn there were three zones with timers already set. She set the dial to manual watering and waited. Nothing happened. She listened for the sound of water and looked for a break in the black tubing. No water. She punched a few more buttons on the control panel, but no water came.

The water to the drip system must be turned off for winter. Annabelle headed to the well house. It was a concrete cylinder in the ground where the well head and pressure tank were located down below the frost line. She lifted the heavy steel lid and shoved it aside, leaving a gap large enough for her to climb down the integrated ladder.

A flashlight lived on top of a breaker box next to the ladder. She turned it on and swung the beam around. A dense spiderweb on the pressure tank held a huge black spider with the ominous red tattoo of a black widow. The bite could be very dangerous, but this spider looked dead.

Annabelle found a small green petcock labeled in black sharpie with "Drip System." She turned it and water sprayed the leg of her jeans and her shoe. She shrieked and closed the petcock. The water had come from a brass spigot, the pipe drain.

"Of course," she chastised herself.

Many footsteps approached the well house as she spun the spigot closed. Six heads looked down at her, blocking out the daylight.

"We're going to the river," Harley shouted. The sound reverberated off the steel lid and around the well house walls. Annabelle winced.

"Have fun. Heath, stay here. I'll be right up."

The heads withdrew and Annabelle heard them whispering. She felt suddenly vulnerable—alone down in the well with Paul not expected home until tomorrow and her phone left in the garden.

The whispering stopped. The heavy steel lid of the well house shifted.

"No, no," Annabelle cried. "Leave that. I'm coming out."

The six heads appeared again. As she peered up at them, she tried to look stern and parental, but the optics were wrong.

"The six of us are going to the river," Harley said with finality. The faces disappeared, including Heath's, and the footsteps retreated.

Annabelle clambered up the ladder and out of the well house in time to see the last head disappear down the arroyo.

# 24

ANNABELLE'S INSTINCT WAS TO JUMP IN HER CAR AND CUT OFF THE KIDS before they reached the river. She would scold them and scold Heath. He knew better than to walk off without her permission.

But before she retrieved her car keys, her temper had cooled. Heath was having fun with friends. They weren't going far, and he was attended by a girl whom—how old was Harley? Eleven?—Annabelle might have paid to watch Heath while she ran a quick errand. If she caught up to the six kids and made a big fuss about supervision from parents, they might never include Heath again. It was important that she nurture his relationship with these kids. They would get him talking, get him playing, pull him out of his head. It was a miracle that so many kids his age were nearby. And they accepted him.

Annabelle, in the dark moments before falling asleep, worried that Heath had become somehow marked by what happened to him. She feared that kids could tell from his solemn disposition and maybe something in his eyes that he no longer played with the same wild abandon that they did. What happened set him apart. This was silly.

She'd had irrational parenting fears before. One pernicious vision from Huntington Road was that the tigers would escape from the zoo.

During the day, the zoo leant a pleasant exoticism to the suburban neighborhood. But at night, Annabelle feared that an escaped tiger might lie in wait for them in the yews. One dark winter, upon returning home from work as she unclipped Heath from his seat, the hungry tiger would pounce on her back and dig in its claws. Prone on the driveway with the tiger chewing her innards, she would kick the car door closed, saving her son as her last act, even as her blood sprayed the windows.

Annabelle went inside. She wrung her hands and paced. It wasn't only that Heath was gone. It was that she no longer felt sure of her decisions. She had never lived in a neighborhood like this one. There were no playgrounds or after school programs. They'd been here five days, and she hadn't met any parents, no adults at all. She didn't know what she was supposed to do.

What were normal parenting standards around here? What about her parenting was evidence-based and what was culturally diffused folk knowledge she internalized through osmosis from the suburban parents around her? What was she willing to budge on and what principles would remain sacrosanct? She knew she couldn't ruin these nascent friendships for Heath with a groundless insistence on a parenting modality out of step with the locals.

When she saw the river, more dribble than rapid, with Heath yesterday, she had relaxed. The Box Elder parents didn't seem as lax and foreign as it first appeared. While the terminology and geography were different, sending your kids to play at this river after school was not much different from sending them to play at the playground down the block in Royal Oak. Of course, she didn't know any parents who sent their five-year-olds to go play at the playground by themselves in Royal Oak. That's what the benches were for, so the parents could sit and stare at their phones and supervise their children. What would Donna say if she knew Heath was at the river while Annabelle sat at home? Donna, who literally kept Stu on a short leash when he was three.

Annabelle considered asking Di, the most practical mom she knew. Di's last message to Annabelle had read, "Haven't heard from you. Did *The Crazies* getcha?" with a gore-covered pitchfork still from the movie. If Annabelle told her that Heath was unsupervised at the river, Di would be positive the crazed locals had gotten to her.

Per her usual self-soothing MO, Annabelle found herself at her computer. Here she learned about free-range parenting. The name came from the practice of allowing farm animals to roam in a wide area, choose their own food, and spend their time engaging in the range of behaviors fundamental to their species. The theory is that free-ranged animals, human children included, are healthier than their cooped up counterparts.

Annabelle didn't care for the comparison of her child to livestock and her role as rancher instead of parent, but the concept validated her current parenting choice. She could tell Donna it was a new theory she was trying.

As a free-range parent, she would encourage her child to develop independence by limiting her supervision. The evangelist for the movement contended that kids need opportunities to stretch and grow and that free-ranging encourages personality formation and builds confidence. Annabelle read article after article until she felt that she had stumbled upon her new parenting ethos.

She and Paul should allow Heath to play with his friends unsupervised. What he needed were boundaries and a set of skills to help him navigate the world on his own. She could teach him those skills. She liked this new vision of herself, not a hovering helicopter but a trainer for an unknown world. She would be like NASA preparing an astronaut for space.

While Annabelle now felt that she could validate her decision to let Heath go, it did not make Heath's absence any easier to bear. She worried. Had they gone to play in the branch of the river that she and Heath had seen? Was there another tributary with rushing rapids and slippery boulders? What about the aggressive bulldog? They had not given her the opportunity to prep Heath for what might happen. Her only solace was that, as Heath had said about Maud, the other kids were born here. This was not their first trip to the river by themselves.

Annabelle returned to the well house to finish what she started: turn on the water to the drip system. When finished, she was careful to haul on the steel lid until it thudded in place. The well house could be a dangerous place for kids to play. She couldn't imagine the horror of being trapped in the earth in the dark.

The rest of the afternoon, Annabelle was incapable of performing any tasks. She paced at the window, praying, and waiting for Heath's red hair to appear out of the arroyo. When his head did appear, accompanied by the rest of the kids, she allowed herself a moment of tearful relief and silent thanks before opening the door. The kids boosted Heath up the side of the arroyo and then returned in a chattering rabble back down the wash.

"Hi Mom," Heath said, climbing the porch steps. He sat at her feet pulling off his shoes on the welcome mat. Annabelle just stared at him. He was coated head to feet in mud.

## 25

ANNABELLE CARRIED HEATH STRAIGHT TO THE BATH. WHILE HE WAS still dressed, she hosed him off with the showerhead, which he found hysterical. She stripped him and left him with the tub filling to put his filthy clothes in the wash. His outfit would get its own load.

While she shampooed his hair and washed the mud from his ears, she asked him about his afternoon. Where did they go? What did they do? Was there anyone else with them? Did they see anyone? Were there mean dogs or raging rapids?

He answered satisfactorily, but he sure didn't seem like the brazen child who walked off while his mom shouted, "No," from a well house. He adopted a desultory attitude as he loaded his floating car ferry. She couldn't get another smile out of him until she got out the shower head.

"Front side, whoop-dupe," she sang, hosing off the muddy bathwater. "Back side, whoop-dupe."

It wasn't until after dinner, when Heath was in his jammies cuddled on her lap with his two pre-bedtime books, that Annabelle felt ready to confront him.

"Heath, you know that you shouldn't have left with those kids today. I told you no, and you left anyway. That is terrible behavior. I didn't want you to go because I thought it would be dangerous. I am trying to protect you."

Heath nodded.

"But I also want to tell you I am proud of you. You have done a great job making friends here. And going to play at the river without an adult is a sign to me you are growing up."

She shifted him on her lap so he faced her.

"I want you to play with your friends at the river, but there are some ground rules. I need to know that I can trust you to follow the rules. Okay?"

"Okay," Heath said.

"You must only go to play at the river where I can find you. You can't go anywhere else, not even to the other kids' houses. If they want to go, you come back home. Right away. You come home the way Maud showed us. I need to always be able to find you."

"Okay, Mom," Heath said. His eyes twinkled.

Annabelle filled with pride. Her son would become a confident, problem-solving, independent little boy. He would escape the helicopter-dependent fate of his cohort back in Royal Oak.

"Are you going to tell me now how you got to be so muddy while building a fort?" Annabelle asked casual and relaxed now that she had handled her parenting business.

"They wanted me to show them what the dead guy looked like when I found him. Harley said I should keep still with my face down in the mud."

"Heath!" Annabelle said, covering her mouth in horror.

She recovered. As she read to him about each little pig being huffed and puffed until it was as dead as a doornail, she debated what to do. She had just granted permission to spend time with those kids and congratulated his ability to make friends with them. She couldn't retract it like she had the dog feeding responsibilities. They were being curious. They were being kids. Death is fascinating to them. She decided not to say anything about his dead guy mime. If she didn't make a big deal of it, he wouldn't think it was a big deal.

As she read, she breathed in his little boy smell. It was now tinged with sulfur, decay, and stagnant water. He smelled like mud.

## 26

HEATH CHASED ANNABELLE THROUGH THE HOUSE WIELDING A chainsaw. It was a child-sized battery-operated toy chainsaw, but it made the noise and the chain really spun. His Aunt Gwen had given it to Heath as a going away present figuring all the other country kids would have been gifted a real version upon birth.

Heath initiated this game by starting up the chainsaw against her leg while she cleaned up from breakfast. It startled her and he ordered, "Run."

Annabelle obliged trying to work out the lasting damage of encouraging her son to role-play Leatherface. Annabelle shrieked and threw up her hands like a scream queen as she ran around the kitchen table and toward the bedrooms. She ducked into the bathroom and hid behind the shower curtain holding her breath while Heath looked for her.

Annabelle huffed the bangs off her forehead and checked the time. She couldn't believe she was three days in to being a stay-at-home mom and was already sick of playing with her child. She couldn't wait for the kids to come this afternoon and take him away.

Something had dislodged in Annabelle. It was like an oil well leaking deep under the ocean. She was gushing with a new desire. It felt dangerous and destructive and she knew that all the oil men in Texas would be unable to cap it. It was a desire, a need, to produce. To build. To create. To grow.

Maybe it was just the urgency of her desire, but it felt darker than all her action verbs could convey. Annabelle felt an awakening, daylight shining through the opening door of her prison cell. She was being so dramatic. It's not like her life in Royal Oak or before that with Paul in school had been full of suffering. She had always been free to make her own choices, but she had chosen wrongly.

Why had she stopped painting? She had been an artist for as long as she could remember. Long after her friends traded in their markers and crayons for play kitchens and bikes with banana seats and later gossip and R-rated movies, Annabelle enjoyed creating art in her basement. She drew with pen and ink and charcoal.

She learned to burn wood. Once she had honed her skill, she personalized everyone's headboard in her family. On her father's side of the bed, she burned in the Murray family crest. When her parents' bed became too loose and wobbly, her father sawed out her design using a tool borrowed from a much handier neighbor, re-varnished it, and kept it on his dresser.

She spent a lucrative year beading jewelry. Her creations were popular with the girls in school and with her mom's friends. She made more money that summer selling her elaborate necklaces and flirty ankle bracelets than she would have babysitting or scooping ice cream cones.

But painting was always her favored form of expression. Her high school art teacher nurtured her talent and encouraged her to approach her work with seriousness. Art classes weren't only for the kids who couldn't hack it in Calculus I. Artists through history had always been intellectuals and Annabelle's realistic style required study and mathematical precision the same as da Vinci dissecting corpses. Like da Vinci, she applied the same diligence to her life drawing class as she did to her study of geometry. And it was in doing this that she found her talent and love for period portraiture.

But while at college something changed. She convinced herself that there was no money in art and that she had to train for a "serious" profession. The customary suburban lifestyle—the house, the husband, the kids—couldn't be stumbled into or fallen back on if the dream didn't work out, but had to be snatched and secured early if it was ever to be. She and her classmates used studying, networking, and interning to battle their way to affordable housing, an income-earning spouse, and the kind of life absent of the disasters large and small that stem from poor youthful decision-making. She bent herself for years to a personality-destroying and prosaic goal. And that meant, after her senior year of college, when her work reached an apex of technique and artistry, she quit painting.

The shower curtain whipped open startling Annabelle from her thoughts. Heath roared like a lion and started his chainsaw. Annabelle stepped out of the tub using Heath's head to steady herself.

"You caught me," she said.

Annabelle checked the time again. She was formulating a plan.

At lunchtime, Heath left with the kids for the river, this time with her blessing and silent thanks. Annabelle would use her period of solitude this afternoon and all future afternoons to fashion herself as a homesteading guru on Instagram.

She had originally signed up for the app out of peer pressure. She followed her friends, liking and commenting out of politeness, not real interest. Her usage had been as a consumer of content rather than a producer.

Her feed transitioned in step with her life. Originally, she followed accounts with photos featuring well-designed living rooms, trends in tailored but casual women's work wear, or popular non-fiction books. Over time, the interior design feeds morphed into ones featuring decorated nurseries and ridiculously expensive designer clothes for infants. Soon after her discouraging visit to Dr. Swarnavishan's office, where the only thing implanted in her was a desire to move far away, Annabelle stopped following the baby topics and began filling her stream with homesteading and gardening photos.

Annabelle envisioned her new persona as a cross between Lynette Jennings with her lovely nails and ever-ready hot glue gun and early

Martha Stewart when she harvested produce for the cameras from her farm in Bedford before the incarceration and friendship with Snoop Dogg.

Using tips from myriad blogs and YouTube videos, she optimized her bio photo, profile, and highlights. She was branding herself @Annabellwether. Rather clever, she thought. She hoped to be a bell-wether for other disillusioned suburbanites who wanted the virtuous rural existence. She could show them how it was done.

Her profile read, "Greenhorn green thumb prescribing clean country living for what ails you," accompanied by a smattering of vegetable emojis. She also listed herself as a robotics engineer with a robot head emoji and an oil painter with a palette emoji. People needed to know she had credentials, and that she walked away from something real when her family moved from Royal Oak. Her photos would support her theme, showing how she creates a healthier life for her family every day.

Crafting this brand for Instagram would make her foray into the domestic arts seem more substantial. Annabelle knew it was a poor substitute for fine art and robotics, but it was a realistic way to earn back her confidence. It was a place to channel her gushing oil before the rainbow slick choked out those around her.

## 27

IT WAS UNFORTUNATE THAT HEATH HAD NOT YET RETURNED FROM THE river when Paul pulled into the driveway that Friday afternoon. When she greeted Paul alone, he demanded to know where his five-year-old was. It was a poor introduction to her new parenting philosophy. *Do you recall those kids you thought were creepy our first night here? Heath is out playing with them. By himself.*

Paul wanted to get in the car and find Heath. He thought his return home warranted interrupting his son's playtime, embarrassing him in front of his new friends. Annabelle considered forestalling this plan by saying she wasn't sure where he was, but that wouldn't sound good. But if she said she knew where he was, at the river, and they drove there and didn't find him, that wouldn't help her cause either.

While Paul paced in front of his books, Annabelle tried to explain the principles of free-range parenting. She empathized with his anxiety because she had felt it acutely too only the day before. But Heath had returned home in one piece. Her experiment had worked.

"If you had only seen him, Paul. He was so proud of himself. He glowed with pride and accomplishment."

This wasn't strictly true. Heath had returned home subdued, even for him. But he was relieved to have escaped punishment and ecstatic that she granted permission for him to go play again. Annabelle knew from reading online the benefits that would accrue from this approach, so she embellished and elided a bit.

Paul wasn't buying it.

"I realize that we moved away from Royal Oak in part to escape the endemic pressure to parent like jail keepers and maybe I am over-reacting because I've missed the past few days here, but what you're calling free-range sounds to me like laissez-faire parenting. Let me finish." He held up a finger. "The difference between laissez-faire and free-range is in the preparation. Heath didn't work up to spending the afternoon alone with his friends; he just went. This wasn't measured and gradual. We haven't increased his capabilities with smaller oppor-tunities for independence and responsibility. You just sent him out into an unfamiliar environment with your fingers crossed."

"You're not giving me enough credit," Annabelle protested. "Heath and I walked together to where the kids play. We established rules. He can't go anywhere else between here and there. He knows we are trusting him to be responsible. And it is not like he is doing this all by himself. He is with other kids that know what they are doing."

"All right. I'm sorry for questioning you." Annabelle snuggled into Paul's chest for a hug. "I can't wait to see our independent five-year-old," he said. "When is he due home?"

Annabelle hid her face in his cashmere sweater. "Yesterday, he got home just before five."

Paul pushed Annabelle away to look at her face.

"You don't have a rule for how long he can be out?"

Annabelle shook her head. She'd just lost whatever credit she had won.

When Heath returned—just before five—filthy and happy, hungry and tired, Paul handled bath time. Father and son had only been chatting in the bathroom for a few seconds when Annabelle heard Paul call her name.

"What is this?" Paul asked her when she entered the bathroom. He displayed a huge tattoo across Heath's bare chest. It shocked Annabelle to see a skull inked in black, but she suppressed her surprise.

"Wow, honey," she said to Heath. "Where did you get that? What is it?"

"The symbol for The Six. It's a skull."

It was a rudimentary drawing of a long forehead with six eye sockets and grinning teeth. The skull was drawn in black sharpie.

"Did everyone get this drawn on them?"

"Yes. Josefina didn't want to lift her shirt, so hers is on her arm. And Harley drew hers on her palm."

"Why are you called The Six?"

"Because there are six of us, Mom."

"So it's like a club?"

"Yeah. We're in a gang."

The tattoo wouldn't bother her if it weren't for the fact that it upset Paul. She remembered doodling in blue pen on her thigh under her desk when she was in school. Was this so different? They weren't indelible tattoos meant to last. Paul had scrubbed away all but the faintest outline with soap and a washcloth. And Annabelle liked that they called themselves The Six. It meant they were intending to continue to include Heath.

Over dinner, Annabelle could sense Paul's frustration. This was not the homecoming meal she had planned. Instead of talking as a family, Paul regaled Heath with the story of his ride on a San Francisco trolley. So that is where he had been for work the last few days. Annabelle, quiet and excluded, sliced her broccoli into smaller and smaller pieces so she wouldn't be the first to finish eating.

In anticipation of Paul's arrival, she had baked bread that afternoon. It was a real hand-kneaded loaf set to rise three times in the sunny deep windowsill in the living room and baked in a loaf pan in the oven. She was trying to outgrow her bread machine and increase the authenticity of her homesteading skills.

She had imagined Paul's impressed expression when he beheld her golden brown herbed loaf. It included fresh thyme Annabelle had identified and harvested from their garden and was crusted with sea salt. The loaf was still warm inside when Annabelle cut into it at the dinner table.

Paul praised the bread, but Annabelle didn't swell with pride in the way she was expecting. The Instagram comments had been much more encouraging.

As soon as Heath was in bed, Paul started grilling her again.

"Who are these kids he is hanging out with?"

"The oldest kid is Harley. She is twelve or thirteen," Annabelle explained, increasing Harley's age a few years to decrease her own feeling of culpability.

"There is a little guy that just turned five," she continued. "He's not in school yet. The other three are in kindergarten now. Two of them are brother and sister, twins. They all meet up when the morning kindergarten gets out."

"Let me get this right. Heath is playing with three classmates he would have had if you had put him back in school." Annabelle winced at this. Of course, genius Paul wouldn't miss this point. "And a pre-schooler that will be his classmate next year."

"Yes."

"And a teenager, unrelated to any of them, spends her time with them instead of kids her own age, and draws skull tattoos on their chests?"

"She's not a teenager. She's a little girl," Annabelle corrected her previous statement now that it was no longer suiting her argument. "Harley looks like she's ten."

"Where are their parents? Is she watching them while they're at work? And why isn't this maybe ten- maybe thirteen-year-old in school?"

Annabelle didn't have any good answers for his questions.

## 28

DAN QUINTANA


Delfina and I are raising Harley, our granddaughter, because our daughter, Dinah, died alone on her couch three doors down from us of a heroin overdose.

We knew that Dinah had used heroin. She started when her husband Trey began his lineman's work. He brought it home to her. About six months into Trey's new job, they moved back to Box Elder into the trailer on Robert Baranowski's property. We were so glad to have Dinah back in Box Elder that we didn't ask the right questions. Why, if Trey is making so much more money, do you need to sell your house? Why is the trailer all you can afford? Why do you want Harley to sleep over with us on the weekends? We were naïve. No, we put our heads in the sand and refused to see what was happening. And when it became obvious, we were too frightened and ashamed to confront her.

We allowed it to happen, her addiction. Harley was getting to school. She was a quick-witted, sassy little girl, just like her mother had been at that age. Dinah made it look like everything was all right. And we believed that it was.

There were signs, though. She had changed. Dinah put up a wall between us. She needed us more than ever to take care of Harley after school, to get groceries, or drive Harley to a doctor's appointment. But she also kept us at arm's length. We attributed her need for constant help to the fact that her husband was often away, and her standoffishness to the fact that she was a grown woman trying to assert her independence. We told ourselves they were a normal, happy family.

Early one morning a neighbor, it was Pat actually, called us to see if Dinah and Harley were okay. I didn't know what he was talking about. He said there'd been a police car and an ambulance at Trey and Dinah's trailer in the middle of the night. Delfina and I slept right through the commotion.

We ran over right away. I was still wearing my pajama pants and slippers. We tried the door. It was locked. We knocked, but no one answered. Trey's car was gone, but Dinah's was there. We guessed the ambulance had taken away Dinah or Harley and Trey followed in his car. In our rush to get to them, we had forgotten our cellphones and the spare key to their trailer. I sent Delfina home to get them. I'm glad I did.

I peered through the window in the door and saw that the trailer was a mess. The dining room table lay on its side, the kitchen countertops were bare and their usual contents littered the kitchen floor, some curtains dangled off snapped rods. For the first time, I noticed that the wooden railing for the porch I was standing on was askew, broken, and splintered. I moved to a side window. Through it I saw my daughter in her robe lying on her side on the couch. Her eyes were open and staring. I could also see Harley standing in the hallway leading back to the bedrooms. She was dressed for school, but she was heaving tears and they had darkened the front of her shirt.

Harley was maybe eight. I hadn't seen her cry in years. I waved to catch her eye, but her mother on the couch absorbed her attention. It was in this moment I realized that Dinah was dead. Somehow the ambulance had missed her, gone to the wrong house. I began to pray for her. But then Dinah moved. Still slumped, she brought her phone to her ear.

With her mom occupied, Harley ran for the door and unlocked it. I rushed to meet her there. She clung to me. I'll tell you I was frozen. I was struggling to catch up with what happened, to recalculate my daughter and her family as people who would find themselves in a broken scene like this. Harley sobbed into the Colorado Rockies shirt that I sleep in. She said, "I'm going to be late for school."

It couldn't have been later than six thirty in the morning. There was plenty of time for Harley to catch the bus at eight fifteen, but her specific concern seemed like something I could fix.

"Let's get you ready for school," I said, crossing the threshold into the bedlam. "Is your dad home?" Harley shook her head and her lip quivered, but she had stopped crying. "I'll make your breakfast. Do you still like Fruity Pebbles?" She nodded. "You go change into a clean shirt."

I could tell it was Delfina that Dinah was talking to on the phone. My wife must have called her daughter as soon as she got home. Thank the Lord she did. I think if I had stood peering through that window at Dinah on the couch, thinking her dead, a moment longer, the shock might have done something to my heart. We didn't need anymore emergencies that morning.

I righted the dining room table. The legs were still sturdy. I tucked in the chairs. This would be Harley's island of normalcy until we could get the rest squared away. Some things are easier to right than others.

The small miracle of the morning was that the box of Fruity Pebbles remained upright on top of the fridge while the other varieties of cereal crunched underfoot in the kitchen. I prepared Harley's bowl and set it and a spoon on the table. I poured a glass of orange juice into a plastic Donald Duck glass. I placed everything in an orderly fashion at right angles. Finding Harley's backpack in the corner, I placed it on the chair next to her place setting.

She returned in a new t-shirt that in a golden cursive script read,

"Diva, no autographs please." She had added a bow clip to her hair. Harley was trying as hard as I was to make this a normal morning. I fried an egg for her. I am lost in the kitchen as Delfina is a great cook, but I could fry an egg. I continued a round of cheerful banter as Harley ate, trying to drown out the sound of her mother sobbing into the phone.

Through my banter, I could still hear some of what Dinah was saying. There had been a fight and Trey had left her. He'd left her for another woman and he wasn't going to be coming back.

Delfina arrived at the door still talking to Dinah on her phone. She saw that I had Harley under control and ran to Dinah. She pulled her up to sitting and hugged her. Dinah's head lolled back, and I considered for the first time that she was not a sober woman. I'll admit I felt a little disgusted with her, falling apart like this when her daughter needed her. But then Delfina took Dinah's chin in her hand and turned her head to the side. A blood-crusted welt followed her jawline and ended with a purple gash on her brow that had been clipped together with a butterfly bandage.

I felt an anger flare in me I had never known. While Delfina examined and accepted her daughter's injury, my fists balled and my jaw clenched. I had stopped breathing. I thought for the second time that morning of my heart.

"Harley and I are going for a walk," I declared. Delfina nodded at me over her shoulder as she walked Dinah back to take a shower.

We set out, I in my slippers, with more than an hour until the bus would arrive to take Harley to school. I held her backpack in one hand and her forearm in my other. We'd traveled a ways before I realized that I had been talking to myself and that I was walking so fast that Harley had jogged beside me. I released her and let her catch her breath.

We were in front of the cemetery. I don't know if seeing my daughter lying there with glazed eyes or knowing what I wanted to do to Trey led us there. If I had been thinking, we would have turned the other way out of the drive and gone toward the river or into the scrubland to throw stones and talk. Out this way, the only place to get off the road was at the cemetery. So I opened the gate, and we walked around crunching on the dry grass and commenting on the headstones.

I knew many of the people buried there, or at least their families, but Harley didn't. She read their names, looked for the oldest birth-date, and cleaned weeds away. She admired the statue of a sleeping lamb placed by the Garcias when their infant son died.

I waited for some explanatory words to come to me, something I could say to help her understand that it would be okay. But I was too confused myself to say anything and Harley was carrying on like nothing had happened. When it was time, we turned back, stopping at the top of her driveway.

I heard the school bus rumbling down the street. I knew Harley hated when anyone waited with her, so I said my goodbyes to her then. I told her she was a brave little girl and that she shouldn't worry, that Abuelita and Abuelo would be there when the bus dropped her off after school. I considered that maybe we should have kept her home from school that day. I thought maybe Delfina could do what I couldn't—explain that last night had been an anomaly and everything would be okay. But Harley seemed eager to be gone from the scene and I couldn't blame her.

That morning, while Dinah slept, Delfina and I cleaned up the trailer. Delfina told me what she had learned. Trey had started drinking a lot lately. He was drinking last night. He got riled up and admitted to Dinah that there was someone else in his life and that the woman was pregnant. They had an explosive fight and Dinah started breaking things and demanding that he leave. He hit her across the face with a bottle of whiskey.

"She thinks it knocked her unconscious," Delfina said. "But she doesn't remember. She told me that Harley slept through the whole thing, but then she admitted that she didn't remember calling 911. It might have been Harley who called. The next thing she knew the police and EMTs were there and Trey had left. She doesn't think we'll ever see him again."

If only that had been the case. Trey was in and out of their lives for a year, a long miserable year during which the police were called again, multiple times to the trailer. But finally, he left for good. It was just Dinah and Harley. And it was then that Dinah told us what we should have already known. She was addicted to heroin. She told us she wanted to stop, and she needed help. With Trey gone for good, she also needed our financial support. We were happy to give her both. That was when we began the phase of our lives centered on Dinah's recovery.

We went with her on a few trips to a drug counselor in Santa Fe. It was the counselor who told us the story of heroin addiction, the story Dinah had always been too ashamed to tell us. He was the one able to explain to us the part of our daughter's life we'd been unable to understand for years.

He told us that Dinah began snorting heroin when Trey would bring it home from his work trips. Trey convinced her heroin wasn't a big deal, and when she tried it, she agreed. They would snort heroin after Harley was in bed and it would make them feel calm and happy. And she wouldn't wake up hungover like from a night of drinking; she would feel happy in the morning too. She thought of heroin as a helper drug. It helped her be a supportive wife and a better mom.

Dinah was one of the few able to maintain a casual relationship with the drug for years, even in the face of Trey's increasing dependency. Trey moved to injecting heroin and began to spend large amounts of money to sustain his habit. His addiction embarrassed her, especially when it meant that they could no longer afford their house in Mountain View. It happened too quickly for her to take precautions; she was always at the mercy of his need for the drug. As long as he could shoot heroin, he was tranquil and loving. She convinced herself it wasn't a problem.

Initially, Dinah refused to inject heroin and ratcheted back her usage when she felt herself habituating. But she knew the checked-out bliss Trey was aiming for and she wanted it too. Heroin bestowed upon her unearned happiness and allowed her to maintain an easy harmony with her husband. She could manage because she wanted a copacetic life for her and her family more than she wanted the heroin.

But when she began to mistrust Trey and their relationship became hostile, she turned to heroin as self-medication. The disconnected pleasure of the drug was better than anything she could feel without it. As she became more ashamed and afraid in her life, she began to only feel like herself when she injected heroin. It was only heroin that could give her beautiful, shining thoughts and replace her constant fear of impending doom with a warm safety. It was heroin that made life worth living. The rest of the time, she was just waiting until she could use it again.

Accepting our daughter's heroin abuse was a difficult adjustment for Delfina and me. It was hard to know that our Dinah looked at her beautiful daughter and chose heroin instead. It was hard to see her as an addict. We felt guilt, wondering where it had all gone wrong, but we also felt hope, believing the worst was behind us. Dinah got a job at the grocery store and she attended her Chemical Dependency Anonymous meetings with fervor. She was even helping a teen girl to recover.

Dinah and Harley came over for dinner a few nights a week, and we helped Harley with homework and watched movies with her other nights when her mother went out on dates. We encouraged Dinah's dating. We thought if she could find a good husband and father for Harley, it would bring stability to her recovery.

Those nights, we'd send Harley home on her own to get to bed. It wasn't a far walk, and she was plenty old enough to be at home a few hours until her mom got in. What we didn't realize was that Dinah hadn't gone out that night, perhaps hadn't gone out any of the nights. Harley found her mom's dead body on the couch. She was cold and blue and had a needle in her arm.

# WEEK TWO

# 29

PAUL WANTED ANNABELLE TO MEET THE PARENTS OF THE SIX, BUT SHE wasn't sure how. The geography and fences and isolation and lack of gathering spaces made it tricky. And she was afraid of looking silly, like an outsider, like someone who didn't know what she was signing up for when she chose a rural life. She didn't want to reinforce any of their city-slicker stereotypes. She wanted to be knowing, local, authentic, trustworthy.

She was afraid to visit the school, lest an administrator try to enforce Heath's attendance and anyway parents didn't seem involved in the school or in pick up and drop off. A yellow school bus rattled down the main road twice a day for the unsupervised transmittal of the local kids. But Annabelle was determined to get acquainted with some Box Elder natives. The least she could do was introduce herself to their only next-door neighbor.

The road bordered their house on one side and the arroyo on another. Across the road was high desert scrubland, sagebrush, prickly pears, and whiptail lizards. Their longest property line bordered a farmer's field already sprouting with greens. Annabelle waved to the man on his tractor when he came to plough deep furrows in the earth, but that didn't leave much opportunity for socializing. The fourth

property line bordered a lot with a house. A tall wooden fence separated their properties. Annabelle frequently heard someone in the
yard on the other side of the fence as she labored in her garden.

The Grangers had never ventured past their own house to see
what lay at the end of their dead-end road. She had allowed the
mystery to continue for too long. Hearing the unknown homebody
talking on the other side of the fence—was she talking to a pet?—
Annabelle resolved to go meet her nearest neighbor.

Annabelle put away her gardening tools and washed her hands.
She changed out of her muddy sweatpants into something more
presentable. Instead of leaving immediately, Annabelle decided she
had better bring something. She couldn't show up uninvited and
empty-handed. She recalled Di Durham, the first neighbor she met on
Huntington Road. Di popped out from the shrubbery, blocking
Annabelle's exit from her garage after work one evening.

"You're coming with me," the woman said. "I know your husband
is out of town. Mine will be working in the city late tonight. It's the
perfect time for us to get to know each other."

Before Annabelle could text Paul or grab her purse, the woman
pulled Annabelle by the arm and shoved her through the gap in the
yews into her own backyard. If it had been anyone besides Di, a five-
foot tall pixie of a woman, her tone and gestures would have led
Annabelle to believe she was being kidnapped. Instead, Di offered her
a cushioned seat at a round table under a covered porch draped with
ivy. She had set the table with small round plates and a three-tiered
serving stand laden with exquisite treats.

"Drink?" she asked. Before even introducing herself, Di introduced
Annabelle to the Paloma, a pink refreshing tequila-based cocktail
made with grapefruit soda. It was Mexico's answer to the rum and
Coke.

Annabelle thought about her first meeting with Di as she stirred a
bowl of cookie dough with her wooden spoon. The gathering would
have been a high tea, except there were no finger sandwiches only
dessert and no tea only cocktails. The desserts on offer were tiny

beautiful squares of cake with a checkerboard pattern. Di called them Battenberg cakes. They looked complicated to create and Annabelle was impressed when Di revealed she made them herself.

"I'm an allergist and the office takes half-days on Mondays. I always spend the time off tackling a complicated recipe, but with Alex working late, I have no one to share these with," Di explained.

She and Annabelle spent many future husbandless evenings together, and they became mothers within three months of each other. It had all started with an almost magical first meeting on that otherwise lonely Monday. Today was a Monday. Annabelle couldn't help but see that as a good omen. Soon she would have a best girl-friend next door. She only had to take the initiative the way Di had when she kidnapped Annabelle from her garage.

When the cookies were ready, she loaded them on a paper plate. It wasn't Di's silver tray, but it would have to do. Before leaving, Annabelle ducked into the bathroom. She fluffed her hair and re-parted it in the way that covered most of the white. She practiced an affable smile in the mirror. It had been a while since she had tried to make friends. As she flipped off the lights and slipped on her shoes, she tried to contain her giddiness. It would be wonderful to have someone to talk to again.

Annabelle couldn't see her neighbor's house until she walked past the fence. It was a hovel. Cable and electric lines swooped in a low dangerous arc before attaching to the rusting tin roof. One portion of the house tilted ajar from the rest. Inside the doorless detached one-car garage that cantilevered to the left were garbage bags and furniture in a heap. A corrugated plastic roof in gray green covered the porch. Garbage and garbage bags were scattered across the porch and tumbled out into the yard. Two giant cats paced amongst the bottles, weed strewn appliances, and other detritus. An enormous woman in a floral muumuu sat in a metal chair on the porch with a puzzle book on a tray table in front of her.

Spotting Annabelle, the woman called to her, "Hello there!" but instead of stopping, Annabelle continued walking down the road with her plate of cookies held high in her hands. Annabelle looked straight ahead, pretending not to hear.

After avoiding the woman, Annabelle wasn't sure what to do. She couldn't return home past the woman's house bearing her cookies for no one, so she continued walking. She passed a chicken coop and a gated property lined with a barbed wire fence with a black dog on a chain monitoring her from the shade. There were no cars in the driveway.

She abandoned her pretense of delivering cookies to a neighbor and cut through an arroyo. Once hidden by the trees, Annabelle set down the plate in the sand and covered her cheeks. She was so ashamed of herself. Why couldn't she go meet her neighbor? How obvious had it been that Annabelle snubbed her? When had she become so judgmental and rude?

It was the shock of seeing the house. The neighbor was probably a perfectly nice woman who had a problem with hoarding. I've seen the shows, Annabelle told herself. She was psyching herself up to march back and introduce herself when she realized that some mud from the arroyo had intermingled with the cookies on the paper plate. Abandoning her resolve, she slunk down the wash to the main road, crouching below the bank so the woman on the porch wouldn't be able to see her retreat.

When she reached the road, ducking around the corner, she realized where she was. She could hear The Six playing in the trees at the edge of the river. The arroyo she had just walked down turned into the dirt road that led to the river. She squinted to see Heath and the other kids engrossed in a construction project. Three of the kids tilted a long smooth branch up against a tree trunk. It must be for a fort. The woman on the porch had a good, if distant, view of her child's favored play area.

Annabelle wondered if, while she worked in her garden listening to the sounds of the neighbor lady talking to her cats, the neighbor lady was watching her child playing. The woman probably didn't have much else to do.

## 30

THE TANTALIZING CERTAINTY THAT ANNABELLE WAS ONE CHANCE encounter away from befriending her mysterious neighbor evaporated when she had rounded the fence. Even if Annabelle could overcome the clear differences in how they kept home and all the associated values and backgrounds this implied, she could never recover from the shame of walking past the woman without a word based on looks alone. It was unforgivable and revealed something about Annabelle that she did not want to further examine. She wanted the whole experience behind her.

She slumped on her porch swing, the undelivered cookies beside her, and scrolled through Instagram hoping for a quick bit of affirmation. Her photo of the waxing moon rising above the neighbors' field had gotten more likes since the last time she checked.

Flicking through her feed, she sought refuge from the messy world. She absorbed the perfect photos of other people's lives: mist in a green field, a bee on a flower, a woman with a basket of rainbow-stalked chard on her hip, a child squatting next to a morel mushroom in a quiet wood, tea diffusing a rosy hue into a clear glass, a bed outdoors under a flower-covered bower with an asymmetrical blanket and an opened book.

Annabelle was drawn to the photos on Wanda Way's profile page. Wanda Way was a forty-something parvenu, a lifestyle vlogger and Instagram influencer sponsored by Anthropologie and Stila. Her brand, The Wanda Way, touted the benefits of simplistic, intentional living. She had iconic dyed gray hair. Her website focused on decluttering one's digital, financial, and domestic life. People called her the Oprah of Instagram.

Wanda used inspirational aphorisms and beautifully produced photos to draw people in to simplicity in food, design, and style. Wanda Way's photos evoked the idyllic country life that Annabelle thought she'd find in Box Elder.

It was easy to get lost in Wanda's world of casual glamour. Her grid was a cohesive, irresistible, soothing world where her house, wardrobe, and meals reflected her aesthetic. The lifestyle she presented looked authentic and livable, cozy even, but so perfect as to be unattainable. There would be no junk drawers, ratty underwear, or frozen pizzas in Wanda's world. She had escaped the entropy that plagued the lives of the ordinary woman.

In her latest Instagram story, Wanda smiled in front of a placid water feature she had installed in a corner of her yard. Two ducks floated on the pond behind her aviator-sunglassed face. The next photo showed giant orange and cow-dappled fish swimming beneath the surface. The third photo was of the pond at night. The fountain was lit purple and illuminated orbs in multiple colors floated on the surface. It looked like a scene out of a Disney movie. So that was how Wanda spent her day: installing a pond that by evening teemed with contented plant and animal life and augmented her photogenic existence.

Still scrolling on her phone, Annabelle absent-mindedly patted the top of Maud's head, then quickly retracted her hand. From the first time meeting Maud back in February when she barked at them as they approached with the realtor, Annabelle noticed that a black crust lined the dog's ears. She'd never been able to convince Maud inside the house, much less into the bath and the weather was too cold to hose her clean outdoors, but it was time something be done.

Annabelle googled. She diagnosed Maud with fly strike dermatitis. The black crust was Maud's dried blood. Flies had bitten the tips of her ears until they bled. The blood attracted more flies that laid eggs, which hatched into maggots. The maggots had chewed her flesh ragged. The cure was to wash her ears with warm water and apply an antibacterial ointment.

So that is what Annabelle did. With a basin of warm water and a tube of Neosporin, she sat next to Maud on the porch washing away the blood. Maud was very receptive to the treatment. She relaxed against Annabelle's leg and blinked back somnolent eyelids.

While Annabelle worked, she inspected the insides of Maud's ears. Something like coffee grounds were spilling out of them. Having applied the Neosporin, Annabelle moved from the floor to the porch swing to google this symptom. The Internet diagnosed Maud with ear mites. They were tiny arachnids that lived in the ears and caused intense itching. They also caused deafness. Is that why Maud couldn't hear? She read that the coffee grounds were mite poop. The mites could not spread to the ears of humans, but they could cause allergic reactions. Annabelle thought of Maud leaning against her thigh and felt grossed out. Maud continued her blissful stare on her couch cushion.

Annabelle could handle this too. The cure was to drop mineral oil down the dog's ear canals. Annabelle washed her hands. She rubbed her phone, on which she had been googling, with hand sanitizer. Then she went to her bathroom to find the tub of unguents she kept under the sink. She found rubbing alcohol, witch hazel, castor oil, hydrogen peroxide, and yes, mineral oil. It was a new, unopened bottle.

She returned to Maud. She didn't have an eye-dropper, so she pushed Maud on her side and poured some down one ear. Maud jerked and sat upright. The dog didn't care for this procedure. Annabelle pushed Maud to the other side and pinned her down. She poured again. Maud shook her head. Oil was everywhere, but Annabelle was confident she had gotten some down the ear canals.

Now she took each of Maud's ears in her hands and massaged. She looked into the dog's face. Maud's eyes went dreamy again. She nuzzled her head against Annabelle's hands. This was likely more physical affection than anyone had shown the dog in months, perhaps years.

With dirty mineral oil running down her hands and threatening to cross the boundary of her wrists to reach her forearm, Annabelle left Maud panting on her cushion. Once inside, she again washed her hands scrubbing to get every mite and mite poop off of her and down the drain forever. Nothing about this procedure or her dog were Instagram appropriate.

## 31

ANNABELLE CRAWLED ON HER STOMACH IN THE GARDEN TO PHOTOGRAPH her kale plants. She would clip the leaves to make chips for Heath. She could overlay the simple recipe in funky font on her photograph for her Instagram post.

As she zoomed, she spotted a cluster of gray bugs. Annabelle examined her kale. Aphids besieged each leaf sucking the sap from her plants. The insects were primally repulsive, a huddled infestation crawling on top of each other. They disgusted her.

In Royal Oak, her kale had always come in a bag and pre-washed. She wiped the bugs onto the concrete patio and then rolled a rock over them again and again to smash them into husks and honeydew. So much for respecting an insect's role in the biosphere. When she saw the extent of the infestation, she prepared for war.

In an instant, Annabelle renounced her previously untested commitment to nonviolence. She accepted now that to become a gardener was to relinquish the precepts of pacifism. A garden plot is a battleground taken by force from the surrounding environment. A gardener, fooling everyone in sunhat and cotton gloves, is a pitiless, calculating warrior.

Her gardening book recommended garlic and water in a spray

bottle as an effective deterrent for many garden pests. She chopped three cloves and doused her kale. Her targeted spray blew clusters of aphids from the leaves. One struggled on the ground. She waited for it to gasp a last poisoned breath. Instead, the aphid righted itself and started crawling.

Annabelle consulted her gardening book again. The organic insecticide recipe called for soaking the garlic overnight in mineral oil and adding Dawn dish soap. Annabelle dumped her solution down the drain and chopped the rest of her garlic bulb for soaking overnight. She knew she had the mineral oil from cleaning Maud's ears yesterday. That had been another project whose goal was the suffocation and extermination of mites. Annabelle was becoming quite the killer.

She staged a photo with an infested kale leaf next to her small glass bowl of soaking garlic. "I'm concocting my chemical weapon. The battle begins tomorrow." She typed her caption and posted to Instagram. While on the phone, she researched garden pest control. Even natural sprays like the garlic mixture deterred beneficial insects and pests alike.

She learned of another option; ladybugs eat aphids. Ladybugs, the familiar red bugs with black spots featured in children's books and on kitchen aprons, eat the pests of the garden without harming the plants. Far from the passive, delicate cartoon-version of themselves, ladybugs were skilled predators feared by the aphids. Annabelle ordered a bag of fifteen hundred live ladybugs to be sent to her house the next day. She was assembling her troops.

Ignoring the kale until her army of lady predators arrived, Annabelle focused on the weeds. Once she began watering her garden, the earth sprouted a sea of celadon plants opening arrowhead-shaped leaves low to the ground. Following her favored identification technique, she tasted a leaf. Edible. But something about the abundance of the plant and the gusto with which it sprang from the soil suggested to Annabelle that this was a weed not a crop. According to this cynical gardening heuristic, thriving, easy to care for plants are weeds and delicate divas requiring constant attention are the cultivars. A helpful soul in a New Mexico gardener's forum identified the plant in the photo she posted.

"That, dear, is lamb's quarter. The good news is that it belongs to the same family as spinach. You can sauté and eat the leaves. The bad news is that it will spread and grow like a weed. It will crowd out your other veggies if you don't remove it. Welcome to New Mexico."

Now that she knew it wouldn't kill her, Annabelle tasted a few more of the leaves. Not bad. Certainly less bitter than some of the lettuce varieties she was cultivating on purpose. But she wanted nothing to invade and threaten her garden.

Squatting between the rows of food, Annabelle pinched each individual plant just above the soil and tugged hoping to remove the root and prevent it from regrowing. She moved down each row targeting and removing only that species of plant from each square foot. As she heaped the wilted, lifeless plants onto her patio she considered herself on a mission of ethnic cleansing.

"More trouble than you're worth," she thought as she single-mindedly eliminated each plant. She snapped a picture of the pile for her Instagram. She captioned it, "The Lamb's Quarter Genocide is complete."

When she finished, her neck and left knee ached. Her body was still acclimating to the high altitude and to the repetitive squatting movements required of the gardener. There was no fitness class that could train one for the stooping required to tend the earth.

Annabelle googled for tips on garden ergonomics. She found several modified garden tools to support her natural wrist flexion and to avoid slouching, but none of them convinced her of their value. Just like the callouses that were forming across her palms, Annabelle figured her body would toughen up through experience. She would transform from new recruit to battle-hardened soldier.

In the meantime, she would have to care for herself. She took a moment to stand in Mountain pose. Finding her breath, she dove into her standing fold, tucking her fingers under her shoes in lieu of grabbing her big toes. She stepped out into Plank for just a moment before lifting into her Downward Dog. With her next exhale, she relaxed into the pose. The space between her shoulder blades expanded. The crown of her head hung toward the earth. She pressed her heels to the ground feeling a taut line run from her Achilles through her spine. She walked the Dog, alternately pressing each heel toward the ground. Feeling sprightly, she hopped her feet to meet her hands and felt the renewed flexibility in her forward fold. She rolled vertebrae by vertebrae up to standing, inhaling deeply and raising her arms above her head.

Looking dreamily at her weed-denuded garden, she brought her hands together in prayer position at her chest. Her fingertips reeked of garlic.

"Now, I am become Death, the destroyer of worlds," she thought, reciting her Gita.

# 32

---

HER GARDENING CRUSADE POSTS HAD NOT GARNERED THE LIKES FOR which Annabelle had hoped. But she was not deterred. She would share with her followers delights from her kitchen. The kitchen in Annabelle's new house was compact and efficient rather than spacious and glamorous like her kitchen on Huntington Road. The cabinets were painted a slate blue and the Corian countertop was brick red. The color combo highlighted the saddle-colored plaster walls. Annabelle traced an L on the floor as she moved from fridge to countertop to stove to sink.

Heath was due home from playing with The Six soon, but he could sit across from her at the breakfast bar drawing pictures for her while she measured, mixed, and frosted. She loved the new lexicon she was learning. Choux, meringue, and ganache replaced servos, actuators, and accelerometers. Now she proofed, tempered, and whipped instead of soldered, cast, and calibrated.

Annabelle looked out her kitchen window at her tiny orchard. The apricot trees were budding. Beautiful white blossoms covered them like a setting for a wedding magazine photo shoot. But it was still early May. Another hard freeze might come and kill those blossoms and ruin any chance of collecting apricots this season. If that happened, she would have to scratch her dreams for making apricot tarts, and apricot jam, and apricot salsa, and maybe an apricot drinking vinegar. Perhaps she could take photos of apricot goodies from the neighbors, if she ever met any, to show her followers the possibilities.

The neighbors would have apricots no matter what the weather held because they were clever enough to string the old-fashioned jumbo-bulbed Christmas lights on their budded fruit trees. The magical effect was not meant as decoration. Sunday had been Cinco de Mayo and usually Annabelle would have prepared for a co-worker's fiesta with guacamole, margaritas, and salted beer with lime. Guests would have worn sombreros with dangling colored poof balls. One might have donned a mustache pushing the cultural appropriation of the gathering from innocently festive to borderline racist. But now that she lived in a predominantly Hispanic area there hadn't been so much as a picado banner strung from a porch. The locals hadn't celebrated. Instead, they were stringing Christmas lights as a practical way to give the apricot trees enough heat on frosty spring nights to save the fruit. Annabelle's energy-saving LED three-mode outdoor lights would not suffice.

Annabelle got the feeling that everything she owned, every purchasing decision she'd made on the basis of health, environment, or corporate social responsibility was all a ruse. It was the ancient Christmas lights she'd needed all along.

As she gazed out the window, her fingers moved through the running tap water. She waited for it to get warm enough to activate the yeast. Her goal was to bake a perfect loaf of bread. The water turned hot, and she had to yank her fingers away. She wiped them on her apron and turned the tap back towards cold and tested the temperature again.

She had learned that yeast was a finicky organism. If the water was too hot or too cold, her bread would never rise. Her last loaf had been dense and doughy. Paul had sliced off an inch thick piece at dinner. He slathered the butter on and took a big bite. But his first bite was not followed by a second. How could he take another? With that kind of denseness, the one bite was like eating an entire loaf. It just expanded in your stomach. No, she would activate the yeast properly this time.

Her recipe was for a braided egg-bread sprinkled with sesame seeds. If she did this right, the photograph would be beautiful. The recipe directed that she activate her dry yeast with warm water. This was a very general instruction. Was warm water the temperature of one's wrist like when heating a baby bottle—98.6 degrees; the temperature in which one bathes—102 degrees; or the temperature for one's herbal tea—160 degrees? Strangely, the Internet had not reached a consensus on this point. If she summarized, water temperatures below 100 degrees would produce glutathione, which would make her braided egg-bread dough too sticky to knead. Water temperatures above 130 would kill the yeast. She filled her measuring cup adding cooler water until her thermometer read 115 degrees, the middle ground.

To prepare, Annabelle had studied YouTube videos of people making bread. The bakers measured or weighed their ingredients carefully, but after that it was all swagger and feel. They dumped their ingredients together, hugged the risen dough in their arms, and transferred it to a countertop to be shaped under a spray of flour tossed with panache like dice at a craps table.

Annabelle admired their craft. Watching people bake bread was soothing. They were very physical, shaping the bread with their hands, their sleeves rolled to the elbows. They were communing with a living organism attuning themselves to the rhythm of the rising dough where time itself was an ingredient. She thought she could be a good baker. It required a combination of precision and artistry, both traits in which she had been trained. She just needed to work on her technique.

From Dr. Watanabe, Annabelle learned more than just Japanese management techniques. She also learned the ikigai life philosophy. It was perhaps the lesson of this philosophy that had ruined her, made her unsuitable for her suburban life. Ikigai refers to one's sense of purpose. It is one's reason to live. It should be a central focus of a life well spent. Annabelle's life in Royal Oak had lost its purpose. Yes, she had had a wonderful husband and son, family close by, a nice home, comfort, and security. But having these things differed from ikigai.

Her life, the movement of her body, her intellect, and her spirit through the day had become something rote and programmed. When her alarm woke her up each morning, she formed a mental image of her to-do list and she executed those tasks for the rest of her waking hours. If there was joy, it was in executing those tasks with efficiency. At first she had believed that she was doing these things in service of her wonderful life. It was only recently that she began to realize she was executing these tasks instead of following her bliss, as Joseph Campbell would say. She was receiving no sense of fulfillment for all her bustling about.

As she kneaded her bread, rejecting the impulse to add more flour which would only toughen the final product, she contemplated her ikigai. Was she blossoming? Could a married mother blossom at thirty-six? She had taken a bold new direction with her life. She didn't miss work at all. What to make of that? Wasn't she supposed to be craving the intellectual stimulation of the workplace and the honest dignity of wage-earning? Isn't that what Paul foretold?

She did miss social stimulation. Annabelle had spent the last week profoundly lonely, and she wasn't sure how to remedy this. There were no apparent book groups, bootcamps in the park, volunteer opportunities, or even—and her mother-in-law would be so glad to hear of Annabelle's interest—junior leagues to join in Box Elder. She had checked. Once the next school year started, she hoped the gravity of the parenting social universe that revolved around the education of their children would pull her in.

The oven timer beeped. Annabelle pulled her hands, stuck with dough and frosted in flour, free from her nascent egg-bread. Keeping her hands up like a doctor prepped for surgery, she tapped on the oven light with her elbow. Her snickerdoodles looked ready. Disregarding the flour that was getting everywhere, she pulled out the cookie sheet and transferred each cookie onto the cooling rack. She wiped her hands on her pants and found her phone. She needed a picture of these for Instagram. The cookie tops sprinkled with fresh-grated cinnamon were riven with cracks that revealed the cooked dough below. So enticing.

Annabelle craved a witness to her work. It didn't feel real without a teacher, a professor, a supervisor, or a boss reviewing and evaluating how she spent her working hours. Over the weekend, Paul had appreciated her meals and praised her blossoming baking skills, but she could tell he didn't approve of how she spent her time. He fell in love with an intelligent, ambitious, talented career woman and this right turn into the domestic arts confused him.

Paul demonstrated a calculated coolness toward her efforts this weekend. He was trying to let Annabelle know that he and Heath did not require her to make them fresh bread to be happy. They would be happy with store-bought loaves and clothes wrinkly from being left in the dryer too long and cars running weeks past their oil change date, if Annabelle was doing something she found satisfying. Annabelle loved him for that. But still, she craved unadulterated enthusiasm for her efforts. She was finding it on her phone whenever a like, comment, or follow appeared.

# 33

On Wednesday, the ladybugs arrived in a white mesh bag. As instructed, Annabelle cut up cubes of sponge soaked in water and sealed them into the bag to help rehydrate the bugs. She was eager to release them and halt the devastation to her kale, but the instructions were clear: the bugs would fly away if released during daylight. They could be fooled into continued hibernation in their bag by keeping them cool. Heath handled the bag to look at the bugs before Annabelle tucked them in the fridge to await dusk.

The ladybugs intrigued Heath, so she turned them into a project they could work on together. They read about how to entice ladybugs to stay in the garden instead of flying away. Ladybugs need a house, something with lots of cracks and crevices for hiding out. While reading about the details of ladybug home construction, Annabelle also learned that lights at night attract beneficial insects. Attracting beneficial insects became the theme of their morning. It would help the garden and it would keep Heath occupied until The Six showed up.

Annabelle gathered the dozen dusty, tilted solar lights staked along their driveway, while she sent Heath to gather long sticks in an assortment of thicknesses to make into the ladybug house. She wiped her solar lights clean of spider webs and bug detritus with a damp cloth and flipped them on their lids to see if the light turned on. For those that didn't, she cleaned the contact points and replaced the rechargeable batteries.

She let Heath place the lights throughout the garden, teaching him first to not step on the plants and sprouts. Forgetting about the dangers of hantavirus, Annabelle scoured the shed for some twine and clippers. Finding them, she bound Heath's sticks into a bundle.

Heath used his hands to dig a hole in which to secure this ladybug high-rise. This was the first time Heath had helped Annabelle in the garden.

Paul had come home last weekend with a complete set of gardening tools for him. There was a spade and a fork and gloves in a canvas carry kit and a child-size shovel and hoe with brightly colored heads. The tools had disappeared with The Six the next day. Heath assured Annabelle that the tools were safe and used every day down at their fort by the river. It was too much work to carry them home at the end of every day. Annabelle didn't mind. But what were the kids doing down at the river?

When the ground proved unyielding, Heath retrieved her trowel and dug again. He furrowed his brow with concentration and his breath heaved. He knew to keep his fingers away from the sharp edge, to lean his weight against the handle, and to set the removed dirt in a pile away from the hole. His determined and competent physicality impressed Annabelle. Neither she nor Paul could be described as sporty. She had assumed she was raising a bookworm not an athlete.

When he finished digging, Annabelle set the sticks in the hole. Heath shoved the dirt around the sticks using his palms like bulldozer blades. He packed in the earth by pushing his weight onto his fists. Annabelle released her hold on the stick bundle and they remained in place.

"Good job, Heath. Your years spent in a sandbox have made you an excellent gardener."

Heath shrugged. "We're digging a hole at the river. It has to be deep enough to trap someone," he said.

"Freeze for the camera," Annabelle ordered.

Heath paused his digging and plastered his "cheese" smile across his face. It looked fake, but the dimples were winning. Her child was adorable.

She took as many photos of Heath as she could before his patience ran thin. She imagined a row of her Instagram grid featuring her son building the stick house, a closeup of a ladybug, and one of her son's muddy boots. She could include information to buy the gardening toolset for children, an instructable for building bug homes, and where to buy beneficial insects online.

"Why are you guys digging a hole?" she asked.

"For strength and discipline."

"Strength and discipline?"

"That's what Harley says."

Annabelle imagined Harley as a drill sergeant commanding her recruits to ever more intense physical feats, thereby instilling camaraderie, pride, and team cohesion. She liked this vision of her son as a valued team member.

That evening, Annabelle sat on the edge of her bed, rubbing cream into her hands. She studied her nails, two of which had been stained green during a weeding frenzy. Annabelle climbed into bed and reached for her book. She had been looking forward to reading it all day. She wanted to learn more about the theory of mitohormesis and gardening. Now that she no longer viewed her gardening as a peaceful rekindling of the mystery and miracle of nature within her and instead planned her garden like a military tactician and executed missions like a power-hungry despot, she was ready to receive the wisdom of the author's words.

Everything wants to eat, but nothing wants to be eaten. It is the most fundamental conundrum of the living. Vegetarianism does nothing to alleviate the dilemma as ripping a carrot from the ground as surely ends its life as the poleax to the beef cow's head. We are all murderers. Even the verdant smell of fresh-cut grass is the odor of traumatic injury to each blade. There is a casual cruelty to existence.

Annabelle understood the difference between the slaughter of a cow and the harvesting of a carrot. But it had nothing to do with cows and carrots. Both endeavored to live. The difference was in the death's effect on the killer. Cows resemble us more than carrots do. They have expressive faces, loving personalities, and mournful lows. A carrot is difficult to anthropomorphize.

Annabelle was familiar with the problem of empathy through anthropomorphizing via a string of YouTube videos showing people "torturing" and "killing" robots. One of her graduate school classes featured a module on robot ethics. They watched the videos of sadistic teenagers flipping dinosaur robots upside down as they cried and tried to twist away. Just watching cruelty to an animatronic creature, even though one knows it is a lifeless collection of electronics, made her and her classmates squirm.

Annabelle knew that there is a flaw in people; they're more sensitive to pain they can imagine for themselves, that they can empathize with, than to an objective measure of actual harm. How many people would eat burgers if they had to slaughter the cow? And how many of us are gardeners, harvesting our yield with pride? Gardens are open-air abattoirs and gardeners dealers of death.

Annabelle snapped her book shut before she had finished a paragraph. She had forgotten to disperse the ladybugs.

She pushed off the covers and scurried in the dark to the fridge. Flicking on the patio security light, Annabelle stepped outside barefoot and in her nightgown and robe with the bag of ladybugs and a pair of scissors. She misted the kale plants with water as the instructions directed and then cut open the bag. She had intended to film the release during the evening's golden hour for an inspired Instagram post, but the video would never turn out well in the dark.

She tried to sprinkle the bugs onto the plants, but few cooperated. They clung to the mesh. In frustration, she huffed her bangs off her forehead. With a nervy determination Annabelle reached into the bag, crawling with fifteen hundred active bugs, and pulled out a nest of dried material. Stepping across her garden with her toes in the dirt, she tucked the nest inside the ladybug skyscraper Heath had so expertly buried.

Despite her delicate efforts to direct them to the kale plants, the ladybugs crawled from the bag onto Annabelle's hand and up her arm. Instead of repulsion, Annabelle felt like a guardian, like a white-robed angel of the garden. She sat on the railroad tie garden border with her bug-covered arm outstretched so she would not smush any of her soldiers.

In her stillness, the patio light, activated by a motion-sensor, went out. Her newly commissioned solar lights sprinkled throughout the garden glowed. In their light, she saw the ladybugs leave one-by-one for the stick house. The evening smelled of mint. Early season crickets stridulated, practicing their mating calls in the distance. She felt ownership, belonging, and pride. Her garden was enchanted.

Once she had washed her feet and climbed back into bed, Annabelle was too dazed to read. She flicked off the light. Pulling one of Paul's pillows into her arms, she sniffed the pillowcase.

She wondered as she started to fall asleep, if she had done the right thing. Releasing fifteen hundred predatory insects into her garden on the basis of some positive Amazon reviews seemed like a bold move.

She knew nothing about the ladybugs. Maybe they were members of some exotic African breed that lay nests in people's ears or swarm the windshields of moving cars. Annabelle knew all about the cane toads of Australia. They too were introduced to eat a garden pest. With no natural predators, the poisonous invasive toads bred and spread creating a cascading ecological disaster for the continent.

In her dream, Annabelle woke to the sound of toads hitting the roof of her house. She pushed back the covers and was horrified to see her legs covered in a pulsing mass of ladybugs.

# 34

ANNABELLE APPROACHED HER INSTAGRAM ACCOUNT WITH THE SAME confident, analytical professionalism that she had used to earn her degrees and in her career. It had always been her determination and can-do attitude that garnered her success, not the specific skills she honed.

She applied her intellect to the business of being a lifestyle influencer. It wasn't monetization she sought, but recognition. If she put herself on the virtual therapist's couch she would say that if others found her lifestyle attractive, then it would help justify her family's move to Box Elder.

Annabelle planned each post. Behind every photo was a handful of minutes spent tweaking the lighting and balancing the staging. Annabelle relied on her artist's eye, which had been dormant for years, to assess the framed scene and resulting photos.

She knew that the artfulness of her photos was as important as the homesteading projects themselves. Her followers would judge not only her lifestyle but the savvy with which she presented it.

She had been meticulous in her use of hashtags. The Instagram specific terms—#instalife, #instadaily, #instagood; the broad descriptors—#nature, #beautiful, #spring; and the shameless—#followme and

#instalike—had all proven successful ways to find more followers. Annabelle added #yum, #eatwelleveryday, and #cleaneating to every photo of a vegetable or baked good and #cleanliving and #rural-lifestyle to every outdoor shot. Selecting the perfect cloud of hashtags was important, but it wasn't rocket science or robotics engineering.

This morning she would apply herself to standing out from all the other part-time wannabes. She had the advantage. She was smart, and she had time to dedicate herself to the task as if it were her job.

Her first step was to identify the influencers in the rural lifestyle and family categories. While rain sprinkled outside and Heath worked on a puzzle, Annabelle researched these market competitors.

She sat at the breakfast bar with her laptop and a half-eaten home-made cranberry orange muffin. That recipe had not proven a favorite with Heath, so she was choking down multiple muffins a day so they wouldn't go stale. She even gave one to Maud. Annabelle hated to waste food, even more so now that she knew firsthand how arduous it was to grow it.

She followed the popular posters using the #parenting hashtags. The ones who used hashtags like #loveofmylife and #mybabyboy were boring. Annabelle had no concerns that Heath was growing up too fast. Nor did she care for the sarcastic parenting accounts—the ones that swore, showed pictures from the 1950s with bitchy comments, and compared mothers to lionesses on the savannah. Their glib approach to parenting engendered an aloofness toward the tribula-tions their offspring suffered, like they weren't engaged in helping their child find a place in the world.

She followed the promising looking frequent posters with many followers and added glowing, hashtagged, emoji-laden comments to a smattering of their posts hoping for a follow back.

The #homestead hashtag was more serious. The pictures featured homemade soap, raising chicks, and eating rattlesnake. Annabelle wasn't ready to contend with this scene of the competent and dedi-cated just yet—her profile called her a greenhorn.

After commenting on some posts and following the posters, Annabelle feared that she had joined a pod of follower-hungry homesteaders. They followed her back and commented and liked every single photo she posted. Annabelle despised this kind of faux adoration. There was showing support and then there was lying. One was showing up at the art opening, the other was shill bidding.

But her flurry of interactions would not be enough. For a short time, Annabelle looked into a company that used artificial intelligence to boost one's followers, for a fee. Annabelle signed-up for the free trial to reverse engineer what they were doing. Companies laid claim to "smart bots" and "AI" by applying the most simplistic algorithms these days. Annabelle didn't get far. The hype words convinced her that the company's application of an AI algorithm to the problem space was perfunctory at best.

The more interesting option to boost her followers was with her very own @Annabellwether augmented reality feature, which would allow her followers to add a face filter to their photos. She downloaded the studio provided by the platform for this purpose to her computer and worked through a few tutorials.

Annabelle was a rusty programmer. It had been years since her work at the lab had required her to write any code, but she could still follow directions and infer the patterns being taught like the A-student she was.

Once she got the rudiments of the process down through tutorials, she wanted to work on her prototype, but what would people want to add to their photos? In a burst of artistic inspiration—she could feel herself firing on all cylinders in a way she hadn't in years—she decided on a bunch of flowers.

She began with a freely licensed bouquet cartoon she found on the web and altered it in her image manipulation program. Perhaps inspired by Warhol or Pop Art in general, she brightened the colors and thickened the black borders of the cartoon bunch. When satisfied, she exported the image to her augmented reality studio.

The studio software allowed developers to overlay images on a photo in relation to the faces recognized. This meant one could add bunny ears on one's head or substitute hearts for eyes or add a rainbow pouring out of one's mouth. Annabelle wanted to add her bouquet under someone's face. It could look like it delighted them to be receiving a bouquet or that they were stopping to smell the flowers. It would catch on, she was sure of it.

After much debugging and trial and error, Annabelle uploaded her masterpiece. She took a few photos of herself, two in her garden and one with the porch and the mountains behind as a backdrop, and added the augmented reality bouquet. It looked good. With no one else at home to try, Annabelle took a photo of Maud, but the application couldn't recognize the dog's face.

She waited for the bouquet to finalize and upload. While she waited, Annabelle wrote genuine sounding responses to the comments on her posts.

In a move more cunning than she would admit, she signed up for an Instagram scheduling service. With this program, she could create extra content during the week and schedule them to post over the weekend when Paul was around. She wouldn't have to face his disapproving eye every time she picked up her phone. She wouldn't have to pick up her phone at all.

The bouquet was ready. The point of using augmented reality was to amass more followers. So she began a follow, like, tag campaign. Users could get the augmented reality bouquet option for their posts if they followed her, liked her post, and tagged three of their friends. She puffed her bangs off her forehead. That had been an incredible amount of work. She waited on tenterhooks for the first follower to try it.

But she didn't have to wait long. Within twenty minutes many of her one hundred fifty-two followers began posting photos smelling her flower bouquet. Her likes and followers began a steady upward climb. It was instant gratification. Not bad for a day's work. She looked up from her phone. Where was Heath?

# 35

THERE IS SUCH A THING AS A SIXTH SENSE—AN AWARENESS THAT extends beyond information gathered through the five senses. Annabelle had heard of solo sailors waking up just in time to steer their boat clear of an oncoming freighter, of the Moken sea people sensing a tsunami long before it made landfall, of shepherds knowing when a wolf was stalking its flock. She had heard that ovulating women could sense snakes in the bush. Annabelle believed these intuitive hunches sprang from the subconscious, which reached conclusions from subliminal clues.

Don't believe what you learned in kindergarten. Humans were designed with several sensors beyond those for sight, sound, taste, touch, and smell. Just like ambulatory robots, humans were equipped with equilibrioception and proprioception—the senses of balance and body movement through space. Our biology gives us a sense of time and the feeling of pain. People have the vomeronasal organ in their noses, which detects minute chemicals including pheromones, the same sensor that leads dogs to sniff each other's pee. People also have pacinian corpuscles in their joints so sensitive to vibrations that they can detect the waves from the ground that foretell an imminent earthquake. These are the same sensors that send other earthquake-predicting mammals running.

Even if we ignore these signals, the data is gathered. If most of the time we neglect the clues of our extra senses, what makes some subconscious messages pierce the aggressive filter of the prefrontal cortex? Why were some people sometimes blessed with keen intuition? Were these presentiments cosmically bestowed upon worthy Noahs and Cassandras to save themselves and those they loved? Did it happen when the subconscious and conscious minds were aligned and attuned to the same goals? Did the shepherd train himself to direct all his many sophisticated sensors toward protecting his flock? Annabelle hoped that is what she had developed for Heath.

When the sprinkles turned to rain, she stepped out onto the porch. Heath must have left with The Six for the river while she was working. She hoped the rain would chase him home. She had a bad feeling.

Maybe it was just the blackness of the clouds and the way the wind exposed the light undersides of the leaves. Maybe it was the national headline she saw that morning of an elementary school hit by a tornado or the trailer on her Instagram feed for a summer thriller about a town whose children get abducted. Or maybe it was her sixth sense shouting to her, pleading with her to pay conscious attention to the signs.

She sat on the porch swing, her eyes trained on the arroyo for the first sign of Heath's little head returning home. Maud got up from her cushion and started pacing the porch. She stopped at Annabelle's lap and panted heavy wet breaths out of her rotted teeth. Annabelle pushed her away.

Maud continued pacing until a flash of lighting rent the sky followed by a roll of thunder. The deaf dog leapt for Annabelle, trembling. She burrowed her muzzle into Annabelle's crotch and shook. Annabelle wanted to pull away, but the dog's terror of the storm was too pathetic. She stretched her sweatshirt over Maud's eyes and stroked her neck. Maud's ears were still encrusted with black fly feces and a dirty slime of mineral oil and her slobber was wetting through

Annabelle's pants. But Maud needed her and she couldn't bring herself to push the old dog away.

Minutes later, still with no sign of Heath's return, the storm intensified. The rain hitting the metal porch roof drowned out all other sound. The gutters poured water, the wood chips in their small xeriscaped yard floated into the gravel driveway, and the farmer's field transformed into a pond.

Annabelle was content to await Heath's return on the dry porch until she heard, and in a sickening moment comprehended, the rushing sound of angry water. She flew down the steps to the driveway to look at the arroyo. It had become a raging river of foamy water the color of chocolate milk. Bobbing branches floated past until the torrent sucked them under.

Annabelle screamed. The rain soaked her clothes and her hair hung in her eyes. She pointed an accusation at Maud trembling on the porch. Maud had taught her and Heath to use the arroyo for a path, and now it was a gushing watercourse.

Annabelle took off toward the river, threading between the trees and weeds and uneven ground above the arroyo. Spines, branches, and barbed wire grabbed at her clothes. She brushed the sodden hair away from her face, but her tears floated her contact lenses and obscured her sight.

When she reached the road, she saw that it too had become rapids. Three cars in a line waited on a slope in the road for the water to recede, their headlights on and their wipers swishing. Annabelle held onto a fence and skirted the water pushing clods of mud from the roadside bank into the roiling water with each step. She hoped the drivers would see her panic and come help her find Heath. She had not thought to signal them.

Sheets of water continued to fall. She reached the dirt road that led to the river. Water from two arroyos converged here and blasted down the road. Knowing she needed to get to the river, to Heath's fort, to him, Annabelle made the foolish and irrevocable decision to step into the water.

The depth was just over her knees, but the ground beneath her feet eroded away before she could risk her first step. The force of the water knocked her down. Warm, chalky water full of debris filled her mouth and nostrils and made her choke. She flipped onto her back.

Annabelle's shoes floated and dragged her downstream as she dug her fingers into the roadbed beneath her. She needed a strong grip to prevent being swept away. Grit and mud pushed under her nails as she clawed. Her progress slowed, but the insistent water kept winning pushing her a few yards further.

A tree branch wedged into the bank of the road snagged her hair and pulled her head underwater. She grasped the branch above her head and held on. If she drowned, Heath would be left alone in this strange place until Paul returned from his trip. Water pushed into her mouth and down her lungs. It burned. She needed to breathe.

Would he go to Harley's house? Would her family take care of him? Or would he wait with Maud on the porch for her return? Or had he already washed away? Was he clinging to a branch somewhere down-stream? Would her body brush his as it rushed past?

That was it. With her head still snagged underwater, she kicked her feet to the bank and dug in her heels. She extricated herself from the arroyo—heels, toes, knees, a hip, an elbow, head last—leaving some hair behind. Exhausted, she leaned her head against the cinderblock wall along which the bank was packed. She gave herself a moment before deciding how to continue to Heath.

But she didn't need to decide. She heard the shrieks and pleas of kids a few feet away. Looking through the branches of bracken she saw The Six standing on the wall next to her. They watched the water rushing past and took turns pretending to push one another. Heath gripped Harley's wrist and forearm as she teased him, guiding his center of gravity over the edge of the wall. He looked terrified and alert and elated. It was the look he had after the wooden coaster at Silver Dollar City.

Annabelle sobbed, hidden along the wall until the rain stopped and the sun came out. A train of cars splashed through the remaining water up on the main road as the arroyos' output diminished to a trickle. Annabelle listened to the kids walking back toward the river.

Brushing back her hair and pulling her sweatshirt away from her breasts, she stepped out into the road. "Heath," she called. She sounded more fierce than she meant to. Heath stopped sword fighting with sticks to look at her. "It's time to go home."

She held out her hand to him. She felt relieved when he dropped his stick and skipped towards her without a fight. He accepted her hand and turned to wave goodbye.

"See. You. Tomorr-oh," he called, adopting Bashful's staccato speech pattern.

They trudged home through a muck-covered wasteland. Tree branches, leaves, and litter were strewn everywhere. The passing cars sprayed chocolate-colored drops across the fences, mailboxes, shrubs, and telephone poles. The mud pulled at their shoes in places and created a slippery skating rink in others.

Annabelle pushed Heath's bottom up the arroyo bank and into their driveway. As she climbed up, she saw Heath run to Maud and throw his arms around her neck. The dog was soaking wet. Her flattened fur revealed each of her ribs and the sunken hollows of her hips. She looked like the ghost of a dog. How far had the terrified dog followed after her?

Annabelle had not closed the door to the house. It stood wide open with the lights on. She picked up Heath and carried him across the threshold, slipping out of her shoes in the doorway. She deposited him in the tub and turned on the water.

Maud, dripping wet and pathetic, stood at the open doorway, but true to form, she would not enter. Annabelle retrieved a stained towel from the linen closet and rubbed Maud down on the porch. Maud seemed to appreciate the attention, but struggled to remain upright against the vigor of Annabelle's rubbing. From her collection of dog treats, Annabelle chose a rawhide bone and gave it to her. It would take Maud days to gum through it.

With Heath cleaned up, she sent him to get in his jammies and choose some books. She promised hot chocolate. After her own ablutions, which involved picking twigs from her hair and coming away with blood on her fingers, she started a load of the sodden laundry.

On her hands and knees, she wiped the floor clean from Heath's bathroom to the front door.

They cuddled happed up on the couch under blankets, with a mug of cocoa each. Annabelle felt too exhausted to talk to Heath about what had happened. Instead she opened a book and began to read aloud.

"There was an old lady who swallowed a fly. I don't know why she swallowed the fly. Perhaps, she'll die."

Annabelle shut the book.

"Let's watch a movie."

She turned on the old Disney version of *Robin Hood* with an anthropomorphic fox in the titular role. This was part of her effort to introduce Heath to the Western canon of children's movies, in other words, those that she had loved as a child.

When she chose the movie, she planned on delighting Heath by being able to sing along to all the songs. Instead, she sat glued to her phone, responding to comments on her posts and on a video that Wanda posted.

The approbation her posts had received was reaffirming. And engrossing. The next thing she knew Heath had fallen asleep next to her under a blanket watching miscellaneous cartoons. The movie had ended. Where had the evening gone? She carried Heath to bed and tucked him in. Had he brushed his teeth? It was too late now.

Annabelle put on her nightgown and climbed into her bed heavy with exhaustion. In the remaining minutes she could keep her eyes open, she marveled at the action taking place on her phone. Before turning out the lights, she confirmed that she had 27,699 followers. She smiled in the dark. *Oo-de-lally, Oo-de-lally, golly what a day.*

## 36

THE NEXT MORNING ANNABELLE STEPPED FROM HER ROOM ONTO WHITE swirls of mud caked to the tile floor. The mess went all the way to the front door in arm-length arcs. It looked like the botched cover-up of a crime scene.

Her efforts last night spent on her hands and knees mopping up the mud—wax on, wax off—had not proven successful. A chalky residue remained. There was nothing else to do. Before Heath woke up, before she put on the coffee, before she even put in her contacts, Annabelle filled her bucket and crawled across her floors once again attempting to repel the mud that was invading her home.

As reward for her drudgery, she checked her phone. Her feed teemed with photos of people sniffing her cartoon bouquet. It was a wonderful feeling to see her art touch so many strangers. Instagram was showing itself to be a better venue for visual art than galleries. On Instagram she could see people interacting with her work. It was as informative as watching Paul read her bio and study her painting at her college art show so many years ago.

That afternoon, when Paul arrived home, he pulled a red bicycle with training wheels out of the back of his Jeep. Heath was ecstatic. Annabelle was grateful that she told The Six that Heath couldn't play until after his dad arrived home. Paul scooped Heath up and twirled him around.

Heath sat astride the bike as Paul clipped a helmet with stegosaurus spikes under his chin. It was a beautiful moment, but Annabelle felt annoyed. She was the one who was supposed to be filling his days with memories.

Paul pushed the bike and Heath pedaled across the gravel of their driveway up onto the dirt road. He walked alongside as Heath operated the bike on his own. Annabelle, sensing a Kodak moment, snapped photos for the family and for Instagram.

Under the hashtag #learningtoridebike, Annabelle found photos of smiling children on sidewalks and paved driveways. In comparison, her photos made it look like they were forcing Heath to ride in the mud of a pig sty.

The road sloped down to meet the bed of the arroyo and became deep, soft sand. Heath rolled his bike into the sand and stopped. He pedaled as hard as he could but couldn't inch it forward. Paul turned him around and got him rolling in the other direction. Heath pedaled, perspiring with concentration, past Annabelle, who was recording a video. She waved. The problem with riding a bike in that direction was the deep ruts. Heath dropped his front tire into a rut and his progress stopped.

"Where is he supposed to ride that around here? This isn't Royal Oak," Annabelle snapped at Paul. It wasn't a nice first thing to say to your husband when he returns from a week spent away earning his family's living, but the surprise bike agitated Annabelle.

"He has to learn to ride a bike. I'll take him to the church parking lot."

"You don't get it."

Heath dismounted and pushed the bike out of the rut. He walked it back down the driveway. Annabelle didn't want to have this fight in front of him, and she didn't have to. Miraculously, The Six called from the thicket.

"Heath. Let's. Gooooo," Bashful called.

Without a second look at his new bike, Heath left. Neither Paul nor Annabelle cared. They were locking eyes, waiting for him to get out of earshot.

"You keep pretending we still live in Royal Oak, like nothing has changed," she said. "You can't transplant your life from there here. Wake up! Look around. It's all different. You don't know because you're never here."

"I'm never here because I'm the only one making money for this family. Your Instagram photos aren't going to sustain us."

"Don't make fun of me, Paul. My education and all my training don't count for anything here. So yes, I'm feeling unfulfilled and unnoticed and unappreciated, so I post to Instagram. It makes me feel good. I know it isn't real appreciation, and it isn't real work, but you know what? Neither was calibrating robots. It was only a matter of time before they approved a robot to do my job too."

"You said you wanted to live in the country for Heath, but do you even know what he is doing out there? Do you know anything about those kids?"

"I know they don't go to a private school and their parents aren't on the boards of any foundations, if that's what you mean."

"That's not what I mean and you know it."

"Should I have done background checks?"

"Every time I come home, Heath is out with those kids. I got the bike so we could do something as a family. I miss him. I miss you."

Annabelle accommodated his shift in tone.

"I know. I'm sorry to make you feel bad about the bike. You're a great dad. It's just, I'm trying so hard. None of this is coming naturally. I almost drowned, you know."

She imagined her obituary headline: *Wife, Mother, and Homesteading Inspiration Found Tangled in the Brush and Drowned in Box Elder, New Mexico.* A three-photo story would be posted to her Instagram account with the Juno filter: one an arranged professional family portrait, another of her smiling healthy and radiant among vibrant veggies in her garden, and the third of her muddy dead body with wet, tangled hair covering her vacant stare.

Annabelle tucked into Paul's chest and clutched his jacket. Why was she starting to blubber? She had never been one to play the martyr. Was she distracting him from her adoption of a dangerously lax parenting philosophy?

"I know. I'm so glad you and Heath are safe," he said, pulling away from her snuffling.

"It wasn't a big deal, but it could have been." Annabelle channeled Jessica Chastain. She couldn't seem to stop playing for sympathy.

"How did Heath handle it?"

Heath, of course. Paul had married a strong, capable, independent woman—a partner. And she had married an invested father for her future children. Paul was supportive of her. When they both finished classes at graduate school, Paul started at the consulting firm right away. He wrote his Ph.D. thesis while working at a real job getting paid real money. But Dr. Watanabe extended Annabelle's prestigious internship for another year. The internship came with a small stipend. It was a pittance. Paul encouraged her to accept the internship even though she couldn't contribute to the household finances, and they had agreed in grad school that as soon as they graduated they would look for a house in a good neighborhood. He never griped about the responsibility of being the sole breadwinner paying off student loans for two. When Heath was born, he was instantly smitten and attentive to their baby's needs. And when she became overwhelmed, Paul responded by stepping up his childcare and housework duties. He was the perfect modern mate.

But Annabelle could admit to herself, her college women's herstory professor be damned, that she sometimes wished Paul would coddle her. The fantasy always began with him saying, "Oh, you poor fragile creature." She wanted him to insist she wear high heels. Something sexy, but impractical that led him to drop her off at the restaurant door while he circled around for the parking spot and to offer his arm while she climbed a broad staircase. She wanted to feel that he approved and protected her footwear choice, not that it lowered their collective fitness. And she wanted him to give her something to swoon over. When she dragged the garden hose from the shed, why couldn't he say, "Let me get that for you, you poor fragile creature?" He could flex his muscles and strut with the hose while she followed behind with admiring comments. She wasn't helpless, quite the contrary. But she wanted him to pretend she was, just occasionally. It would be belittling and demeaning, but also kinda hot.

## 37

DAN QUINTANA

We should have done more to guide Harley. Those first months after Dinah died were a dark time for us. We were all grieving. We were all getting used to the new living circumstances. Delfina and I went from being retirees to parenting.

I tried not to think that Dinah would never find love again. That she would never see Harley graduate and get married. That she would never have the pleasure of becoming a grandparent.

But it was Harley who had the hardest time. It was she who was abandoned by her father and who found her mother dead. Those first months were a horrible time for her. That's why I cut her so much slack. That's why she's turned out the way she has. I can only blame myself.

It was three months after we buried Dinah that Delfina noticed mats of long black hair in the laundry and in Harley's brush. The hair loss was a huge source of fear and embarrassment for a young girl. Harley had always had thick, long hair, and it somehow remained untangled and smooth despite all her outdoor antics.

Each day she found disturbing clumps of hair on her pillow, in her brush, in the shower drain. It was terrifying. Of course, it is the treatment not cancer itself that causes hair loss, but I couldn't help but fear that Harley was terminally ill and would be taken from us too.

Her pediatrician assured us she was healthy. He said the hair loss was telogen effluvium. That was just a fancy way of saying the stress of her bereavement had caused her body to choke out nutrients to her hair and so now it was falling out. He assured Harley, who had taken to wearing a pink knitted beanie with crocheted flowers even to bed, that her hair would grow back.

Her classmates, who had been charming and supportive and uncowed by the stigma of early death that kept some of Box Elder's adults away from us, couldn't miss the opportunity to make fun of her. I'm not a fool. Harley, who was born self-assured, had been a bit of an *aprovechada*, a bully, at school. She did not mince her words, and she had a way of getting what she wanted. She had a tendency to run over others, especially the quiet, sensitive ones. I think the kids saw an opportunity to get back, and they did. Unfortunately, Ben Cordova led the charge. He was a boy much older than Harley that she had a crush on.

Ben collected the hair that fell on her classroom seat, presumably over a few days to get so much. During lunch in the cafeteria, he came out with her hairs clipped to his. He performed a mime of her trying to cover her head with the little hair she had.

Now if you ask me, those were the misguided actions of a young, stupid boy with a crush, but Harley wouldn't believe me. I told her I used to kick Grace, Delfina's sister and my first crush, in the shins when I was in second grade to express my undying devotion. Grace never caught on and instead stood away from me with her friends between us.

Anyway, that day in the cafeteria another kid sang the chia pet song at Harley. Who knows how she knew it. I haven't seen a chia pet in a decade. It became a—what do they call it now?—a meme? Every day for the next week, kids said, "Cha-cha-cha-chia," and sniggered when Harley walked down the hall.

Delfina thought of a solution. She booked an appointment with Stella at her salon. If Stella cut Harley's hair short, Delfina figured, then it wouldn't look like she was losing so much each day.

Harley looked forward to the appointment. She had never gotten her hair cut in a salon. Dinah had always cut it on their porch. The place wasn't much, just a room off Stella's garage, but it had the chair and the mirrors with the lights. But when Harley sat in the chair and Stella brushed her hair, so much slid to the cape that Harley began to cry. She was inconsolable. She cried for her hair and for her mom and for the tragedy that would permanently mark her life. And she cried out of embarrassment for crying.

Stella gave her a great chin-length haircut with a section that came down over her eye. It made her look older and the shorter hair made for smaller clumps on her pillow.

But that didn't stop the teasing at school. Her scalp peeked through her hair no matter how she parted it. It became sunburned and flaked. Someone—she doesn't know who, but thinks it was Ben— left a bottle of Head and Shoulders in her locker. A teacher's assistant, an older girl, graded her biology exam and when she got a question wrong wrote "That was flaky" with a winking face in red marker. Kids feel so uninhibited when the opportunity to be cruel presents itself.

We only found out about this when the school called us because Harley missed her study period. She told us she spent it hiding in the handicapped bathroom stall. I didn't know what to tell her except, "Your hair will grow back soon."

But it didn't grow back soon. She'd lost half of her hair before the shedding tapered out. It's been six months and only now have we noticed new wispy hairs growing at her temples. That was a lifetime for a self-conscious girl who had just lost her mother.

Harley stopped wanting to have friends over. She no longer felt comfortable with anyone her age. The kids who came to our house in support after Dinah passed stopped coming around, but they used Harley as an excuse to be out after school. No parent can scold a late child who was spending the time consoling a grieving one. There was a mild rash of trouble-making as these kids used their Harley alibi to pull pranks like throwing water balloons at cars, stranding cats on the roofs of sheds, and stealing beef jerky from the gas station.

At first, Harley didn't want the kids to come over, but soon, she didn't want to go to school at all. We indulged her now and then, let her take the day off from school. We spent it as we did our weekends, working in the yard or on a house project and then playing Widow Whist and watching movies. But somehow, and I can't account for how it happened, Harley stopped going to school at all. We would wake her up and get her fed and out the door for the bus, but she wouldn't get on. Or if we drove her, she would never go in the schoolhouse door.

I am ashamed to say that we told the principal, a well-meaning woman who I should never have yelled at, to stop phoning us. I told her we were managing the best we could and if Harley didn't want to go to her school, which was populated by heartless mongrels, she didn't have to. The calls stopped. I think she must have understood because the police haven't come on a truancy charge.

Harley never stopped pretending to go to school even though we all know, without admitting it to each other, that she hasn't been going. We still wake her up in time for the bus and she still leaves and is gone all day. We know that she hangs out with the half-day kindergarteners and one even younger than that. Harley is a bossy little girl, which means she needs people to boss. She used to have her friend group under her control, but that all changed with the hair incident. Now she has this group of loyal little ones.

It's not right that she spends her time playing with kids so much younger, but she comes home with a smile. It is a wonderful sight. And I like that they go play at the river, building forts in the bosque, digging tunnels, and making believe. It reminds me of my youth.

But I have made a dreadful mistake. I should have intervened. When I realized her break from school wasn't going to last a few days, or a few weeks, or even a few months, I should have stepped in. Next school year, Harley will be in attendance at school every day. I swear it. Her education is vital to her future and she can't hide from her peers forever. They will have forgotten about her hair.

I should have done something earlier. I just can't stand to see that little girl upset. Or maybe I am just not strong enough anymore to be the parent she needs. I am grieving too.

# 38

ANNABELLE DID NOT RECEIVE MANY PERSONALIZED EMAILS ANYMORE.
Her work email account had been shut down before she had even left
the building on her last day. She didn't know anyone's email address
in Box Elder, so there were no party invites, nor any requests to
carpools or playdates. Mostly, she received bill notifications,
TheSkimm, and other newsletters to which she had subscribed. But
on Saturday morning she received an email that made her sit up
in bed.

*Hello @Annabellwether,*

*Wanda Way requests a ten-minute interview with you for her lifestyle outlets
on Monday, May 20th at 3 PM Eastern. Practice your Wanda Wave in
advance.*

*Please RSVP with a headshot and bio and your Skype handle.*

. . .

*Doric Diamondis*

Annabelle screamed into her pillow and kicked her feet with glee. It was like being a teenager with a hot date. Wanda Way wanted to talk to her, Annabelle Granger, after two weeks of Instagramming. Who else had Wanda Way talked to? The chef who opened the cooking foam restaurant at the Bellagio, the actress playing the mermaid in the new Showtime series, and the anchor who quit Fox to become a beauty blogger. The woman had a book deal, *The Wanda Way*. You could pre-order now.

The Wanda Wave that Annabelle was to practice was an Instagram gimmick where Wanda or whoever she was interviewing would sweep their arm in front of their face. Through simple video editing, the gesture served as a transition from a before to an after scene. So for a Sephora + Moschino makeup tutorial the video would show Wanda without makeup and then she would Wanda Wave and it would show her face made up to perfection.

When demonstrating The Wanda Way for making one's bed, the video showed her sitting on the corner of her bed with the covers tossed aside. After her wave it showed her among layers of crisp white sheets, stacks of white pillows, a white coverlet, and an Indian stripe afghan arranged at a jaunty angle over the upholstered footboard.

The Wanda Wave was one of her signatures and, Annabelle admitted, it was a crafty way to entice people to watch her videos. Whoever did her editing was good.

If Annabelle could pull this off, she would achieve the impossible: merge motherhood and success. If she became Instafamous, she could earn money and garner recognition by sharing her satisfying, self-guided projects that both challenge her creatively and directly contribute to the health and happiness of her family.

This was it. This was the opportunity she had been seeking all those listless months in Royal Oak.

Annabelle would dedicate her day to responding to Doric and preparing to make the most of her interview with Ms. Way. If there was an Oprah bump, there was a Wanda rush and Annabelle would be there to capitalize on her new followers.

The only hurdle was Paul. He wouldn't see the interview for what it was, a giant, flaming opportunity for Annabelle to re-establish herself as a woman in command. When Annabelle wiggled her phone with Wanda's email in front of his face, she was skipping with excitement. Her excitement was infectious, and he took the phone from her eagerly. But his face changed as he read the note.

"Can I assume this means that Heath will receive even less of your attention this week?"

"Do you know who Wanda Way is? This is big."

"How is this big? Two minutes on some woman's Instagram?"

"I give Heath my attention."

"If I'd known you yearned to join the chattering classes, I would have introduced you at the Sports Grill at the Club. At least that's a respectable place to be seen."

Annabelle snatched the phone back from him and stomped out the door, pulling her coat from the rack as she went. With nowhere to go, she stalked to the shed to be by herself. Paul could make Heath's breakfast today. Or he could fly Heath to the "Sports Grill at the Club," if he thought that was so great.

## 39

PAUL GRANGER

Paul still thought of Annabelle as the radiant electrical engineering major who executed paintings with mathematical precision and featured people with alien eyes. When he was an inexperienced college lad, he didn't know that the world made women like Annabelle. But then Paul had not met many women. He had always been a driven, focused student. He had paid little attention to girls. That was until his senior year.

The student housing gods led Paul to answer an ad posted to the campus online message board when the lease on his initial apartment fell through one month before the start of the semester. Paul couldn't remember the exact phrasing of the ad, but it went something like this: *Ladies! Rafe and Steve-o need a housemate. Three-bedroom house just off campus. You get your own room or can stay in one of ours. Act fast, we can't stay single for long. Send us a photo.*

Desperation and a hint of curiosity about potential friendship with the carefree bros that would post an ad like that led Paul to respond. He wrote an uncharacteristic response: *The ladies will be all over you with a wingman like me.* He sent a photo of himself wearing nerd glasses with white tape wrapped around the bridge. Rafe and Steve-o thought his post hilarious and, knowing no sane woman would reply, invited Paul to become the newest resident of The Cock Pit, their name for the once-charming rundown Victorian a block from campus.

Paul spent the summer before his senior year working at his father's accounting firm as he had the summer before. The experience broadened his résumé. But Rafe and Steve-o lived all year long in The Cock Pit. It had been their home since sophomore year. So when Paul arrived two days before the start of the semester, the house was already in full swing. Paul had only to set up his twin bed and his laptop with speakers in his room.

The mottled, squishy carpet on the first floor reeked of beer. The front door was never to be used. A gravid tarp hung from the ceiling against the door. By tradition, every time one popped a beer, they would toss the cap into the tarp. If a person were to open the door, three years of bottle caps and the associated rancid residue would rain down on them. This booby trap remained even though they spent most evenings on the front porch. Going inside meant walking along the driveway and through the kitchen door. It amazed Paul that none of the revelers who passed through The Cock Pit ever opened the front door. They somehow knew. Perhaps it was the armchair and box of broken electrical equipment and associated wires on the porch blocking the door that alerted them. The place was a firetrap.

It was a small school, and Paul already knew of Rafe and Steve-o. They were hard partiers, goofballs, and inseparable. But Paul also knew that they applied themselves academically. Rafe was on a tennis scholarship and Steve-o was pre-Med.

Rafe exuded Latin sexual energy. He walked with his hips thrust forward and his chest up. He had wavy, silky black hair that brushed his shoulders. If he woke up with bedhead, Steve-o teased him he better check his Farrah Fawcett in the mirror. He was fit except for a slight beer belly and he liked to wear his college-logo sweatband when drinking on weekend nights. It was part irony and part pride.

Steve-o got satisfaction breathing life into a party. He knew every drinking game and cultivated playlists to keep a party bumping. By issuing a crowd-pleasing dare, he could turn a wallflower into the evening's hero or condemn him to obscurity forever. There were no repetitive nights when Steve-o was around. He also liked to fight. The fights always began with him head butting someone, most often a preppy guy who thought all the chicks were for him. They usually ended with a piece of furniture breaking. Rafe and Steve-o kept their cordless drill charging on the mantle next to an elective art class pottery bowl full of screws to effect quick but ugly furniture repairs. Their school was too small for fraternities, but Steve-o wished that one day his antics would appear on the homepage for the website collegehumor.

Paul learned that the fellow he replaced as housemate, a guy Rafe and Steve-o referred to only as The Captain, had dropped out of school when his binge-drinking began looking more like advanced stages of alcoholism than college buffoonery. Paul couldn't remember ever meeting him. Rafe told Paul his priority had never been putting in appearances on campus. The guy spent his days heckling people in the park and his afternoons and evenings wearing a Captain's hat and drinking from a giant plastic cup on the porch. His party trick was to drink any alcoholic concoction poured into his cup. PBR, Guinness, vodka, and some girl's peppermint schnapps? He chugged it down. It was a savvy, if disgusting way to drink for free. The guy was cool, but always a little frightening, even to the inveterate drinkers.

The Cock Pit had rules. The boys wore shower shoes because no one ever had or ever would clean the bathroom. All empty cans and bottles were to be left lined up on the porch railing after a night of drinking. They would magically disappear by morning. In reality, a homeless guy they called Sorry Charlie collected them for their ten cent deposit. It was The Cock Pit's way of giving back. Another rule was that no one in the house would accommodate studying. If the music was too loud, leave. In effect, this meant that Rafe, Steve-o, and Paul studied on campus in the library and student lounges and almost always together. Rafe and Steve-o became not only his housemates, but his constant companions. The other rules were as complex as the chivalric code and all related to the goal assumed to be shared by all three that they were on the constant lookout for pussy.

Paul hadn't initially been on the constant lookout for pussy, mostly because he believed acquiring pussy required a great deal of effort. He thought he needed to show an uncommon charm, lavish the pussy's owner with gifts, and show evidence of an undying fealty. He wasn't ready to expend that kind of effort. There had been a girl, Allison with the backne, whom he made out with after they studied together. He had never been sure how to categorize her.

But Rafe and Steve-o showed him that girls were just like guys. It's not that they were on the constant hunt for cock, but, just like the guys, they wanted to be noticed and chosen and to have an unusual experience they could tell their friends about. All he had to say to any given girl at one of The Cock Pit parties was that the house they were in was his, and not like he owned it, just that he was renting a room for the school year. Girls were interested in the type of guy who would allow his home to be overrun with drunk lunatics every Thursday night. They were interested in being a part of the wild night.

Paul's confidence soared. He knew what made him charming and what made the ladies swoon and he used this knowledge to his advantage over and over. The nights he spent partying with Rafe and Steve-o were the best of his college years.

Then, two months before graduation, he met Annabelle. She wasn't the sort to attend house parties, so he had never had the pleasure of using his moves on her. Her crowd preferred to smoke pot and drink wine sitting on the floor around a secondhand coffee table in a room with too many houseplants.

The thought of bringing her to The Cock Pit terrified him. He thought she would think his lifestyle juvenile, rather than a temporary excitement in what he planned to be a life of hard work and responsibility. He thought she would think Rafe and Steve-o, his closest companions in the world ever, pigs both in terms of hygiene and their views on women. He thought that if she disapproved of the spectacle that was his senior year, she would disapprove of all of him. She would be unable to see his other smart and reasonable and worthy choices. It would be over.

So he panicked when he saw her standing one Thursday night a few weeks into their fledgling relationship on the sidewalk in front of his house. He waved to her from the porch. Annabelle took her time walking to him, stopping to hug a few girls talking on the steps. She'd brought her own drink, a half growler filled with some hoppy craft beer she carried with one finger through its handle. She said nothing to him.

Paul left her side to get her a clean Solo cup for her beer. It was a long walk along the driveway and into the kitchen where the keg and stacks of red cups were waiting. As he went, he cursed himself. Why had he decided to live in The Cock Pit? He could have found a clean, quiet housemate somewhere if he had kept looking. It was on this walk that Paul realized how much he liked Annabelle. He would give up Rafe and Steve-o and his whole eye-opening, debauched year if it meant she would stay with him.

When he returned to the porch, it was his worst nightmare. Annabelle was still there, but she was with Rafe and Steve-o. They surrounded her as she leaned against the railing. They looked aggressive. His housemates were not taking kindly to Paul's total infatuation with Annabelle to the exclusion of other pussy. It broke the code and brought the fear of the impending end of their senior idyll too close to home. He was lifting the spell. It was not time to settle down; it was time to double down.

As he approached, he heard Steve-o say to her, "Well if it isn't Grungy Granger's hoe. Blessing us with your presence?"

To the throng on the porch he called, "Everyone. Everyone. We've got a guest. How do we show hospitality at The Cock Pit? The beer bong."

As Steve-o produced the homemade device from a table littered with cigarette butts and wounded soldiers, Paul had panicked. He had no idea how to get Steve-o to back down once he started with the peer-pressure theatrics. The crowd on the porch cleared a circle as they waited to see Annabelle's reaction.

Paul squeaked, "You don't have to," just as Annabelle, without breaking eye contact with Steve-o shoved her growler into Paul's stomach and took a knee. The crowd cheered.

Steve-o accepted three cans of Natty Light and emptied them into the beer bong—a basin made of an empty laundry detergent bottle with a plastic tube connected to the bottle's opening by fraying duct tape. Steve-o held the tube in a U above the bottle to prevent the three cans of beer from draining out.

"Ready?" he said to her with surprising gentleness.

Annabelle nodded.

She accepted the open end of the plastic tube and wrapped her mouth around it, but not before beer sloshed out and wetted her neck and shirt. Steve-o held the detergent bottle high. The crowd watched the level of the liquid in the clear tube drain lower as Annabelle chugged.

Steve-o loved the show and her acceptance of his challenge. With a smirk, he produced for the audience a bottle of Everclear. He poured one, two, three glugs of the alcohol into the beer bong's basin. Annabelle remained steadfast. The crowd cheered again as they watched the remaining beer and then the clear one hundred ninety proof alcohol disappear into her mouth.

Paul grabbed for Annabelle's elbow to help her up, but she sprang up like a boxer both arms in the air. Steve-o patted her on the back. Paul couldn't help but admire her. This was a girl who could hold her own. This was a girl who rose to a challenge. This was a girl who didn't need rescuing.

Drunk Annabelle wasn't like any drunk college girl Paul had met before. She didn't adopt an annoying laugh, cry, talk too much, or lean her head on his shoulder. Instead, Annabelle searched The Cock Pit for a hose clamp. She rooted through their bowl of screws on the mantle and in the kitchen cabinets and the pantry, before finally finding a hose clamp discarded on the basement floor in a heap of mortar dust next to the furnace. Returning to the porch, she replaced the duct tape on the beer bong with the hose clamp and secured it using a bottle tab as a screwdriver. No more leaks.

Had Paul mistaken Annabelle's resolute acceptance of every challenge presented to her as grittiness when it was something more clinical than that? His wife had mutated lately. She was still Annabelle, but like in *Body Snatchers*—a scarring movie Paul had seen hiding behind the couch as his sister watched—, she might be an alien clone. She sure had been acting like a soulless, egocentric pod double. Or was Box Elder a harmless incongruous interlude for Annabelle, like The Cock Pit had been for him?

Rafe's only comment about her, Paul recalled, he made the next morning over giant bowls of Lucky Charms. "Nice choice, dude. She's got a huge rack and a sweet ass."

They all graduated some weeks later and moved out of The Cock Pit. Paul moved with Annabelle to Ann Arbor, and just as they had feared, he lost touch with his housemates. He knew that Steve-o married a slim, delicate Korean girl with a dirty mouth he met in med school in Baltimore who was studying to become an anesthesiologist. Rafe married Heather, a blond Californian with whom he'd been on again off again with his senior year. Her father was an orthodontist who sent her to college in Michigan to make her more wholesome. He never suspected Rafe lurked amongst all the corn-fed Midwesterners.

Aside from some rude, but work-appropriate Facebook comments the boys posted to each other now and then, Paul had lost track of his friends. His Cock Pit interlude ended.

When would Annabelle's end? Paul had an idea. It was Mother's Day on Sunday. It would be the perfect time to help Annabelle remember her way.

# 40

PAUL WAS AN ENTHUSIASTIC CELEBRATOR OF HOLIDAYS. HE WAS THE ONE who remembered their anniversary. He was the one who chose and sent their Christmas cards each year. And it was Paul who planned her first Mother's Day celebration at a restaurant—with an eight-month-old. Annabelle was hoping for toast and a magazine in bed while Paul took Heath for a stroll around the block. Instead, she had to find a clean bra and pull on pants without an elastic waistband to match Paul's natty weekend style. He'd made a reservation, so they had to hurry. Chop. Chop.

When Heath had turned eight months old, his behavior shifted. He became full of restless energy. Where before Annabelle could leave Heath on a mat on their kitchen floor while she made dinner and took tiny, guilty sips of Paul's beer while they told each other about their days, now Heath scooted out of sight the moment she released him.

The first day he figured out his new trick, Heath got rug burn on his chubby legs. Paul's sister Gwen (whose son had taken his first steps), sent non-skid rompers and anti-slip knee pads. These gave Heath the traction needed to scoot across the tile and Berber carpet in the time it took Annabelle to open and close the refrigerator door.

Heath's ambulation made her uneasy. She had to step up her

parenting game to keep him safe. He did not stay where she set him and that meant everything became a timed exercise. With Heath on the living room rug, she could run to get the laundry from the dryer before he got to the wrought iron standing lamp. She could check the meatloaf before he tried to scale Paul's bookshelf. Her house had become the set for a game show brought to you by the creators of "Supermarket Sweep." *Can Annabelle finish her household chores before Heath finds the glass-blown Christmas ornament that rolled under the couch last season? Find out after this word from our sponsors.* They had a playpen, but Annabelle hated to coop him up.

That was also the age at which Heath became very attached to her. Since he turned six months old, he had gone every weekday to the natural play childcare center. The handoff from mother to caregiver had always been smooth and without issue. But at eight months, Heath began to cling to Annabelle. She would have to pry his pudgy hands from her clothes as she passed him off. He cried real, fat tears as she ran to her car desperate to get out of his sight and to be alone to wrestle with her parental deficiencies and weigh the lasting harm of child abandonment.

On the drive that first Mother's Day, Annabelle bemoaned the dirty looks they would receive at the restaurant when Heath threw his spoon, or smacked his hi-chair table, or became a vocal child. Paul laughed at her.

"On Mother's Day? Everyone loves family togetherness on Mother's Day."

Still Annabelle felt her tension ratcheting up at every stoplight. Couldn't he surprise her instead with time to sit by herself alone in the house for a while? Wasn't that the true spirit of the holiday?

When they pulled into the parking lot, Annabelle assessed the restaurant and realized that this was more than a Waffle House. Heath would surely be an intrusion to the other diners regardless of whatever ridiculous holiday invented by Hallmark and florists was being celebrated today.

Annabelle huffed the bangs off her forehead. As she unclipped Heath from his car seat, she started whispering. "Oh, Heath. You better be on your best behavior. This is a grown-up restaurant. The patrons aren't going to want to hear from you."

When she saw Paul toting the diaper bag with Heath's driving wheel—which made an annoying noise for every button pressed and sometimes in the late evenings when she and Paul sat on the couch watching TV made noises in its toy bin all by itself—Annabelle smacked her free hand to her forehead. This was going to be awful.

But Paul, all swagger and confidence, had something up his sleeve. Annabelle holding Heath on her hip followed the hostess to a private room. The highchair was already in place. They sat, just the three of them, at a table for ten overlooking a window box of budding daffodils. Heath played with his driver's wheel and ate organic Cheerios and struggled to pull diluted apple juice from his new sippy cup while Paul spoke appreciative words to Annabelle. She drank a mimosa, even though she was breastfeeding. Whispering into her ear, Paul convinced her that the wee bit of alcohol would help Heath have an extra-long morning nap. She swung a leg over his lap.

Annabelle's favorite breakfast was eggs Benedict, but Paul was hopeless with sauces, so he chose this restaurant for its famous hollandaise. She ordered and devoured a crab cake Benedict and they luxuriated over the empty plates disappearing without their intervention. Restaurant meals had become a thing of the past since having Heath. They sat drinking Zingerman's coffee, the kind they drank throughout their grad school days at U of M. The familiar taste left them reminiscing over their early years together. Their intertwined life story followed a happy arc: budding romance, commitment, marriage, mortgage, pregnancy, promotions, and parenting. And in that moment it all made so much sense, their life together with Heath in Royal Oak with their demanding, well-paying jobs. Annabelle had won, and this was her prize.

The Grangers spent all four of the next Mother's Days at the same restaurant in the same private room. It was a family ritual marking the changes over the past year and the constancy in their lives. Annabelle had never come up with a reciprocal Father's Day tradition that fit them so well.

This year, for the first time, their new home in New Mexico upset the usual Mother's Day routine. Annabelle assumed, given the hostility with which Paul had been treating her this weekend, that this meant the day would be marked with Paul pitching in with meal prep and maybe taking a few family pictures under the apricot trees for their families back in Royal Oak. Nope.

Annabelle woke up on Sunday to the blare of an alarm clock. That was unpleasant. Paul bounded into the room full of good cheer and informed her of the plan. They would drive into Albuquerque for breakfast and a special outing afterwards, wear sunscreen. Annabelle found this unpleasant too, but she dressed and applied sunscreen like a compliant hostage.

That day marked their two-week anniversary in their new home. During those weeks, Annabelle had rarely been in a car and when she had they traveled at sedate, county-road speeds. In that time, she had become a nervous passenger. With her entire family strapped into Paul's Cherokee, Annabelle felt vulnerable to all the strangers buzzing past, driving I-40 way too fast for a Sunday morning. It's not like the drivers were late for work.

Annabelle clutched the Jesus handle like Paul was performing drastic maneuvers down the freeway instead of ten-and-two-ing it as always. She tried not to think of headlines: *Mother's Day Misfortune for Brunch-Goers*; *Family of Three Wiped Out in Spectacular Car Fire*; *Traumatized Five-Year-Old Sole Survivor of Twelve-Car Pileup*.

They made it to the restaurant in Albuquerque's Old Town without incident. Annabelle hoped she would feel the same affirming transformation she had with Paul and Heath that first Mother's Day. She wanted to feel a sense that her choices were right and inevitable and all was as it should be. But that was not to be.

Annabelle saw right through this little outing of Paul's the moment she saw the menu. The restaurant was known for its eggs Benedict. In fact, a local rag had voted it as having The Best Eggs Benedict in Albuquerque. Paul was attempting to recreate their life in Royal Oak. As she choked down an odd interpretation of her favorite dish involving cornbread instead of an English muffin and smoked cayenne hollandaise, Paul drummed up suspense for their special outing with a guessing game.

Annabelle guessed it was a visit to the National Nuclear Science Museum. Paul had dropped the fun fact, as he parallel parked, that the museum had an Atomic Annie, a cannon designed to launch a nuclear warhead. Paul had watched a video online about the cannon and was dying to see it in person.

Instead, Paul unveiled that their special outing was to be a trip to the zoo. That's when Annabelle knew for sure he was recreating a semblance of the home she'd torn him from. As Heath cheered and concentrated through an elaborate high-five with his dad, Annabelle stared out the restaurant window. The zoo?

As Paul drove to the zoo, Annabelle sank into a pensive funk. She thought her older, wiser sisters would tell her she was overreacting, reading too much into the day. Paul chose the restaurant because he thought she would like the food and the zoo because that is a fun, family way to spend time with a five-year-old. Be glad he planned something, her sisters, both approaching twenty-five years of marriage, would say. But Annabelle knew Paul's chosen outing revealed a much darker yearning. Paul wasn't trying to recreate the refreshing family harmony they found every Mother's Day—the genotype, let's say. He was recreating the phenotype, the look of a happy family doing the things that happy families do.

Paul was struggling to adapt to the foreign environment, which she could understand. Annabelle was struggling too. The only one who took to it like a duck to water was Heath. But at least Annabelle was embracing her struggle, seeking the good, restyling her life. Paul was clinging to his old patterns and his old choices. And like a comfort blanket, he sought the familiar, in this case, the exotic fantasy land across from which their house on Huntington Road sat. He sought the zoo.

# WEEK THREE

# 41

THE PRESSURE WAS ON. WITH HER WANDA WAY INTERVIEW IN ONE week and Paul refusing to see Box Elder's potential for the Granger family's long-term home, Annabelle had to act quickly.

She pulled out her notebook and made a list.

*The perfect family*

*1. Lives in a clean, functional, organized, cozy, and aesthetically pleasing home,*

*2. Eats wholesome, varied, appealing meals,*

*3. Engages in stimulating, hands-on creative work,*

*4. Relaxes together with peace, understanding, love, and humor.*

These things didn't happen on their own. They happened when a homemaker cleaned the house and prepared the meals. They happened when the environment provided activities for work and play. These things happened when a family adopted a simple, low-budget country lifestyle.

The domestic arts existed for a reason. It plowed the energy expended by one partner back into the family. The time spent gardening produced fresh food and exercise. The need for firewood, pruned bushes, pest control, and to attract beneficial bugs, bats, and birds provided educational and enriching activities based in nature and the seasons. How different from a suburban weekend spent trolling the parking lot looking for a space close to the coffee shop, trying on trendy clothes at the mall, and then queueing to buy the latest model phone.

It had all made so much sense.

"Can I play outside until The Six come today?" Heath asked her.

Her first response was to chide him for thinking he could play in their unfenced yard without her supervision. Then she remembered that he played outside every day without her supervision. Why did it seem so much more dangerous for him to play alone in their yard than at the river with The Six?

She smeared sunblock under his eyes and sent him out.

"Look out for him, Maud," she told the dog on the couch cushion who brightened at the sight of them.

Annabelle went to the kitchen window and watched her son lose himself in an imaginary world. He weaved among the fruit trees gesticulating and mouthing sound effects until he twirled around dramatically and fell to the ground. He laid on the wood chips looking up at the sky. He looked so alone.

Annabelle added another point to her list.

*5. Relies on their community for support and camaraderie.*

Where was Annabelle's support and camaraderie? Lately she couldn't even get that from her husband. She imagined what she would do if the man on the tractor who plowed his field were to knock on her door and introduce himself. The name on his mailbox was Quintana. He would be sitting now at the breakfast bar, embarrassed in his stockinged feet because she requested he remove his boots before entering her house.

"So Mrs. Granger, what brings you to Box Elder?" he would ask.

First she would say, "Oh, please, we're neighbors. Call me Annabelle."

She would pour him a glass of fresh-squeezed lemonade with sprigs of lavender clipped from the plants in front of the porch as garnish. And then she would tell him what happened to Heath in the marsh that day.

"It sounds like you made a brave decision moving your son away from the contaminants, both chemical and social, of the city and choosing a more wholesome life. Not everyone has the guts needed to move away from what is familiar for the sake of one's family. Annabelle, I'm proud of you."

As she topped off his lemonade, which he would find delicious, refreshing, and distinctive, she would wonder for a moment about the state of her bathroom. If he needed to use the facilities would Mr. Quintana find Heath's dribbles all over the seat and a dirty pair of SpiderMan underwear cast off in the corner? Did Annabelle keep house to a standard that could receive an impromptu guest?

In her house on Huntington Road, they'd had a powder room that she forbade Heath to use. Dishes in the drying rack, toys in the living room, even an errant Cheerio on the floor could be excused, but a guest having to tango with your child's urine? That was a different category altogether.

Annabelle went to the pantry for latex gloves, wipes, and a basil-scented bathroom cleaner—because everyone wants a whiff of the old country before doing their business. As she knelt in front of Heath's toilet, she considered how she would introduce herself now that she was no longer a robotics engineer. *I'm a stay-at-home mom* wouldn't do. Nor could she tell Mr. Quintana with a straight face that she was a homesteader, not to the man who got here via tractor.

By choosing to brand herself an expert in rural living, she had alienated herself from her neighbors who would only roll their eyes at her bombast. The only people she could fool would be those she never met. She hoped the locals weren't fans of Wanda Way. Annabelle had moved on from bathroom disinfection to gathering laundry to do a load of reds when her phone pinged.

"Excuse me, Mr. Quintana. I need to check my phone. All that pinging means people like my most recent Instagram post. Are you familiar with Instagram? I'll show you my page."

In her imagination, Mr. Quintana sat rapt at her breakfast bar, one hand on his lemonade while she showed him the app on her phone. She would set a dessert plate with two star-shaped linzer cookies stuffed with raspberry preserves in front of him with a linen cocktail napkin on which she had embroidered the Granger "G." Clumps of drying mud would fall from the cuffs of his jeans. His cowboy hat sitting on the seat beside him would remind her of where she was, how far she had come.

While Annabelle scrolled through her Instagram, Heath opened the door.

"I'm going to the river," Heath told her, sticking only his head inside so he would not have to remove his boots.

"Tell her," Annabelle heard Harley command.

"I'm going to be home after dinner," Heath said.

"Okay, sweetie. Have fun," Annabelle said.

She continued to scroll through Instagram, explaining to Mr. Quintana why one post received more comments than another. She showed him strangers using her augmented reality bouquet in creative ways.

"Why, Annabelle, did you make these cookies yourself?" Mr. Quintana would ask after taking his first bite. "Your husband and son are lucky to have you."

Mr. Quintana would push back in his chair and grab his hat to leave.

"Please stay," Annabelle said. "Let me cook a meal for you. There are things I need to say."

Annabelle began assembling the ingredients for homemade meatloaf with a savory topping containing ketchup, Worcestershire sauce, and horseradish. The breadcrumbs would be real crumbs from one of her crusty loaves, not that stuff that comes in a bag. She would accompany it with a salad containing greens from the garden and a special honey mustard salad dressing she had learned to make.

As she squeezed the ground meats between her fingers, she told Mr. Quintana about Tim. While she blended the topping, she explained her struggle to get pregnant and produce a sibling for Heath. With the meatloaf shaped on a cookie sheet and baking in the oven, Annabelle told him about her soul-sucking former job at which she excelled that also earned her a big salary and gave her social esteem. She'd always thought social esteem a dismissible trifle until now, until she had to present herself without it.

"I think I've made a mistake moving here, Mr. Quintana. What should I do?"

Her phone pinged. It was the evening check-in text from her husband. She looked out the window at the slanting sun. Where had the afternoon gone?

The text read, "How are my two favorite people?"

When she looked up, Mr. Quintana was gone. In her mind, she heard the front door click shut on his departure. Mr. Quintana couldn't help her. But Wanda Way could. Wanda Way sowed social esteem like wildflower seeds in a garden. Annabelle had one week before the interview to make her family Wanda Way perfect. She looked at her five-point note for a happy family. She could do this with or without Paul's support.

Annabelle frowned at the slice of plated meatloaf. What was she thinking? Meatloaf isn't photogenic, even if she harvested rocket leaves, green onions, beets, and miniature carrots from her garden to add a side salad. Annabelle took a photo of the meal and texted it to Paul—"eating dinner," she wrote—and skipped uploading it to Instagram. She pushed the plate aside. She poured herself a bowl of Special K and ate it standing over the sink looking out at her apricot trees.

# 42

ANNABELLE EXAMINED HER FACE IN THE MIRROR. SHE LEANED CLOSE TO examine the now permanent creases around her eyes, the inconspicuous mustache above her lip, and the dimpling skin under her jawline. With her elbows propped on the bathroom counter, she pinched at some whiteheads on her chin and in the crease of her nose.

She had read somewhere that the oil produced in the nose crease was similar in composition to the oil sharks produce and that sharks don't get cancer and so something something something nose sebum cures cancer. Even Internet loving Annabelle could recognize that this bit of trivia required more research, but she couldn't help that it had lodged in her brain as a fun fact.

As she picked at her face, a habit she found soothing, Annabelle recognized in herself a stark loneliness. It had never mattered that Paul traveled all the time when she was at work, but now the days stretched out before her. Even though there was so much to do, so many plants to tend and weeds to pull and skills to learn, it all felt like empty busy work without Paul and Heath or anyone around.

The Wanda Way interview would be one of the biggest events of her life. She was being recognized for her homemaking and in such a short time! She brought to her Instagram feed a technical bent that others didn't have. New technology did not daunt her. She could thrive as an Instagram influencer and yet she didn't have anyone to share her news with.

After a few minutes spent lost in the zone of sliding through photos and videos, she changed to the texting app. She needed to hear from someone real, someone who would respond and validate her existence. Scrolling through her contacts, all people back in Royal Oak, she saw Tim's entry. She'd sent him an email with a few photos of the new place when they'd arrived, but the conversation had tapered.

Did she have a carnie joke she could tell him? Could she tease him about her retirement from the fair? Even if she had a brilliant witticism to text him, it was past seven in Royal Oak. Tim couldn't very well text her while sitting on the couch next to his wife, could he?

There were some mommies she could have texted. They would be jealous of her Wanda Way interview, but she knew she would have to pretend that her decision to uproot the family and move to the New Mexican desert had been a perfect, prescient, and wise decision. She was not up for feigning bliss. She couldn't possibly reveal that her privileged position at home while they worked meant that she was bored and lonely.

The last text from Di said, "I've seen your Insta, so I know you're alive. Just tell me: Do the Hills Have Eyes?"

Di seemed intent on ridiculing Annabelle's choices forever and the woman had an inexhaustible supply of horror movie references about normal people meeting terrible ends at the hands of rural folk. Why was that even a genre? Di would send in the National Guard if Annabelle even hinted to her that she wasn't happy.

Without knowing what she was doing, Annabelle unbuttoned some of her flannel shirt. It had been laundry day, so her three sturdy bras were drying on the rack like spatchcocked game hens. She was wearing a black lacy thickly lined number usually reserved for date nights and funerals.

She held the phone up high for one of those teenaged kissy-lipped selfies. Catching sight of her splotchy, picked at face, she instead snapped a single photo of her lace-lined cleavage. She watched herself, disembodied, scrolling through her contacts. Was she about to sext Tim? No, she stopped at P and entered a message for Paul: "Hey lover, miss you." Annabelle had noticed that sending texts with photos took longer on the spotty cell connection she got at this house, but the message sent.

What kind of juvenile attention grabbing was that? She put herself on the virtual therapist's couch. She was relieved that she had not just sent a text to her former colleague and work-spouse Tim. Maybe that infatuation had died a natural death with distance. But why had she sent that text to Paul?

She thought about his reaction to receiving it. Annabelle knew not to bug Paul at work. He was a busy man and her job now was to handle the household. Calls and texts during work hours were for emergencies only. But maybe, if she sent him a sexy text, he wouldn't mind being bothered at work? Was that why she did it? She needed his attention and felt the only legitimate way to request it was by photographing her cleavage. Annabelle groaned. What was going on with her?

She checked the time, too embarrassed to wait for his reply or for no reply at all to come. Her only chance for human interaction would be if she left right now to check her mail. She'd noticed that the good people of Box Elder congregated at the bank of mailboxes at five-thirty each weekday afternoon. Annabelle buttoned her shirt and hustled for the door. She tossed a squirrel-shaped, homemade frosted dog cookie at Maud so she would know to stay on the porch, a food-based communication system they had been perfecting over the weeks.

Annabelle had accurately predicted the socialization patterns of her neighbors. Three women gathered at the side of the mailbox bank, the place where locals posted notes about garage sales and lost cats. Annabelle unlocked her box, listening for an entrée into the women's conversation. The Granger's only mail was a postcard from Verizon for a limited time offer. Nothing to start a conversation with there.

Then she heard a woman say, "You take that back. Her boyfriend is a sweet young man. He wouldn't have anything to do with something as awful as this."

Now Annabelle was interested in their conversation. She joined them. "What's going on?"

"Are you Grumpy's mom? My little one is Bashful."

This surprised Annabelle. She knew that the kids had adopted the dwarf names she had given them, but didn't know that it had spread to the parents.

"Yes, I'm Annabelle. I'm sorry about those names..."

She stopped short when she saw the poster the women were looking at. It said, "Help us find Alinda Green. 14 y/o, 5'1", brown hair, brown eyes. Last seen Monday, May 13 wearing jeans and a white hoodie with butterflies after being dropped off by the school bus."

There were two pictures of Alinda. One was a school photo, and the other showed her looking much older with tousled hair, makeup, and a skimpy top cuddling a small white cat.

"Oh, how awful," Annabelle said. She was shocked. She believed she had moved her family far away from this kind of danger.

"I wouldn't worry about it," Bashful's mom said. "The police are convinced she ran off with a boyfriend."

"She was going out with the Cordova boy and he's still here. Says he don't know nothing."

"Oh Adina, keep up. That ended months ago, before Christmas. She must have been dating someone from the city, lying to her parents about it."

Bashful's mom waved her goodbye saying, "Welcome to Box Elder."

The friendly farewell sounded ominous.

Annabelle studied Alinda's face in the photos as the other women headed off. She didn't recognize Alinda Green and she couldn't recall anything unusual happening on Monday. Annabelle backed away. She wanted to find Heath.

# 43

ANNABELLE NEEDN'T HAVE WORRIED ABOUT HEATH. WHEN SHE returned home, he was sitting on the porch swing talking to Maud and waiting for his mother to unlock the door.

"I'm sorry, sweetie. I just went to get the mail. Were you waiting long?"

"No."

"What do you say we go out for dinner?" She felt a need to get out of the neighborhood. Alinda's disappearance was disturbing, and she wanted a new setting. "Do you have to go to the bathroom?"

Heath shook his head.

"I'll just get my purse."

Annabelle returned with her purse and a cup of kibble for Maud. She turned on the porch lights before locking the door. There was a taco stand up the road. Annabelle loved their shredded beef tacos with guacamole and red hot sauce and Heath could get a cheeseburger and fries. The patrons ate at picnic tables outdoors, so Heath's mud-caked clothes wouldn't be a problem.

Annabelle clipped Heath into his car seat and wiped his hands and face with a wet nap. He accepted the intrusion into his personal space with limited squirming. She wanted to ask him about Alinda, but she wasn't sure where to start. Once on the road, she glanced at his precious face in the rearview mirror. He smiled out the window.

"Heath, have you heard about a girl from the neighborhood named Alinda?"

"I know Alinda."

Annabelle wasn't expecting this. She thought she needed to bring up the disappearance with Heath in case he heard the kids whispering about a missing schoolmate. She never considered that he would have known her. The girl was fourteen!

"You've met Alinda?"

"She came to play with us at the river after school."

Annabelle panicked. Maybe Heath knew something that the police should know. She did not want him involved in another police investigation.

"You didn't tell me this. Why didn't you tell me she was playing with you guys? Does anyone else come and play with you?"

Heath shrugged and continued to look out the window. Annabelle took a deep breath and tried a new tack.

"Alinda is missing. Her parents are worried about her."

"Her parents shouldn't worry. Death has touched her. She's gone to a better place than she could find on earth."

Annabelle's mouth hung agape at her son's comment when he said, "Mom! Look, it's Dad's car. He's home." He was pointing out the window toward the church's parking lot.

Annabelle ignored him and said, "Heath, why would you think she's dead?" But she caught the reflection of Paul's distinctive red Jeep Cherokee in her mirror. The car was parked out of sight from the road behind the church. Instead of waiting for Heath's answer to her question, Annabelle wondered what Paul was doing home two days early and parked in an empty parking lot. Without looking in her mirrors she turned around and drove into the lot. She pulled her car up to his and wound down her window. He looked up from the phone in his lap and wound his down too. He looked pleased to see her.

"Hey, babe. I'm home."

"What are you doing here?"

"The client canceled. Half their office has been home with the flu all week."

Annabelle nodded. "But what are you doing here?"

"I just pulled off to check my messages."

Annabelle nodded again. "Well, we're going to dinner at Paco's Tacos. Do you want to come?"

"I sure do." Paul tucked his phone in his jacket pocket and wound up his window. He locked his car and leaned in the window to kiss Annabelle. He slipped her a little tongue and said, "I'm so excited to spend the rest of the week with you guys." Annabelle thought of the chesty text she had sent him earlier that afternoon. There'd been no reply.

Paul opened Heath's door after Annabelle flicked the locks. "Hey, buddy. It's great to see you." He rumpled Heath's hair and engaged in some odd choose a hand for a pinch or tickle game that they had been playing lately. He settled into the passenger seat and Annabelle ferried her family to dinner.

She was distracted through the whole meal. When Paul knew he was coming home, why hadn't he texted her? And why stop to read messages one minute from their house? Annabelle felt like a fool. At some point in their marriage, she had stopped keeping track of Paul's business trips. She rarely knew what company he was going to work for in any given week much less the hotel in which he was staying.

Periodically, they would watch a disaster flick—a volcano erupting all over the western US or a tsunami wiping out the eastern seaboard —with ballsy displaced family members going on cross-country quests to find each other. Afterward, Annabelle would make Paul write down his travel itinerary and hotel before he left. But that never became a habit and they would both forget for his next trip.

Annabelle worried, like all wives who have learned their husbands are lying about their whereabouts, that Paul might be having an affair. It would be so easy for him. It's not that she wasn't interested in his life, it's just that they had parceled out their division of labor so completely that if they didn't talk about it, they assumed it was going well. Annabelle didn't like the thought of Paul having an affair if only because that meant he had lost some of the ardor he felt for her. She depended on his continual admiration for her self-esteem. If he saw something in her, then there must be something there.

But then a worse thought struck her. What if Paul didn't come home early? What if he never left? Alinda went missing on Monday. Annabelle thought of Alinda's photo holding the cat and trying so hard to look grown up. She might have caught his eye. Paul could have been skulking around here waiting for her. But that was ridiculous. Paul was not a kidnapper or lurer of children and not a murderer. Of course, that is what Mrs. Bundy thought too.

## 44

The next morning Annabelle burst in on Paul while he was in the shower. She leaned against the bathroom counter and folded her arms.

"Are you having an affair?" she called to him over the sound of the shower spray. It was the same tone of voice she would use to ask if he preferred a bagel or toast with breakfast. There was a long silence from the shower. During this time, Annabelle began to tremble. How had she let this happen?

Paul turned off the water and pushed aside the shower curtain.

"Why would you think that?" he asked. Even dripping wet and naked he didn't look vulnerable.

"You're not even going to deny it?"

"I do deny it." He pulled a towel from the bar and dabbed at himself. "But why would you think that?"

"Where were you this week?"

"I told you. I flew Monday morning to Las Vegas. I met with the client in the afternoon to do our preliminary presentations and data gathering. The next day, half the office called in sick. I sat alone in their conference room handling my emails and writing up a report. The next day when I went in, even more people were out sick. The manager requested that we cancel the rest of the week. I got the earliest flight I could back home."

"Why didn't you tell me you were coming home?"

Paul sighed. He pushed past her to rub deodorant into each armpit while he studied himself in the defogging mirror. With his towel wrapped around his waist, he left the bathroom and Annabelle trailed after him. He grabbed the bedpost and swung around.

"We made the decision to move here together. It wasn't your decision; it was our decision. You keep trying to prove something to me. I was afraid that if I told you I was coming home, you would spend the whole day completing the chores for the week and fixing a vegan three-course dinner with a fresh-baked dessert. You don't have to play Holly Homemaker because you stopped working. It's enough for Heath to have his mom around."

He took Annabelle's hand and kissed it. She always hated that. There was no way to kiss a hand without it being smarmy. He proceeded to his dresser, oblivious.

"But why stop at the church parking lot?"

"I see why that looks weird, but I needed to call my office to let them know what had happened in Las Vegas and I had to cancel my flight on Friday and update my expense report with the changes. I wanted to have that all done before I rolled into the driveway so I could turn off my phone and enjoy my time with you and Heath."

He pulled her into him and kissed her neck. "And that's exactly what we're going to do."

Annabelle couldn't help but smile. She wrapped her arms around him. It was so good to have Paul home.

They spent that day and the next alone together in the house while Heath played with The Six. It was like a second honeymoon sans campervan. They snuggled on the couch and watched *It Follows* one afternoon and *Don't Breathe* the next—Annabelle got her horror flick fix and Paul his chance to shout at the screen when he saw a shot of Detroit he recognized. Is there anything more luxurious than watching a movie at home in the afternoon?

Paul polished off her tub of Curaçao no-bake booze balls while they watched. This was the highest compliment he had yet paid her new kitchen skills. They swayed together in the kitchen when Lady Antebellum's *Just a Kiss* started playing. This had been the song for the first dance at their wedding, although it wasn't a favorite of either of theirs. Leave it to Paul, Mr. Sentimental, to remember that. They made out on the couch. They made love in the shower and on top of the covers in broad daylight. It was like they were in grad school again.

But a doubt lingered in Annabelle's mind. Why hadn't Paul come down with the flu?

## 45

"THERE'S A GIRL MISSING," ANNABELLE TOLD PAUL. IT WAS SATURDAY and Annabelle couldn't pretend any longer that she thought everything between them was fine.

"Missing?"

"Yes. From around here. She hasn't been home for a few days. The police are involved. No one has seen her since Monday."

"How terrible for her parents"

"Were you really in Las Vegas on Monday?"

"You think... me?"

She nodded.

"Jesus, Annabelle."

"Were you?"

"Yes, I told you. I was in Las Vegas. Why would you think...? Because I came home early? When did you become so—"

"So, what? When did I become so crazy?"

"I was going to say fragile."

Usually at this point in an argument, one of them offered the other a conciliatory tone, and the other accepted. They both would state what they would do differently and apologize for the confrontation. Hugs were exchanged. Annabelle would feel heard and appreciated.

But not this time. They fought like they had never before in their entire marriage. They dropped all pretense and civility. They forgot the rules. They went for the gullet. No one knew Annabelle better than Paul did, so no one could insult her with the precision that he did. And she did not spare his feelings either. Their marriage was supposed to be based on an agreement that they would help each other grow and fulfill their dreams. Paul was supposed to support her self-esteem and her self-actualization. He was not supposed to make her feel like a bad parent because she used Instagram for her creative outlet.

Maybe it was true what he accused; maybe she had never loved him the way he loved her. Aside from a crush on Jason Hornbury in middle school, he of the curly hair and sideways smile, where she ached, she spied, she giggled, she walked around in a haze, the love bug as popularly depicted had never bitten Annabelle. And Annabelle was positive that her feelings for Jason Hornbury had everything to do with pubescent hormonal surges and nothing to do with True Love.

Annabelle hadn't been swept away in her romance with Paul, but she didn't find this to be a lacking in herself and she didn't find it to be a shortcoming of Paul's. Quite the contrary. Annabelle understood Paul, and she knew what she was getting when she chose him to be her mate. What could be a higher compliment? I see you and I want you. It was an analytical decision perhaps, but those seemed more likely to last than ones based on surging hormones and the romantic abandonment of one's personal goals.

Perhaps her love-struck peers would groan at her, accuse her of *being* a robot not building them. But she never thought for a second that hers wasn't the better choice. As soon as the goo-goo eyed woke up, they would find themselves trapped without the tools to improve their situation. But she and Paul were smart. They knew, for example, how to have a fight. The purpose was to stick to the disagreement at hand, not to bring up every peripheral nit-pick and foible. And *ad hominem* attacks were off the table. Emotions must be controlled. One had to remember that their spouse was a trusted partner who wanted the best for the relationship. She could do that. Paul could do that. And they had, many times before.

But not this time. The argument deteriorated.

"I hope it was you who took Alinda because it would mean you're more interesting than you seem."

"Jesus, Annabelle. I have a reputation to uphold. How is that going to work if my wife thinks I murdered a child?"

"Aha! No one said she was murdered. For all we know, she is just missing."

Paul grabbed Annabelle's accusing finger and twisted her into him. "This isn't *Law & Order*. You can't catch me in a lie I'm not telling." He pressed her arms to her sides as she attempted to twist free. "Stop this!" he said through gritted teeth. "Stop this now. You act like more of a child than our own child does."

"Let. Me. Go!" Released, Annabelle twirled back on him, her accusatory finger back in action. "You don't have a reputation to uphold around here because you don't know anyone around here. Neither do I. The only one making friends and settling in is Heath, and he's five."

"Exactly. He's five. And where is he right now?"

"So now we're back to this? If you're so worried why don't you go get him? Oh, wait! I know why. Because you're just biding your time until something goes wrong and I see the light and we can move back to Royal Oak to live like normal people."

The recriminations continued from there.

"Paul, you're such a boring traditionalist. You feign this snooty cosmopolitanism when really you're just like a big homesick baby at sleep-away camp. You pretend to be fine, but you're counting the days until you can go back to Michigan and to your mommy and daddy."

"Well you're a selfish, self-absorbed housewife whose novel excuse for child neglect is not because you're working three jobs or are mentally ill but because you've become addicted to an app popular with teens and the people who market to them."

They'd reached an impasse. The rest of the day they scowled at each other and communicated in polite expressions of regret: *Sorry, I should have put the milk back; Forgive the intrusion, but I heard your phone vibrating.*

Even in bed, the mood was frigid. Paul read his book, another biography of George Washington, without a glance in her direction. She made a show of organizing her pillows and opening her book, but she couldn't read a word. Keeping her eyes on her book, she listened for the intermittent turning of Paul's pages and waited for him to finish his chapter and turn out his light. This kind of tension was antithetical to the good sleep hygiene she was fanatic to maintain in their household. Eventually, he turned off his light and rolled to his side with his back to her. He didn't say goodnight. Annabelle felt a hard lump in her throat. She too put away her book, turned off the light, and set her back toward her husband. She waited until she heard the throaty rumbles indicative of Paul's sleeping breaths before she allowed herself to cry into her pillow.

But her self-pity didn't last. Wide awake, she got up. The bedroom hallway was lit with a nightlight, but after that she moved through her still new house feeling her way in the dark. Her hand left the hallway wall while she walked across the tile to the kitchen. The white of the paper towels in their stand on the counter guided her. She tore off a sheet and blew her nose. Sliding on Paul's wool jacket, she stepped outside. She tucked her crumpled paper towel in the pocket. Maud's white fur glowed in the starlight. Annabelle crept toward the porch swing, hoping not to awaken her.

When she sat, she realized that Maud was already awake. The dog lay like the Sphinx panting in the chilly night air. It occurred to Annabelle that Maud might never sleep. She might carry through day and night in a blurry haze of pain. It hurt her arthritic joints to walk. It hurt her worm-ridden circulatory system to breathe. It hurt her nubby gums to eat. Annabelle thought about euthanasia. Is that what she was supposed to do? Put Maud out of her misery?

But was physical pain the same thing as misery? Maybe for an animal. Annabelle knew from her college physiological psych classes that animals weren't capable of a full emotional repertoire. They didn't have the sentience to feel the emotions they displayed. The puppy with his tail between his legs in front of the rummaged-through kitchen trash wasn't feeling guilty; he was responding with submission to his owner's anger. The orca mother swimming with the dead calf she delivered days ago wasn't grieving, but merely stuck in an instinctual behavioral pattern. Annabelle knew the rule: humans are the only conscious beings. But she also knew people felt threatened by sophisticated robots and always strove to diminish their accomplishments. Sure the robotic arm is a more talented surgeon, but it needs a trained doctor to monitor it. Couldn't the same defensive diminishing apply to the animal kingdom?

Annabelle thought she understood Maud. She experienced physical pain, sure, but then there was the emotional kind too. Maud missed her former owners. She was a dog recovering from bereavement. It wasn't time for euthanasia because she was a complicated beast and her lot could yet improve. Annabelle thought Maud's dignity in the face of hardship set a good example. She soothed Annabelle and made her forget Paul's painful words. They sat together companionably that night, looking out at the glowing white pattern of the remaining snow on the distant mountains.

# 46

On Sunday, Paul set a passive-aggressive example for her. He became a super-involved parent intent on getting Heath to laugh and learn new skills. The two of them identified and colored pictures of each of the three bugs Heath had kidnapped and stored in his terrarium. They learned the caterpillar with a threatening orange spike on its tail was a tomato hornworm. If Annabelle had allowed the caterpillar to stay in her garden, it would have feasted this summer on her tomato plants still sprouting in their soil-filled grids on her dresser.

Next, Paul read to Heath fun-facts about their new home state. There is a state park—Annabelle sensed an imminent field trip— where one could walk alongside dinosaur tracks imprinted in rock. The New Mexico paleontological record was riddled with novel finds. The bones of North America's largest dinosaur, who was one hundred thirty feet long, were discovered here. And a 16-year-old had discovered a Heath-sized variety of T-Rex, only three feet tall. Down south, one can sled in shorts and t-shirts down dunes composed of pure white sand, that is if the park isn't closed for a missile test. And most interesting to Annabelle, in 1947 an alien spacecraft may or may not have crashed on a ranch outside Roswell. A UFO museum in the town displayed artifacts from the crash site. Perhaps they would like to display in their lobby her oil paintings of costumed aliens in domestic scenes?

Annabelle overheard all this while she planned for her interview with Wanda tomorrow and made a shopping list for her intended recipes. It was hurtful to feel excluded from her husband and son's Sunday morning activities, but she was relieved to be left alone to prepare. From her kitchen window, Annabelle delighted to see The Six climbing out of the arroyo and approaching their front door. She couldn't wait to see how Paul would handle them.

Heath heard them approach and abandoned the Lego pirate island he and Paul were building to run for the door. He struggled to turn the knob and Paul got up to block the door. He squatted down to Heath's level and looked him in the eye.

"Do you want to go play with those kids or stay here with me today? I can send them away."

"Go play."

"Are you sure? I'm leaving tomorrow for work."

"I want to go play."

Paul considered his next move. The kids called to Heath, and knocked, and kicked at the door.

"Oh, for God's sake, Paul," Annabelle said. "Let him go."

Paul opened the door without a word to the kids and ordered Heath to be back in an hour. It was a pointless stipulation. Heath didn't have a watch and had zero sense of time. But Paul looked appeased. With a scowl tossed at Annabelle, he retreated to the spare bedroom to read his book.

When an hour and a half had gone by, Annabelle saw Paul stomping down the arroyo. He was going to fetch Heath. His funeral, she thought, glad to be nowhere near that violation of trust. Paul had taken a few steps when he cocked his head and climbed back to the driveway. Annabelle thought he was abandoning his plan. Maybe he would begin cleaning out his car with the hand-held detailer vacuum that Annabelle had thought got left behind in Royal Oak with all other tools of pretension. Instead, Annabelle, running through a series of windows, watched Paul march out their driveway and toward the home of their hoarding neighbor next door. Annabelle wiped her hands and ran outside. Was he planning on doing something drastic? Was he going to invite that woman to dinner just to prove that he was attempting to settle in?

Annabelle ran to the road in time to see Paul disappear past the woman's house into the arroyo in which she had first sought comfort with her plate of cookies. Listening, Annabelle understood why. The Six were screaming and shouting in that arroyo the way kids do. She waited on the porch with Maud for their return. She couldn't wait to see Heath's face, having been pulled from his friends. When she heard their steps crunch down the gravel she popped out to greet her son, but Paul made the first move.

"Want to ride your bike?" he asked Heath.

Annabelle watched Paul strap Heath's spiked helmet to his head and heard his mock casual tone.

"Hey, Heath. What were you guys doing to that poor cat?"

"Nothing. We were just inviting him to our meeting."

"To your meeting? Whose cat is he?"

"I don't know."

"Well, where did you find him?"

"We tricked him to get into the cage with tuna fish."

"Heath, did you let the cat go?"

"Yes."

"Hold on. Big push. Ready? Weeeee." Heath's bike rolled down the slope of the dirt road into a morass where the arroyo intersected the dirt road. They had invented a game where Paul's pushing power would send Heath slaloming around obstacles on the slope before coming to a halt in the deep arroyo sand. They were playing on the road, but few cars ever drove past and when they did, it was at a sedate, rutted-road-enforced speed.

Annabelle tried not to feel annoyed, but it upset her that Heath was having such a good day with his dad. She had hoped he would throw a tantrum when he was pulled from The Six. She felt like she was losing an argument and she felt jealous. That is until Paul's phone rang—on a Sunday—and he called to her to take over pushing Heath.

Then she felt put upon, like no one was taking her preparations for Wanda Way seriously.

Annabelle took over for Paul, walking beside Heath as he pedaled. Heath didn't care for Annabelle's pushing style, so he turned away from the arroyo and headed the other way down the road under his own steam. He pedaled farther than Annabelle wanted, past the neighbor's fence, and got stuck in a rut. Annabelle had no choice but to go help push him out of the rut before he bent his training wheels for good. Leaning over him with both her hands on his handlebars, she peeked to see her neighbor, ever-present in her porch chair. Annabelle smiled and removed one hand to wave before getting Heath settled back toward home. The woman made a strange signaling gesture that Annabelle just caught out of the corner of her eye and called to her. It sounded like she was saying, "My cat," before Annabelle slipped beyond the fence.

# 47

SOMETHING WAS TUGGING ON HER BLANKETS.

Adrenaline sent shivers through her veins. She took stock. She was in bed, in the new house, Maud wasn't barking, and the house was quiet. Paul, asleep next to her, was definitely not planning on knocking off his wife who had figured out that he murders teenage girls. She had been sleeping on her side facing the open bedroom door, but the tugging was coming from behind her. It had to be Heath. She willed herself to roll over and face the tugging.

"Mom. Why can't you heal from death?"

It was an ominous question to be asked at your bedside in the middle of the night. Like something a possessed child would say before jamming a battery-powered turkey knife into your throat.

Blurry-eyed and disoriented, Annabelle tossed off the blankets and swung her legs out of bed. Her commitment to sleep hygiene meant they had a strict no-sharing-mommy-and-daddy's-bed policy. All soothing happened in Heath's bed. She got up and directed him back to his room, using furniture and the walls to guide their way. Heath, ever compliant, climbed into his bed and Annabelle pulled up his covers. He looked wide awake, but Annabelle hoped that by not saying anything, she would lure him back to sleep. She headed back to her room, but at his door she stopped.

*Why can't you heal from death?*

It was happening now, in the middle of the night. Heath was ready to talk about what happened in the marsh that day. After a moment's hesitation, Annabelle returned to sit on the floor at his bedside. She tucked inside his bed tent and found his ankle under the covers. To make sure she had heard his question correctly through her sleepiness, she waited for him to ask it again. She could see in the starlight that he was staring at her.

Annabelle sighed and pulled the throw from his rocking chair. The spring nights were much colder in Box Elder than they were in Royal Oak, probably something to do with the lack of humidity and the altitude. She wrapped the blanket around her trying to figure out how to begin, wondering what it was he needed to hear to soothe his worried little soul.

Heath started the discussion for her. "Remember when I hit my head at the good park?"

Annabelle remembered. Heath liked to go to a playground about twenty minutes from their house in Royal Oak that he called the good park. It was good because, frankly, it was unsafe. It was full of classic playground equipment: tall swings that let the kids go way high, monkey bars held in place with concrete footings poking out of the sand, jumbo teeter-totters that lifted kids too high off the ground, and an actual merry-go-round. This park had never seen high-density polyethylene or shredded rubber ground cover. It was not the kind of playground where the worst injuries were static shocks.

Paul liked to take Heath there. It was a mildly disobedient adventure for Heath, as Annabelle had declared the good park off-limits. Most of the time, they both came home sweaty and content, but on one occasion, that did not happen. Paul had been pushing Heath in the swing. Heath liked to sail up so high that the swing skipped a little as it fell back down. He also liked to dip his head back towards the ground on the return arc. She couldn't blame Paul for what happened because Heath's thrill-seeking impetus came from her.

As Paul told the story, they had decided to go to the teeter-totters. Paul was getting ready to grab Heath's hips to slow him down when instead, as the swing reached its penultimate position, Heath jumped free. Heath had shown off his swing jumping skills before, but this had always been on the smaller swing set at his preschool.

Paul told Annabelle—and they laughed about it because everything had all turned out fine, but it must have been terrifying at the time—that Heath launched through the air like he had been shot from a cannon. As gravity pulled him back to earth, his arms and legs flailed and his hair raised up off his skull. He landed, what felt to Paul like minutes later, forehead first at the edge of the merry-go-round. When Paul reached him, the blood was already pouring down his face and soaking his t-shirt. The doctor at the urgent care removed some splinters and washed clean what turned out to be a bad scrape.

But if children can contemplate their own mortality, this was the incident that did it for Heath. The seconds of free falling through the air and then the blood clouding his vision despite Paul's cashmere sweater pushed against the wound, was Heath's very own *memento mori*.

"Yes, I remember, sweetie."

"There was so much blood, but then the doctor cleaned it and it was fine. I didn't die."

"That's right. It was just a big boo-boo."

"But a person can have a boo-boo in their head and it bleeds a lot and they die."

Annabelle remembered Miss Sara's description of the dead gang member in the marsh.

*He was shot in the face. The back of his skull was missing. There was gore.*

Annabelle stroked his ankle under the covers and dove in. "Sometimes injuries are so bad that a person can't heal and they die. That is why we are always emphasizing safety. Your dad and I work very hard so you can't have accidents that your body can't heal from."

"But what about if it's not an accident?"

Here we go, Annabelle thought. Heath knows that kid in the marsh was murdered. It is this fact more than the death itself that has been plaguing him.

"Heath, there are some bad people in the world who don't care if they hurt or kill other people. One reason we live here in Box Elder is to be away from bad people." No, that wasn't right. She didn't want to scare Heath off from traveling and experiencing the world. She didn't want to raise a child who reached old age having never ventured farther than Santa Fe.

"Heath, there are bad people everywhere, but—"

"Can a bad person ever go back to being a good person?"

Ah, now they were on some interesting philosophical ground.

"Yes," Annabelle said without equivocation. "This is a very important thing to learn. It is one of the most powerful parts of being human. A bad person can become a good person if they know what they did is wrong and they say they are sorry in their hearts and to the people that matter."

"I'm sorry, Mom," Heath said with a snotty sob.

"What do you have to be sorry for?"

"I don't want to be a bad person."

"You're not a bad person, sweetie. You've done nothing wrong. What happened out there wasn't your fault. It wasn't your fault."

Annabelle scurried off to get a tissue and a cup of water. When she returned Heath was sitting up in bed. She handed him each item in turn and kissed his forehead. When he laid back down, she rubbed his back.

"Your dad and I love you very much, Heath Granger. And so does Mr. Rex." She pressed Heath's spittle-browned dinosaur into his arms.

## 48

DAN QUINTANA

On Sunday, Delfina and I went to visit the Greens to express our condolences. I trembled as we walked up the footpath. Delfina carried a jar of her homemade vegetable soup and a bag of just-baked dinner rolls and I edged my fingers around the rim of my hat. Though Alinda is missing and not presumed dead, the act of meeting with Amy and Gary was very difficult for me. It dredged up acute, searing memories of the time following Dinah's death.

I remember Pat and Melinda visiting us after she died. I watched them approach from the kitchen window. Pat held his hat and Melinda bore a food dish. Their visit, usually a joy, and on this instance supposed to bring comfort, filled me with dread. I am ashamed to say, I would have hid in the pantry if Delfina hadn't been there to let them in.

Facing my best friend as a failed father was like meeting Pat in disguise. I feared he wouldn't recognize me anymore. I avoided eye contact and waited for the relief that would come when I could sit by myself again. I surrendered to the conventions of the scenario, not allowing myself to take part. Sitting on the couch beside Delfina, I nodded when appropriate and tried not to stare out the window too much. I hoped to make it through Pat and Melinda's visit without allowing any acknowledgement to pass between Pat and me. He knew me so completely and for so long; I was afraid one sympathetic look from him would be my undoing.

But something happened during that visit. Something did pass between us as hard as I tried to maintain my defenses. Pat said, "Remember Dinah's cat?"

"Disney." Delfina whispered the cat's name.

"You all had baby chicks in the barn that spring, so when Dinah found that kitten you said she couldn't keep it, so she secretly kept him in our shed," Pat said. I had forgotten the story of how Disney became our cat.

"She didn't want our boys to adopt him, so she told them a ghost haunted the shed. When they heard the noises of the cooped up cat running around, they believed her. That's how we found out. Matthew wouldn't go in the shed to get the hoe. It terrified him. As the days went on, they caught Dinah going into the shed with food. She told them she had a special relationship with the ghost and would bring him food so it wouldn't hurt her. Our boys were so gullible they believed her even when she came out with scoops of cat turds in the kitty litter we kept in there for sanding the porch steps in winter."

Delfina said, "That's right. And when you told us, Dan felt so bad for the kitten and so proud of Dinah for taking care of him, that he bought a bag of cat food and toys."

Despite myself I joined in. "I told her, 'I saw this felt mouse at the country store and thought you might like it,' and that I'd gotten cat food in case the chickens wanted to try some. The best was the scratching post I made. Dinah helped me with it. I think she thought I knew about her secret cat. When we were all done, I said, 'There now. Don't you think all the mice in the barn would like to play with this?' Oh, you should have seen her face. I set it up in the barn and walked away. It wasn't there the next morning. Everything ended up in your shed."

Pat continued, "And a couple weeks later, when the chicks were bigger and you all were over for dinner I made a big show of getting something for you out of the shed. Dinah tried to distract us. And when we opened the shed—well, the cat shot out of there like a sailor on shore leave—but Dinah had turned the place into some kind of cat paradise."

"She used every one of her sweatshirts to build beds for the cat on the various shelves with ramps in between. It took me several washings to get those clothes clean," Delfina said.

"And she hung a ball from the rafter for him to swat at," Melinda said. "I don't think our boys ever stopped believing a ghost haunted the shed. Dinah could be very convincing."

We all laughed and smiled even as thick tears streamed down our faces. It was a revelation, that. I didn't think laughter was possible when I felt so hollowed out and miserable. Most of all, I didn't think I could interact as I had before with the people closest to me. Pat helped me to remember Dinah as I wanted to, as the happy, wily, creative, and loving person she was. He helped me to recognize that others would remember her that way too.

Pat and Melinda's visit took place after Dinah's funeral. We had no doubt that Dinah was dead and never coming back. The situation was different for the Greens. Alinda had been missing for six days. Gary's heart told him during those dark days without her that Alinda was gone for good. He was working through the depths of full-blown grief.

Amy though, she still boiled over with frantic energy. She held on to hope that Alinda had run away and was off on some Rumspringa and would return home with a butterfly tattoo and a hangover any day now, or that a lonely, gentle person had kidnapped her and was keeping her warm and fed until Alinda could claw his eyes out and escape. With another poster or another TV interview, Amy believed she could bring Alinda home. I couldn't blame her, but she was in denial. She still thought they could resolve the situation in a comical way that would leave them all laughing about the misunderstanding.

I felt for them. I wanted to give the Greens something, the way Pat and Melinda had when they visited us. I wanted them to feel again the memory of their daughter, but surrounded by happiness. So I told them a story of Alinda, the best one I had. She was not a young woman I knew well. I told them the story of Alinda and Harley.

When Dinah died, this community rallied around us, even though our daughter represented a scourge that has overtaken the rural parts of New Mexico like a contagion. Dinah's death was the first time Box Elder had to contend with the fact that heroin had arrived here too. We were not immune.

Friends picked up our mail and dropped it off at our door. They invited us to dinner. Neighbors hailed us from our common fence-line anytime they saw us out. They were all checking to be sure that the grief wasn't eating us alive. As much as I wanted to, we couldn't surrender to our emotions because we were now raising Harley.

The community was kind to her. Harley was essentially an orphan with her mother gone and her father blowing in the wind. We never heard from Trey after he moved out for good. He may not know that Dinah is dead. In the weeks following her death, Delfina tried to find Trey to let him know he had a daughter that needed him. Delfina even hired a private detective to find him. His services only lasted three days before I put the kibosh on that. I don't care if Trey never sees his daughter again. I convinced Delfina that the last thing we want is the drug-peddling louse who took our daughter to take our grand-daughter away too. I hope to never set eyes on that man again.

The community, knowing that we were past our child-raising prime, sent over their children to play with Harley. She was never alone from morning til bedtime those first months. Neighborhood kids arrived at our door to walk her to the bus in the mornings. They played together after school. Some nights we had a rabble of kids eating dinner with us and some nights Harley did her homework and ate at another's house. The thought of those parents' and kids' extraordinary empathy still puts a lump in my throat.

We have always raised the kids around here to be independent.

When I was young, we walked to school and home for lunch with our siblings and other kids from the earliest age. Our parents taught us to be responsible. I fed the sheep and let them out to pasture before I was tall enough to see over their wool. I learned to plow my grandfather's field when I was eleven. By the time I was thirteen, I drove the tractor a mile down the road plowing the fields of my grandfather's friends for a couple of bucks. There was less traffic in those days and people drove with more caution. Drivers then were as likely to encounter around the next curve a thirteen-year-old on a tractor, or an eight-year-old with a ball, or a mama dog with her litter, as another car.

But a laxness developed when the local kids came to play with Harley. Instead of requiring all kids home by dinner, their families decided that spending time with Harley was a community service. Parents granted their kids special dispensation. This made Harley especially popular. The parents figured that as long as their kids were with Harley, there was no need to worry. One person who took advantage of her parents looking the other way as long as she was with Harley was Alinda Green.

Today, Harley spends her time with the group of young ones who now call themselves The Six. It makes them sound like a rogue band of gunslingers. The reason a fifth-grader insists on spending her time with a bunch of kindergarteners goes back to Alinda.

# WEEK FOUR

# 49

WHEN PAUL KISSED HER FOREHEAD ON THE MORNING OF HER WANDA Way interview before he left for the airport, Annabelle pretended to stay asleep. She didn't move from her somniferous curl until she heard his car crunch its exit on the gravel driveway. Then she spread out to the center of the bed. She stared up at the ceiling like a frozen snow angel and allowed her brow to furrow.

On a scale of one to ten, how likely was it she had married a murderer? She thought of Paul in graduate school. During those days, they spent nearly all their time together. If they weren't in class or at the lab, they were studying together, or taking long walks around Ann Arbor, or swimming in the pool and sweating in the sauna at the natatorium.

They were both very busy, dedicated students. They didn't socialize much. They shared a common group of friends who got together at each other's houses to play board games and drink. If he was sneaking off to murder people, it had to have been that he was skipping class and that seemed unlikely given his grades and the admiration his professors had for him. And if he had a secret predilection for murdering young women, why hadn't she made the list? Perhaps she was a little long in the tooth now, but she was confident that, in graduate school, she could have captured a murderer's imagination.

If she hadn't married a murderer, perhaps Paul had become one. Just as she had transformed herself into a homesteading homemaker and Instagram influencer, maybe he had channeled his mid-life angst into kidnapping teen girls. Paul hadn't seen her transformation coming, but he had embraced it and supported her. Was she to do the same? Perhaps, Alinda Green had been his first victim. Did that make it better? Was she willing to cover for him if she was his first and last?

Annabelle tried to envision what happened. Maybe Paul didn't have a client at all last week. He pretended like he did because he didn't want to poke around the house or spend time with her. He drove off as if headed for the airport, but instead he got a hotel room in town under an assumed name. The name he would choose would be stupid, something like Skip Nasterjack, because he couldn't help himself.

Maybe he sat around in his hotel room all day reading his book in his underwear, but he got bored and lonely and decided to come home. He would criticize himself as he drove. All he wanted was a successful career, check, and a family he would love to spend time with, wah-wah. Now he was staying in hotel rooms to avoid them—morose Heath and his ambition-less wife. He would be upset and frustrated, but then he would see Alinda Green get off the bus and it would be like the sun coming out from behind the clouds.

What followed would be so smooth for him, like all his training to charm and dazzle strangers had been for this moment.

"Hey," he called to Alinda as he wound down his window. "I just found mountain lion cubs. They're all alone. I think we should rescue them. Can you help me?"

Sweet kitten-loving Alinda hopped in his car. She clicked on her seatbelt because she intended to be safe and live a long healthy life. He drove her down an isolated road where no one would see his bright red car. He led her out into the scrubland, chatting with her about school and volleyball, until they were far enough for no one to hear her scream. Then he pointed under a piñon tree.

"They're just under there," he said.

As she left the car and kneeled to look, he hit her with a rock, but just to daze her. Paul did not like blood. Then he used a stick to press down on her wind-pipe, one hand on either side of her cheeks. Her eyes bulged and her skin turned red and clammy. Drool ran from her mouth and tears from her eyes. It was a silent, slow process, but one full of intense meaning. He was present and intentional. Getting into it, he added his knee to the weight pressing on her slim neck. Her bloodshot eyes clouded, and he knew it was done.

He removed his red v-neck cashmere sweater Annabelle had gotten him for Father's Day last year and hung it by its tag from a branch of the piñon. He gathered rocks and set them on the body. He set them with care not wanting now to hurt her. The rocks of the desired size became sparser nearby, and he had to travel further to find them. He only carried one in each hand, refusing to dirty his shirt by loading them in his arms.

It's a lot of work, this murder business, but worth it, he thought, smiling to himself. And just like that, once again, he was happy to come home to his family. We would feel like safety to him. We would feel like people who could accept him and love him for whoever he chooses to become.

This was an eerily plausible scenario. Paul didn't suffer from a lack of opportunity to pull off a secret crime. Unlike in grad school, Annabelle rarely saw Paul. He was accountable to no one. There could be a trail of dead girls in every corporate town in the country. His job was a perfect cover. If he were smart, and Paul was smart, there wouldn't be anything to connect him to his crimes or his crimes to each other.

On Thursday and Friday, when Paul had held her hips and swayed with her in the kitchen, or taken her foot in his lap for a rub while they watched a movie, or snuggled into her back as he fell asleep, all she could think about was how she and Heath could get away from Paul, if indeed, he had done something to Alinda Green. But now that she was alone, staring at the ceiling in their bedroom, smelling his pillow, Annabelle wondered if she could absolve him. He would first have to confess to her. Annabelle didn't care for lying, especially when it was a hard-to-believe story of some super-flu wiping out an office.

The truth was, Annabelle would understand if he told her he had been murdering women to alleviate the banal soul-wearying routine of the corporate world or to fill some existential-hole he had hitherto missed in the guiding logic he called his life's plan. She would understand because she too felt soul-wearied by an existential hole. The only difference was that she hadn't felt like murdering anyone...yet.

## 50

WITH HOURS LEFT UNTIL HER INTERVIEW, HER CAR WAS PERPENDICULAR to the road and inoperable. The accident had been minor, stupid really. But now they were stuck. Rain pelted her car, sliding down the windows like streaks of alien blood—all cloaking technology and no gore. She couldn't see out. The wipers swiped clear the windshield, but it was her side window she needed clean. She wouldn't be able to see an oncoming car. Still, Annabelle made no move to protect them. Her anxiety, perhaps not entirely attributable to the accident, left her paralyzed.

Annabelle took this mud-snared moment to excoriate herself. She wasn't handling this like the empowered woman she knew herself to be. What would her former self, the pert grad student installing a Helium-Neon laser, think of the trembling, unemployed, confused woman she was today? Lassitude did not become her.

Her Saab had fishtailed on a stretch of slippery mud turning off the main road onto the country lane. She steered into the skid, but the back end didn't respond—even with the new set of all-season tires rated "excellent" at the shop—and the car slid with no traction at all sideways and partially off the road. It was a slow-motion slide and would have been no big deal. She would have been able to continue on her way but for the drainage ditch that paralleled the road. Her back tires were mired in this ditch, which was flooded with rainwater. Her front tires clung to the road while the water rushing through the back ones rocked the car. The dutiful swipes of the windshield wipers told her the car was running, but her Saab wagon had no ability to power forward out of the ditch.

Annabelle couldn't summon the will to recover from this. She thought of the groceries defrosting in the back. The sticks of butter for her lavender buttercream frosting would soften from rigid bricks to flaccid logs. Her fresh herbs were wilting, her milk curdling. The condensation forming on the eggshells was extending safe harbor to *Salmonella*. It wasn't fatal. The food didn't have to be safe to consume. It just had to look good for her Wanda Way interview this afternoon.

They were so close to home. If it wasn't pouring rain, she would be able to see the green metal roof of their house. They could abandon the car and walk, but Annabelle didn't want to trudge with a child through the rain and the muck. So instead she turned to her phone for solace. Paul did not pick up. Too busy murdering a local cheerleader, perhaps. Annabelle hung up when his voicemail turned on and tossed the phone onto the passenger seat. She narrowed her eyes at it. She willed Paul to call her, confirm his location (supposedly consulting this week at a minor tech firm in San Jose), and tell her what to do. These were three things that Paul never did.

She glanced in her rearview mirror to see Heath strapped into his booster seat. She couldn't help but recall seeing him sitting there with his cookie-stained fingers following what happened. Heath stared out the rain-streaked window lost in his own thoughts, perhaps reliving his trauma over and over again, an animated GIF of brains and gore, perhaps thinking about the terrarium they were building at home. She couldn't tell.

When they slid off the road, she had asked him if he was okay. He replied, "Harley likes your hair, Mom. You can never go to the river."

"Why can't I go to the river?" Annabelle asked.

"It's a secret."

They sat now in silence, fogging up the windows with their breath.

A knock on her car window woke Annabelle from her reverie. She wiped the glass to see an older gentleman peering in. She wound down the window. Rain drops from the roof of her car entered.

"Hey there, *chamaco*," he said, spotting Heath in the back. "I've got a winch. I can get you outta that barrow pit and back on the road," he said to her. The rain magically stopped as if her rescuer was also in charge of precipitation. She kicked open the door, extending her leg until the hinge caught. The door threatened to slam shut from the cantilever of the car.

"Stay here," she told Heath.

She stepped down, pushing herself against the door so it wouldn't swing back on her, and her flats sank three inches into mud. She bunched up her toes to keep from losing her shoes to the suction. The shoes were a lost cause. Suede was impossible to clean, but they could at least keep her feet covered until she made it home. Her every step involved an extraction. For balance, she extended her arms like a tight-rope walker.

The man offered her his arm, but she waved him away.

He had a deeply wrinkled face with a white mustache. He wore loose dark jeans and a tucked-in collared shirt with checks. A light white cowboy hat sat on his head. By stepping out of his truck to come to her aid, he had allowed mud to cake his boots and the bottom inches of his pants.

If they had been back in Royal Oak, Annabelle wouldn't have allowed a stranger who wasn't with AAA roadside assistance to touch her car, but they were in the country now where folks helped each other (and a AAA tow truck was likely an hour away; she needed to get home to prepare for the interview). Besides, she was eager to meet an adult, a local, a neighbor. She was eager to introduce herself even though—mud squelched between her curled toes—the circumstances did not flatter her.

But the man moved with nonstop efficiency. After pulling on thick leather gloves, he attached a bow shackle to the recovery point under her bumper.

"Stand clear," he directed her.

Annabelle stepped aside. She adopted the role of someone who didn't know about mechanical advantage, someone mystified by gear assemblies and cowed by a line under tension.

He started the winch until the wire pulled taut. He then hung a soggy coil of rope from his truck bed over the wire.

"So if it snaps, we aren't cut in two," he told her with a smile.

He started the winch again. For a moment, nothing happened. She imagined the snapped wire shooting at her abdomen like a cybertronic tentacle disemboweling her in front of Heath. And then the winch overcame the resistance in the system and her car slid back onto the mud-coated pavement.

"I'm Dan Quintana. Welcome to the neighborhood," he said, unhooking his shackle. "If you need anything, my wife and I are just down the road." He gestured toward a field. This was, in the flesh, her imaginary Mr. Quintana. She had so much more to tell him.

"I'm Annabelle Granger. We moved here from Royal Oak, Michigan."

*I can build robots.*

"My husband, Paul, is away for work and that's my son, Heath, in the car."

*Paul may be a murderer.*

"We're very happy to be living in such a peaceful place."

*Follow me on Instagram.*

# 51

ANNABELLE UNCLIPPED HEATH FROM HIS BOOSTER SEAT. EVEN THOUGH he knew how to operate the seat belt, Annabelle made it a rule that she was the one to unlock it. The opening scene from *Dead Calm* had been forever imprinted on her mind and she did not want such an incident to occur in her family. She was no sailor.

Maud sniffed at the soggy grocery bags Annabelle ferried into the house. She wasn't a dependable guard dog. She consistently failed to alert them with a bark when The Six arrived on the porch, but she never let a grocery bag pass without an olfactory inspection. Perhaps, in a past life, she worked for the TSA.

Heath settled in at his small table with the terrarium. She had purchased a jade plant at the store for him to add to it. The plant came in an adorable itty-bitty terra-cotta pot. When Annabelle told Heath it was a lucky plant, he carried it with him, holding it in his lap on the car ride home. Annabelle was glad she'd bought the plant. It would keep him occupied while she baked.

It had been impossible for her to complete any preparations for her Wanda Way interview over the weekend with Paul hounding her about her lifestyle choices. Her car accident had taken time from her preparations, and she needed a focused morning to get ready before her interview at one.

Her phone rang. It was Paul. That was unusual. Normally, she was lucky to receive a text of his safe arrival. He coughed into her ear.

"Annabelle, I caught the flu."

"Oh, no!" Annabelle said. She was genuinely alarmed, not by the news, but by the fear that Paul might return and spoil her interview.

"I fell asleep on the plane and when we landed I woke up sweaty and delirious. I didn't bother with a rental car and just had an Uber take me to the hotel."

"Oh, good." He was at the hotel.

"I must have caught it in Vegas. I'm afraid I will get everyone sick when I go in tomorrow."

"Oh, no," Annabelle said for the same reason.

"I'm like the rats on the ships spreading plague to every port city in Europe, only it's the flu via planes to tech hubs, but you get what I'm saying. You can call me Typhoid Mary. I've got NyQuil in my Dopp kit. It's kicking in now. I'm just going to sleep until my alarm goes off tomorrow morning."

"OK. Well you stay put. We hope you feel better," Annabelle said.

She hung up. He did sound sick. Did that mean he hadn't killed Alinda or was he phoning in an alibi like a kid scamming a sick day? He'd said a lot of extraneous details—an Uber? Wasn't that a sign of prevarication? Perhaps he was sick in a hotel awaiting a consulting gig. Perhaps he was burying a local freshman down a well. Annabelle didn't have the energy to care. All that mattered was Wanda Way.

With Paul away, she was free to work, but now Heath was not cooperating. Heath moped about and tried to get Annabelle interested in his project.

"Mom. Mom. Mom. Hey, Mom. Do you want to help me with my terrarium? Look. Hey, Mom, look. Is this the kind of caterpillar that makes cocoons? When will it make a cocoon? I'm going to take the stinkbug out of the terrarium. Hey, Mom. I'm going to take the stinkbug out."

Annabelle was too preoccupied to rise to his bug-based threat. She was washing her vases—repurposed glass bottles—with vinegar to make them shine. The well water here was so hard it left a white film on everything. She wouldn't cut the flowers for the vases until the last minute to be sure they looked perky and fresh.

She set up her camera and laptop on her kitchen island. The scene in her kitchen captured by the camera had to look Instagram perfect. She had already polished her cabinets with beeswax, degreased and buffed her oven and range hood, and changed the bulbs in her under cabinet lights.

The lemon cake was baking in the oven and would be ready for a lavender buttercream frosting as soon as it cooled—that reminded her she needed to wipe her glass cake stand with vinegar too—and a bowl of herb bread dough was rising under a tea towel in the windowsill.

She had already chosen her outfit: dark jeans, her favorite pair of Scandinavian knitted socks (no one would see these, but they would help give her confidence), and a designer baseball-cut t-shirt in dove gray. The t-shirt flattered her bust and her skin tone and the color wouldn't clash with her blue cabinets and red countertops.

Her hair was twirled into damp nodules dotting her head and secured with pins. Annabelle hoped when her hair dried and she released the pins, her hair would fall in loose waves. In college, they'd called this beach hair even though they were two hours from the lake. She'd not tried to get her hair to do this since her wedding day and then it was handled by a professional. It was yet another thing she would have practiced and perfected if Paul had supported her.

The makeup would be tricky. It was important not to look tired and washed out. Her casual clothes would appear sloppy if her hair and makeup didn't elevate the look. It had been a long time since Annabelle had worn much makeup. Tapping around through Instagram she learned that redheads were wearing nude lipstick and tinting their eyebrows to make them thicker these days. Annabelle hadn't had the opportunity that morning to peruse the makeup aisle for new products. Her perfect pink CoverGirl lipstick would have to do.

The key was to look casual and natural. It was the kiss of death for any part of her chosen lifestyle to look like drudgery, but even worse for it to look like she was doing it just for show. Wanda's fans wanted to believe in her authenticity.

Just before noon, when The Six usually arrived to take Heath off her hands, he dropped a bomb. "I don't want to go with The Six," he said.

Wanda would call in one hour and Annabelle still needed to arrange the flowers, frost the cake and place the candied arugula flowers—a thing she had just invented—in an artful array across the top, and get dressed.

"They're your friends, honey. Why don't you want to play with your friends?"

She squatted down to his eye level and checked his forehead temperature with the back of her hand. No fever. She sat seiza style on the tiles and pulled Heath onto her lap. He was getting just heavy enough to squash her. She rocked him a little, and he gripped her shirt in his fists and hid his face under her chin.

"Ah, Heath. I know this move has been a lot of big changes for you. Your dad travels more often and I'm home all the time. I know it's been hard. You lost your routine, but we are doing well as a family. And you are doing well, too. I'm so proud of you. You've made new friends. And you're showing me you're growing up and ready for big boy responsibilities by being safe and trustworthy when you're out there with your friends."

Annabelle tried to push him away to look at his face, but he clung to her.

"I have a big meeting today, Heath. It's important for me. That's why I've been distracted this morning and didn't play with you. It's nothing to do with you. I love you very much. How about tomorrow we spend all morning working on your terrarium and if you don't want to go out with The Six then, we can tell them together? But today, I need you to go."

At that moment, the doorbell rang over and over and over and there were knocks and kicks to their front door. "Heath!" someone yelled. The Six were here.

Heath looked at her solemnly and nodded his head. He wiped the boogers from his nose with his sleeve. She had taught him not to do that, but some of his manners were regressing. It was the influence of The Six. Her family rules were now clashing with what was cool. It was a small price to pay. While Heath pulled on his alligator rain boots, Annabelle got his backpack, already loaded with snacks and toys, and slipped it over his small shoulders.

She wondered for a moment what Heath's little display had been all about as she watched the heads of The Six disappear down the arroyo.

## 52

WHEN WANDA WAY'S SKYPE CALL SANG THROUGH HER SPEAKERS, Annabelle was ready. Her kitchen was shiny clean. The food and flowers formed a fetching display. The kitchen shade had been lowered to block out the blanching natural light. She was lipsticked and tousled.

"Hello? Can you see me?" Annabelle waved into her camera. She was concerned that their slow Internet might cause problems for a video call, but Wanda's silver hair and dazzling smile were delivered to her screen without a pixel out of place.

"Annabelle, babe. We can see you and your adorable kitchen."

Behind Wanda was a white-washed shiplapped sunporch. Diaphanous curtains covered the windows and multitudes of green plants in glass containers at varying heights offered verdant spikes of color. A mirror reflected a hallway with a tidy cupboard and artfully arranged sepia-toned photos along the wall. Annabelle compared this with what Wanda was seeing. Her kitchen with its shiny plaster walls and colorful cabinets seemed kitsch in comparison.

"So you really did it, huh?"

"Did what?" Annabelle asked.

"You pulled it off. You unplugged, dropped out, purged your

consumerist demon. I gotta say I'm impressed. It may look like I live in a pastoral wonder world, but my house is three minutes from the mall. I've got an addiction to Cheesecake Factory. Tell no one. But I guess with Amazon now you can still get whatever you want even in the middle of nowhere. We all lead the same lives. Really, I'm impressed. You bought into the whole intentional living thing one hundred percent. And good for you."

Annabelle straightened and smiled, trying to interpret what Wanda said as a compliment. She wasn't sure if she should inform Wanda that this life—with the besieging mud, the quiet country folk with whom she had nothing in common, and the lack of public spaces —was not at all like her former life in Royal Oak. Two-day Amazon delivery did not modernize rural America. She held her tongue.

"Let's get started," Wanda began. "Hello friends. I am here today with my guest Annabelle Granger in her home in Box Elder, New Mexico. Annabelle was a robotics engineer in Michigan until a couple months ago when she chucked it all to be a stay-at-home mom on a farm property in the hinterlands where she lives with her husband and five-year-old son. She started a lifestyle Instagram, which some of you may follow, @Annabellwether. It features her fabulous adventures in growing food, baking, and crafting. Annabelle, do you make your own clothes?"

"Not yet." Annabelle smiled and willed herself not to look down at her shirt self-consciously.

Annabelle had expected Wanda to read the bio she had written for the interview last week. She struggled to update her self-presentation to match the version of her life Wanda had just introduced. Hearing herself described as a stay-at-home mom in the hinterlands helped Annabelle understand why she had felt so forlorn. This description was a far cry from the one she had provided: "Annabelle Granger is a former robotics engineer who traded the lab for the kitchen and garden to pursue her entrepreneurial spirit. She's a bellwether for harried moms and dads and unfulfilled worker bees everywhere leading the way to clean eating, healthy living, and meaningful simplicity. Follow her for tips and inspiration for adding nature to your life."

Wanda continued, "Tell us, what made you go all in? I think many of my viewers make conscientious decisions daily to live a cleaner, simpler life, but you've taken it to the extreme."

"Hi, everyone. Thanks for having me, Wanda. I don't think of what my family did moving out here as extreme. For several years, I felt a little niggling in my soul. I felt it when standing in line at the grocery store, or vacuuming, or going through the car wash. It was a little voice that said that it doesn't have to be like this. Your life can be different. It started coming with flashes. I imagined scenes of Heath, my five-year-old, building a fort or wading in a pond looking for frogs with his pants rolled up to his knees. I saw us picking strawberries and watching asteroid showers. We could do those things in Royal Oak, but it would exacerbate the real problem. Get in the car to go to the u-pick strawberry place. Get in the car to drive out where it is dark enough to appreciate the stars."

Annabelle's hands were gesticulating without her permission.

"I'm lucky. By selling our house and buying a cheaper one in New Mexico, we wiped out our debt. My husband travels for work, so he can live most anywhere. With our simpler lifestyle, we can live off his salary alone. It wasn't an extreme decision, it was a pragmatic one."

"Good for you. Tell us about that cake I see there."

The rest of the interview passed in a blur. Annabelle hoped her tendency to draw attention to her hands didn't mean that she looked like Vanna White when she exhibited her baked goods. And was she adding a twang to her voice?

"Well thank you, Annabelle, for sharing your kitchen with us today and thank you, friends, for watching. Next week, I'm talking to Tess of Tess Tosses, the closet organization company in Laguna Beach. See you then. Bye."

There were a few seconds of silence where both she and Wanda smiled at each other in the cameras.

"That's it?" Annabelle asked. "I want to thank you, Wanda, for the opportunity to present my channel to your followers. It's been a little isolating—"

"It's no problem, babe. I always love to give back." Wanda smiled at her and then yelled, "Doric! You're needed." Wanda got up from her repurposed steel keg upholstered stool and wandered into the camera's distance.

A pale man with gelled hair, presumably named Doric, sat in Wanda's seat. "What I'm going to need from you is three videos we can use for framing shots. Do a slow pan, and I mean it, a super, super, su-per, slow pan of, one, your garden, two, your quaint little kitchen there, and, three, a charming scene of you and your family outside doing something wholesome. Do you think you could get those uploaded to me by the end of business today? We want to get your piece posted tomorrow."

"Oh, well," Annabelle hesitated trying to think of who she could rope in to pretend to be her family. Doric arched an eyebrow at her. "The thing is, my husband is out of town and my son is at a friend's house all afternoon."

"Fine, just the garden and kitchen then. Send two files. Name one 'garden' and the other 'kitchen.' End of business today please. Thanks." Doric twiddled his fingers goodbye. An unflattering shot of his wet, open mouth close to the camera as he leaned in to end the call remained on her screen.

The let-down was intense. Annabelle didn't know what she was expecting to feel, but the word "salvation" came to mind. Instead, Wanda with her offhand comment about buying into "the whole intentional living thing" made Annabelle sound like she was the dupe who sent money to the Nigerian prince with the email pleas. Annabelle reminded herself that she chose this rural lifestyle first and then she marketed her embrace of it. It wasn't the other way around. Authenticity-craving fans hadn't forced here her. This is what she wanted.

It's true that she couldn't die her hair silver, or go to Cheesecake Factory, or have someone named Doric help her manage her image, but those things aren't important. What's important is spending time with the people you love. Annabelle paused at that thought, recalling that she could not provide Wanda with a video of the Grangers spending quality time outdoors. This was a distressing contradiction, and she put it out of her mind.

Annabelle picked herself up. She had just taped an important interview with a major lifestyle brand and she needed to capitalize on it. The first task would be to take some photos of her "set" with the laptop in place in front of her cake, herb loaf, and flowers. She would upload the photos to Instagram with her thanks to Wanda Way for the interview and her excitement about its release tomorrow. Once the likes started coming in, she would feel happy again.

Annabelle waited for her "garden" and "kitchen" video uploads to complete. Perhaps she had gone overboard spending three minutes on each video panning su-per slowly but also zooming in on her cake, her flowers, the lacy carrot tops in the earth, and a tiny praying mantis on a leaf. The slow Internet speed was frustrating her upload efforts, but she kept her cool because likes and new followers were pouring in. Her phone was constantly pinging. It was the Wanda rush.

Annabelle was about to send her email to Doric with links to both videos when she paused. There was something so lonely about her "garden" and "kitchen" videos—silent, immobile cakes and bugs and plants.

Annabelle reconsidered. She could go to the river and film a video of Heath playing. What could be more indicative of the authenticity of her new life than a multiethnic, multi-aged group of children playing out in nature?

She could either tell Doric that her family had been away all day, or she could give her fans what they wanted. Annabelle headed to the river.

# 53

## PAUL GRANGER

"I told you. I canceled the rest of my business trip because I caught the flu. When I got home, my son was there, but my wife was gone."

"Is that unusual for her?" Officer Alvarez asked.

"Yes, it is unusual for my wife to leave our five-year-old home alone."

"Could she be visiting someone? At a friend or relative's house?"

"She didn't take her car, her keys, or her purse. *Or her son.*"

"I see that you're upset, Mr. Granger."

"Dr. Granger. And yes, I am upset. My wife is missing."

"What kind of doctor are you?"

"No. This is not about me. I want to know what's going on around here. Did you find Alicia Green? Did you even look?"

"Alinda Green."

"Yes, I'm sorry. Alinda. Did you find her?"

"Alinda Green is still a missing person. We suspect she has run away from home."

"But what if she hasn't? What if someone is kidnapping women?"

"And what does your wife have in common with a fourteen-year-old high school student?"

Paul made a sour face. This was not going as he imagined. A policewoman approached the desk where he and Officer Alvarez were dueling. She stared at Paul as she approached. It made Paul uncomfortable. She tapped Officer Alvarez on the shoulder without breaking her stare and handed him a manila folder.

"Excuse me a moment," Officer Alvarez said to Paul and began reading the contents of the file. The policewoman broke her stare and retreated. Paul shifted in his squeaky roller chair while he waited.

Photos in frames cluttered the back third of Officer Alvarez's desk. There was a large professional photo of Alvarez with a wife and two grown children, a boy and a girl. Another photo showed the boy smiling in a football uniform, taking a knee on the grass with his helmet under his arm. In an elaborate frame, his daughter in a wedding dress held hands with another young man. Tucked into the frame was a small photo of a beautiful puckered baby swaddled in a white blanket. It looked like Officer Alvarez had recently become a grandfather.

Paul studied the new grandpa's face as he read the file. He had a bulbous nose scattered with blackheads and wild, thick black eyebrows. He looked like a nice man, even if he was deploying an arsenal of psychological intimidation maneuvers on Paul instead of issuing an APB, sending out a car with a sniffer dog, and reviewing footage from traffic cameras. Did he really think Paul didn't realize he was playing games with him? Or did Officer Alvarez believe the tricks would work even if Paul knew?

He didn't want to think like this, but it occurred to Paul that the way he dressed, his waxed SUV, his manner of speech, dare he say his breeding, was not being well received at this rural police outpost. Officer Alvarez thought him a pathetic, pampered yuppie with a cuckolding wife. He was not empathizing with Paul's panic. Paul was not coming off well.

When they first moved to New Mexico, Annabelle had called Paul a snob, and maybe he was. The officers' condescending dismissal of him was raising his ire. The place probably didn't see much action. They were most likely glorified traffic cops more used to pulling over drunks and speeders than investigating missing persons cases.

In fact, the GPS guiding him to this station had been incorrect. He weaved past anonymous government buildings, a run-down economic development center, a tractor sales lot, and a U-Haul rental facility before parking next to the police cars in a lot without signage. He and Heath had to circumnavigate the dark brown concrete block building on foot before they found the front door. The GPS was unaware of the existence of the black ribbon of fresh pavement that took him to the public entrance of the station, which Paul surmised had been built in the last two years with some kind of rural policing grant money.

It was true that Paul spent most of his time in the big urban centers of America. It was true that his clients feted him like royalty sending cars to pick him up at his hotel so he wouldn't have to navigate an unfamiliar city, hosting elaborate dinners for him in fancy restaurants that had been written up in magazines, and serving catered lunches in their conference rooms with vistas of the skyline. This had made him incompatible with his rural counterparts, who frowned upon displays of wealth, who favored the traditional approach over the hot new things, and who trusted locals more than outsiders.

Not that he begrudged the rural folk their customs. In many ways, he respected it more than the fast-paced superficiality he encountered throughout his workweek. Paul never spent more than a single consecutive week at any one client's office. He returned to some clients every month, but rarely for more than a year. His was a life of short-term relationships. He admired the people of Box Elder who could live together year after year and generation after generation without lunging at each other's throats.

No, it wasn't the fact of rural life that bothered him; it was that he didn't know how to behave. For all his swagger and charm, Paul was an introvert. He had adopted a learned set of behaviors that won over people in his business. He learned these behaviors over the years, starting with the incorrigible social animals Rafe and Steve-o. But his repertoire had long become entrenched. Sure, he could update his in-jokes with the latest scandals and corporate gossip. He could drop his casual slang learned at the tech companies of the west coast for the classier graces preferred on the east coast. But when it came to social interaction, he was set in his ways.

He could have, one supposed, dropped the pretense and been himself. But after years of consulting, years of being *the* Paul Granger, he wasn't sure there was a self left to be. And this was dangerous because he needed these police officers to believe him.

Officer Alvarez looked up from a manila folder. He said, "It's interesting you should bring up Alinda Green."

"Interesting how?"

"Your son told one of my officers you were pretending to go away for work, but instead lived in your car behind a church. He told her that his mom found out and you and she had a fight. Did you pretend to go away the week Alinda went missing?"

Paul looked at Heath. He sat perched on the edge of the chair along the wall, swinging his feet in his alligator rain boots. He was talking with the policewoman, showing her their secret handshakes. So much for keeping secrets, Heath.

## 54

DAN QUINTANA

When I told the Greens the story of Alinda and Harley, I whitewashed the tale. I told Gary and Amy that they were thoughtful to let Alinda play with Harley after her mom died. It meant the world for an older "cool" girl to spend time with her. I did say, as delicately as I could, that at first Alinda used her generous curfews to hang out with the kids her age under the veterans bridge. I only know this because I saw Harley sitting on a rock next to the bridge when I went across the river to pick up a flat of Big Jim pepper sprouts from Maevis Pacheco.

I stopped my car at the side of the road and fumbled down the sandy incline to see what Harley was doing by herself. Boy, was that a mistake. I had happened upon the teen hangout spot under the bridge. I don't know who was more surprised and embarrassed. The girls had tucked their shirts up to expose their midriffs as they stood around looking bored while the boys practiced skateboard moves on the minuscule piece of smooth concrete sloping to meet the piles of the bridge. Harley was too young to know how to interact with this motley crew and sat apart from them.

I'm sorry to admit I beat a hasty retreat to the car. I left Harley there, at the river, with the middle school kids too afraid any words from me would mortify her beyond forgiveness.

But eventually Alinda and Harley developed a real friendship, based perhaps on their fondness for mischief. Alinda never seemed like a girl content to sit around with her belly button peeking out from under her t-shirt when there were pranks to play or competitions to be won.

I think we all heard of the obstacle course they built at the river because that is where the poor Cordova boy broke his arm. Alinda and Harley used old tires and rusted poles, barbed wire, logs, and a few tarantulas they wrangled. They called it the Ultimate Cojones Test Run. After school, the boys would come to test their mettle lured, I'm sure, by the chance to impress Alinda who was born more beautiful than most. Harley timed the contestants while Alinda watched for infractions.

The boys tested their balance by walking along a cottonwood branch, jumped across to another branch, swung on a rope, crawled under barbed wire amongst the tarantulas. I don't know what all they did, but the stories Delfina heard at church and at the mailboxes made it sound like something from those prime-time TV shows—*Fear Factor* meets *Ninja Warrior*. I saw none of this in person and I didn't know a thing about it until Ben broke his arm and put an end to the whole endeavor.

Harley and Alinda spent most of their time away from the house. But the story of Harley and Alinda I wanted to share with the grieving Greens was this. One evening, while Delfina was cooking dinner, and I was reading the paper in my den, Harley with her pink crocheted hat covering her sparsely haired head, appeared beaming at my door with Alinda behind her. Her smile was a welcome sight.

Harley asked to use my tape measure. Now—and I asked Gary and Amy to forgive me for saying this—these girls were always up to something. I couldn't let them use any of my tools, not even a tape measure, without an inquisition. They followed me to the soterrano where I pulled out my tape measure, but I played a little game before I handed it to Harley, reaching out and then retracting it, reaching and retracting until they gave me the information.

"Oh. Abuelo. Hand it over."

"What are you going to do with this?"

"I just need to measure something."

"I figured that. What are you going to measure?"

"You can see if you want."

At this Alinda pulled her ponytail holder from her hair and turned her back to us. Harley measured the length of Alinda's hair from her chin to the tips.

"Oh, it's only nine inches," Harley grumbled. "Is this thing right?" She shook the measuring tape like it was a Magic Eight Ball and could give her a better answer.

"Don't worry. My hair grows fast."

"What's all this about?" I asked the girls while I put away my tape measure.

Alinda said, "I read that I can donate my hair when it is ten inches long. I just go to Stella's and she will cut it to my chin and they can make all the rest into a wig for Harley."

It took me a moment to process what she was saying. I hustled them away so I could shed my tears alone in the cold of the soterrano. I couldn't imagine being a pretty young girl willing to cut my hair for a friend, and not a true girlfriend, but a little girl three grades younger, a tag-along. I couldn't believe the generosity and selflessness she showed and I still can't. And that is what I told the Greens.

It had the intended effect, my story. The Greens set aside their misery for a moment to feel the warm glow of their love for their daughter. They could feel her familiar presence around them. Wherever she may be, they knew that they raised a child with a good heart. That was all I could give them.

The rest of the story of Harley and Alinda is more tragic. Alinda should be forgiven for having reneged on her promise of cutting her hair for a wig for Harley. It all happened slowly, as slowly as hair grows. Once the other kids' parents demanded the girls decommission the obstacle course because they didn't want to foot the bill for any medical expenses, Alinda and Harley drifted apart.

Alinda started dating Ben Cordova. Maybe he asked her to sign his cast. She was going into ninth grade and the differences in ages between her and Harley became too great. It was at this time that Harley's thinning hair became known by the kids at school and her real period of teasing began. Soon after, Harley refused to attend school, and she started to spend her time with the kindergarteners.

You have to understand that from Harley's perspective when Alinda grew apart from her, she couldn't see it as the natural consequence of their age differences and their youth and divergent interests. Harley saw it as a betrayal. I'm not making excuses for what she did. She needs to be punished. But she is a little girl. She needs to be understood too.

I'm not sure when I knew. When Delfina delivered the news that Alinda Green didn't make it home after school the night before I can admit that we smirked, believing she had become a handful precociously. When two days passed without word from her and the police posted a bulletin featuring her photos, Delfina and I wiped the smirks from our faces. We were worried for her and wondered together, out of earshot of Harley, what could have happened.

The talk was that Alinda had a boyfriend in town, but no one knew who that would be or why she wouldn't have called by now. It all seemed like empty conjecture. We thought of the construction on the highway and wondered if she had somehow caught the eye of a worker in that crew. We thought about Tim Fines up the road. He was a sex offender in his younger days, but he had lived in Box Elder without causing trouble for a decade since serving his time. We thought about the new young couple that moved from Michigan into Pat and Melinda's house. Sally next door said she heard them fight like cats and dogs every weekend, but what that has to do with a missing girl I can't tell you. It is more just fear of the unknown and gossip. That red-headed young woman I helped out of the barrow pit wouldn't be mixed up with a predator.

Our unease over Alinda's whereabouts filled our days, but we kept it from Harley. She didn't need to suffer anymore sadness over the important people in her life vanishing from it. She didn't go to school, so it was possible she wasn't even aware that her former best friend was missing. But as the days passed with no word and it became clear that Alinda was not voluntarily away, Delfina and I talked to Harley about it over dinner. I let Delfina take the lead.

"Honey, Alinda Green is missing. She hasn't been home for four days and her parents are very worried about her."

"Alinda's not missing. She's gone."

Harley's manner sent a chill down my spine.

Delfina must have missed it because she asked, "What do you mean gone? Do you know where she went?"

"She's better off now. The Six are waiting for me," she said, sliding from her chair. "Thanks for dinner, Abuelita," she called over her shoulder as she ran out the side door. We let her go. It's what we had been doing the whole time she had lived with us, it was too late to stop her now.

Delfina shrugged. "Well, that didn't go as I expected." Delfina talked about her worry for Harley and how God needed to send some help for that little girl, as I cleared the dishes and she loaded the dishwasher. I was not a good conversational mate. Delfina asked if I was okay. I was not okay, but I nodded and smiled. We spent that evening in the den.

I stared at my paper while Delfina watched her murder mystery show while working on her crosswords. The show featured a pale white corpse with disturbing open eyes. I wondered how my dear, sweet Delfina could watch these macabre shows. The body on the show lay beneath a white sheet until the next commercial break, a benign piece of living room furniture that the other characters gossiped and sipped tea around until the detective would arrive to restore order. I wondered how Delfina, who always guessed the murderer before he was revealed, could have sat at the same dinner table I did, but not conclude that her granddaughter was dangerously troubled.

I couldn't help but think about how Harley might have done it. With a rock to the head? By pinning her face into the cold river water? With the gopher poison I kept in the soterrano? I assumed that if I went to the river, if any adult had gone, it would be easy to find Alinda's body. Harley, in some kind of manic rage, might be able to kill, but not to dispose of a body. Alinda was probably lying where she'd been killed, maybe with a sweater over her face because Harley was sorry for what she'd done. The river was territory ceded to the kids. I hadn't been there since we drove down to watch the August gully-washer carrying away all the sins of upstream in a torrent.

In bed that night, with Delfina sleeping next to me and Harley asleep in Dinah's childhood room down the hall, it took all of my self-control not to slip out and walk to the bosque to find Alinda. I feared if I did that someone would discover me. The neighbor's dog would bark, or a security light I'd forgotten about would click on, or a policeman would be spending his patrol tucked in his car under a tree. I couldn't go find Alinda because the only chance Harley had was if decomposition destroyed the evidence. Now who sounded like a TV detective? That, combined with the sheer unlikelihood of a child being a murderer, could be her only hope.

In the morning, I knew I had overreacted. I'd drank too much coffee. I was all wound up. Harley was a damaged, but gentle little girl. I thought that right up until I watched Harley in the entryway mirror fill in the bare patches of her scalp with black Sharpie marker. I winced, and she saw my reflection in the mirror. Her face told me what I needed to know.

## 55

PAUL GRANGER

When he and Heath got home from the police station, Paul was at a loss for what to do. He couldn't remember a time when he was at home without Annabelle. Too tired to remove his jacket or shoes, he stepped out of the entryway and slumped at the breakfast bar. Annabelle would snipe at him for his shoe transgression if she were here, but she wasn't here.

"Go get your pajamas on," Paul ordered Heath.

"I haven't taken a bath."

"We're skipping bath time tonight. Go get your pajamas on." Looking at the Kamishibai board he shouted after him, "And brush your teeth."

Paul listened to the sounds of Heath getting ready and stared dull-eyed at the board. All of Annabelle's evening chores were red—unload the dishwasher, wipe up floor, feed Maud. Maud. Paul could barely remember the meaning of the word. He got up and opened the front door. Maud's old couch cushion sat empty. Leaving the front door open, he stepped down the porch, calling her name.

"Maud." He began with a stage whisper.

He looked around the side of the house. Annabelle's garden lay trim and tidy with moist soil, labeled paint sticks, and thriving greens. No Maud. Paul called again, louder this time. Soon the whole neighborhood would know he lost his wife. What was the shame in adding the dog to this list?

He opened the door to the shed. Perhaps she had gotten trapped in there? The shed screamed of Annabelle's touch. She had run tube lighting down the shelves. They glowed, illuminating bins of gardening supplies labeled in chalk. Along the back wall hung tools, each one with its own hook and label. None were missing. Annabelle's hand tools hung within easy reach from the inside of the shed door and clothespins affixed to the wall held her gardening gloves. It was a paragon of organization, ingenuity, artistic flourish, and electrical know-how. It was his wife.

She had labeled the only empty spot on the shelf "Heath's tools." Paul recalled the kit he had brought home for Heath. He'd never seen it again, but Annabelle had told him how much use Heath was getting out of it. Paul wondered where those tools were. It wasn't like Annabelle to allow Heath to leave his toys out.

The last place Paul could think to look for the old dog was in the arroyo. Maybe she had fallen into the arroyo and broken her hip and had been yelping for Annabelle until exhaustion overtook her. Paul peered over the edge of the driveway down into the arroyo. He looked both ways, but did not see his dog, injured or otherwise.

The rope swing hung above the arroyo. He noticed that a four-foot length of green hose now surrounded the frayed yellow rope. Paul recalled Annabelle's story of soaking Heath's hands and removing plastic splinters after his first day out with his friends. Annabelle had sprinkled her thoughtful, inventive touches and her earnest, hard work all over the property.

The cold feeling for Annabelle that he had been carrying in his chest melted away and all he could see was her virtue. He had to find her, bring her home.

Paul ran back in the house. He found Heath in his bathroom,

standing on his stool in his dinosaur pajamas brushing his teeth. Even with his mother missing, even having been left home alone for who knows how long, even with an absent, uninvolved father, Heath could be relied upon to do as he was told. He was such a good kid.

Paul knelt down and held his son. He let the dribble of toothpaste from Heath's foamy mouth stain his jacket. He held him for a long time. Paul felt a determination to fight for his family. He grasped Heath by the shoulders and asked him, "Where's Maud?"

# EARLIER

# 56

THE DRAMATIC WESTERN LIGHT SHONE. THE GOLDEN RAYS WOULD enhance her video, minimizing shadows and bathing the scene in a warm glow. Heath would be so surprised to see her. She'd never been to see their fort in the cottonwoods. She buttoned up her plaid shirt over her "homemade-looking" baseball-cut t-shirt and pulled on her Wellies over her good luck Scandinavian socks. She scratched Maud behind the ears and left her with a bowl of kibble, so she could escape without the old lady limping along behind.

Spring in Box Elder, New Mexico had meant mud, more mud than Annabelle had ever contemplated. It was like something out of a newsreel about a mudslide with thousands of lives lost in a Central American country. Mud sprinkles covered her car. Mud residue coated her tile floor. Mud stained Heath's clothes. Its smell pervaded her washer, so now her sheets and towels exuded the perfume of the chocolate-milk colored sludge. She had grown attuned to the distinctive odor and now smelled it in her well water when she drank, when she showered, when she brushed her teeth.

Spring in Box Elder, New Mexico had also meant beautiful vistas of fields, riparian forests, and snow-capped mountains. And sun!

Everyday sunshine and clear blue skies. The spring rains came like a blitzkrieg. Dark clouds blew in, dumped rain, and cleared out. The weather was nothing like the dreary Michigan winters that clung onto spring just to test the mettle of its residents.

They lived on the edge of a desert and yet life sprung up every-where—weeds poking through the gravel driveway, lizards doing push-ups in the woodpile, cotton-tailed bunnies hiding behind sage-brush, and coyotes howling in the night. The natural environment insisted that one take heed. It had sent her car skimming off the road and nearly drowned her. She had learned so much in her few weeks here.

Annabelle followed the arroyo down to the river and its copse of trees. The leaves of the cottonwoods shimmered in the breeze. As she approached, she saw glimpses of the kids running in the woods. She realized she was sneaking up on them, but curiosity overtook her. It was easy to approach without being noticed and peek from behind the thick trunk of a cottonwood.

She saw Heath, easily identified by his copper top. He was shirtless and covered in red mud. The other four little ones were just as dirty and disheveled. Annabelle wondered how their parents got the smell of the mud out of their clothes. The kids gathered under the most magnificent cottonwood tree in the woods. Branches as thick as an elephant's leg arced out of a deposit of mud that had buried the forest floor in a past flood. An intrepid kid could walk up them. The five little ones were dancing under a tree branch howling like coyotes. Clumps of mud were somehow raining down on them. Harley was nowhere in evidence.

Annabelle crept closer. The kids were too entranced by their own imaginations to notice her approach. She wrapped her arm around the trunk of the cottonwood and began to film them with her phone. She wondered if this was too wild a scene for Wanda Way.

The leaves rustled above. Harley was lying on her stomach up high in a tree branch. She was cutting at something with a knife, letting clods of mud fall on her delighted flock below. Harley's knife was serious. It was short-bladed and shiny. If she dropped it, she could wound one of the kids. Annabelle controlled her impulse to bring order to this situation.

She ducked under a leafy branch to see what Harley was working on. Her body reacted with a shudder before her mind processed the horror she saw. The skinny, lifeless, mud-caked body of a child hung under the tree branch, strapped to it at the neck, the waist, and the ankles with strands of the orange plastic rope used to bind hay bales. In a panic, Annabelle counted. There were six children including Heath on the ground and Harley in the tree. How could there be a dead child? Annabelle looked again and noted the filthy white hoodie with butterflies. Alinda.

Annabelle covered her mouth in horror and disgust and retreated behind the tree trunk. Harley completed her task and walked down the tree branch, hopping off onto the soft ground. The knife, secured with a lanyard, swung at her wrist and in the other hand she raised a pelt in victory. Only it wasn't a pelt. It was Alinda's scalp.

Harley swung the scalp around and around above her head sending clods of blood-colored mud through the air. She sat on a log and laid the scalp over her knee. She combed her fingers through the long, dark hair. And then Harley removed her beanie and placed Alinda's scalp over her head. The skin hung over her eyebrows. With one hand holding the scalp to her head, Harley used the other to brush and fluff her new long locks.

It was a grotesque scene, but the kids clapped and danced around her. Harley strutted amongst them like a fashion model, pinning the scalp to her head when it threatened to fall off.

Annabelle was rooted in place, terrified. She felt terrified for herself, for her illicit witnessing of this private scene, for her inability to retreat without being noticed. She felt terrified for her son, who was broken worse than she could repair on her own. She felt terrified for Alinda and how horrible her death must have been.

Mud rained down from Alinda's body. The mud obscured her face, making her look like a scarecrow, not a murdered young girl.

Josephina trailed behind Harley, trying to touch the hair, but Harley jerked away. "No, it's Heath's turn next," she said.

Standing on a tree trunk, she removed the scalp and lowered it toward Heath's awaiting head.

## 57

"No!" Annabelle called.

The Six turned to see her. She backed away and then turned to run. She only made it a few steps before she felt herself falling through the forest floor. She landed on one knee with her neck bent back by the wall of the pit into which she had fallen. Stunned, she took a moment to realign her body and assess her injuries. Her neck was okay but her knee throbbed.

The pit was narrow but deep, over her head. River stones filled the bottom, and she had crunched her knee into one. She also noticed now that the spines of a prickly pear pierced her right hand. Blood oozed from the perforations. She dragged the paddle of cactus along the wall to dislodge it from her skin. The pricks in her palm burned.

She needed to climb out. Her hands and forearms reached the ground above, but her elbows were pinned to her ears. She kicked along the wall to power herself up. Her head popped above ground. The blood pounded in her temples as she struggled to pull herself out. She thought of all the pounds of mud she had shoveled in the past few weeks, of how strong her arms and shoulders had become. You can do this, she told herself before sliding back down into the pit.

"Guys, I think I'm stuck in here," she called out to The Six. She would pretend she hadn't seen anything until she could get help. The kids had been struggling to pull something toward her when she had popped her head out. Perhaps they had a means to save her.

"Hi, Heath," Annabelle said, looking up at her filthy son as he tugged at the corner of a blue tarp. He didn't look down at her. They pulled the tarp over the top of the pit, blocking out all the daylight. She recognized that tarp. The Six had asked to borrow it a week ago.

The tarp collapsed into the pit under the weight of the silted earth it held. The mud crushed her to the bottom. They were filling the pit with earth to help her climb out. She could hear their straining breaths as they worked hard to pull the tarp out from under the mound of mud. They were whispering to each other to coordinate her rescue. But they said nothing encouraging to her. They said nothing to her at all.

They retrieved the tarp. The cold, wet earth fell heavily on the back of Annabelle's neck. It filled her hair and her ears and her nostrils. It ran down her shirt and into the back of her pants.

"I don't think this will work, you guys," Annabelle called as bravely as she could.

She wiggled and strained against the compacting soil. It was so cold and so wet and so insidious. She planted her one free foot on the ground and used it to push her body upright. The effort caused dribbles of piddle to leak out and dampen her underwear. Her plumbing had never been the same after childbirth. She pulled her arms from the dirt and wiped it away from her eyes and nostrils. Her head and shoulders and arms were free, but the mud sealed the rest of her body in place. With her palms on the ground, she tried again to pull herself up.

"You guys, this isn't working. I'm being buried."

Once again, The Six pulled the tarp over the pit. It collapsed with the weight of more earth. They pulled the tarp away. The mud now buried her up to her neck with just her arms extended over her head free to move.

"Kids, now stop it. Enough. This is serious. I'm hurt and I need help to get out. No more mud." She tried to take a parental tone, but the weight of the mud activated claustrophobia and a primal panic overtook her reason.

She put her hands on the ground. Then she saw Harley standing at the edge of the pit leaning on the shovel from the kit Paul had gotten Heath. Harley took a full golf swing and whacked Annabelle's searching hand with the blade of the shovel. The force bent Annabelle's fingers backward. Annabelle yowled in pain and retracted her arms. She screamed for help. She screamed as loud as she could in wet, anguished, throat-ripping cries. Heath returned with a five-gallon bucket and placed it upside down on her head. He sat down on the bucket. Now when Annabelle screamed, it echoed.

"Please stop," she begged. Dirt fell from her hair into her eyelashes. The Six buried her arm with the broken fingers. With her free arm, she reached for Heath. She found his soft little ankle. She stroked it.

"Heath, please help your mom. I'm hurt honey. I'm not mad. I shouldn't have snuck up on you. I'm sorry. Please get help, Heath. I need you." She thought it might be working. She continued, "We'll go home and you can take a bath and I will make you fresh whipped cream and you can have two scoops of chocolate this time and I will read to you. Doesn't that sound nice? Please, Heath."

He stood up and walked away, pulling his leg free from her grasp. There was another whack of the shovel to her grasping hand. She screamed. Dirt and tears and snot filled her eyes and nostrils and mouth. The Six covered her arm with a mound of packed mud. Annabelle grew exhausted. Her screams died in her throat and she blubbered.

The Six remained. Someone continued to sit on the bucket. Annabelle could hear them talking, but not what they were saying. Annabelle found her energy and screamed again as loud and long as she could. The Six responded by whacking the bucket with the shovel. The noise was deafening and the threat of the shovel hitting her face terrifying. She fell to a sniffling silence. They put a heavy rock on top of the bucket and left her.

Annabelle guessed it was five in the afternoon. The Six were going home to their parents like nothing was wrong, like they hadn't killed the missing neighborhood girl, like they hadn't left Annabelle buried in mud. The parents wouldn't suspect anything, just like she hadn't. Annabelle feared she was to be their macabre project tomorrow.

Somewhere nearby, dropped in the leaf-litter, her phone pinged with each new like, comment, and follow to her Instagram.

---

## 58

ANNABELLE AWOKE. CLODS OF MUD THAT HAD FORMED FROM THE DUST and her tears sealed her eyes shut. Snot hung from her nose and itched. Mud entombed her arms and her crippled hands were useless to dig. She couldn't even brush the hair from her face.

The earth had cooled. It pulled the heat from her body. Her teeth chattered. The sound of her ragged breath echoed off the bucket. Her throat was inflamed and she could not scream anymore.

The only movements available to her were wiggling her toes in her shoes, rotating her neck, and opening and closing her jaw. Otherwise, she was frozen in place.

When she summoned the energy to fight for freedom, her hopeless immobility spiked her panic. She kicked, bucked, and strained within her clothes until her temples thudded and drips of urine escaped. The claustrophobia overwhelmed her. She struggled to catch her breath.

But once calm returned she could muster a sense of peace. Being trapped, suspended in the mud, was almost like floating, like drifting off untethered through the frigid darkness of space. The bucket was her helmet and Houston wasn't responding.

Night must have fallen. There was no longer a warm orange glow emanating through the bucket and her sealed eyelids. There was no warmth at all. The crickets had taken up their nighttime stridulation. She thought she could hear the river trickling past and the susurrous cottonwood leaves shimmering in a breeze she couldn't feel.

Oh, Heath! What have I let happen to you?

Annabelle, contemplating her decisions, felt a tidal wave of regret. She was owed no loyalty, not even by her son. When was the last time she demonstrated any true compassion and care to those around her? She was a lousy actress playing the role of wife and mother, stilted and without feeling. They would be better off without her parenting blog guidance and her marriage rules gleaned from women's magazines.

Annabelle imagined Heath and Paul moving back to Royal Oak. Heath would finish kindergarten and start in the first grade in the fall with his old friends. They would visit his grandparents and the zoo. Maybe this winter Paul would teach him how to downhill ski. In time, there would be a new Mrs. Granger. It would be awkward at first. She wouldn't know what to do with Heath, but she would feel her way because she would love him. And Heath would almost never think of his mom lost in the mud of Box Elder.

She heard someone's approach, sticks snapping and leaves crunching. She should have called out, this was her chance, but fear gripped her. She knew they were returning, sneaking from their beds to finish her off.

There was nothing she could do. She waited.

The steps approached. The bucket moved.

She envisioned the executioner's shovel coming down on her skull. Despite herself, she made a terrible cry. What were they waiting for?

The bucket jostled again, but it was not removed. This wasn't The Six. This was an animal, something sniffing the desperate smell of her panic coming to chew on her face. She heard the animal's wet breathing. It was a big animal. It knocked the bucket and almost tilted it off her head. A cold, wet nose brushed her ear.

It was Maud.

# EPILOGUE

## 59

THE APARTMENT WAS QUIET, THE ONLY SOUND THE DRONE OF THE refrigerator and the blips and bongs of Paul's phone as he worked. Heath sat at his small table, which wobbled now having traveled by moving van for the second time that spring. He colored intently at the table pausing occasionally, perhaps to consider his mom's paintings from college hung on the wall in front of him.

The buzzer rang. Heath startled.

"That will be Grandpa and Grandma Granger," Paul said to him getting up.

"Oh," Heath whined. "Why do they have to watch me?"

"I have to fly to San Jose for work. We've talked about this," Paul said over his shoulder as he opened the door for his parents.

"But why can't I be with Mom?"

"I can't take care of you by myself." Annabelle walked into the room, her arms crossed in slings and each finger wrapped individually in foam casts.

"Ah, Annabelle, you're looking much better." Judy kissed her daughter-in-law on both cheeks. Ross behind her set down two suitcases and waved. They would be staying in the guest room of the new condo during the next four days while Paul traveled for work. Annabelle, with all ten fingers broken, needed help with everything.

"We thought we'd take Heath to the zoo this afternoon and bring home dinner so you can rest," Judy said.

It had been three weeks since they'd moved back to Royal Oak. Annabelle remembered her last evening in Box Elder in her nightmares every time she slept. The cold mud, the dark, the reverberation of her breath on the bucket, the throb of her mangled hands. It was her neighbor, Dan Quintana, who'd found her that night.

Annabelle winced. Judy thought it was from the pain in Annabelle's hands, but it wasn't. It was pain from the memory.

"You know what you have to do," he'd said, after clawing the dirt away from her neck and shoulders and torso. "I've already left a note. Tell the police what I did."

While she wiggled and strained to free herself the rest of the way, Dan Quintana sat on a log under Alinda shaking his head and sobbing. Then he put the gun between his eyes and fired. Annabelle could still hear the echo of the gun's report.

She'd stumbled home, Maud limping by her side. When Paul whipped open the front door as she climbed the porch steps, she'd been able to cover her surprise to see him home early because he hugged her and wept. She'd invented her story quickly.

Their neighbor Dan Quintana, the guy who had pulled her car from the ditch, drove into their driveway shouting that Heath was in trouble. Annabelle got into the truck with him and they drove to the river. Dan told her that Heath was through the trees. Annabelle rushed out of the car and fell into a prepared pit. The rest was more or less the truth except she put Dan, not The Six in the starring role.

She'd told the same story to the hospital staff and Officer Alvarez when he interviewed her. By then, they'd found the bodies of Dan Quintana and Alinda Green at the river. Later, they found his suicide note. He'd admitted to killing Alinda. The letter didn't mention his granddaughter Harley, or The Six, or their afternoons spent at the river. And neither did she.

Paul pecked Annabelle's cheek and headed out the door with his spinner bag. He felt the burden of carrying their house in Box Elder—which following the kidnapping, murder and suicide would take forever to sell—, the rent in Royal Oak, Heath's tuition, and her medical bills. And he was flourishing under the pressure, working harder than he had before and loving every high-flying minute of it.

Ross and Judy hustled Heath out the door for the zoo. They'd been so glad when her family moved back to Royal Oak, so grateful that Heath hadn't been affected. If only they knew. But Annabelle wasn't telling.

When they closed the door, leaving her and Maud alone again as they'd been most days in Box Elder, Annabelle went to Heath's table to clean up the crayons he'd left out. Their household had become more lax since moving back to Royal Oak. Neither she nor Paul knew quite how to discipline Heath anymore, though for different reasons. She'd not told Paul about The Six and she'd never talked to Heath about it. If he'd been surprised when she walked in the door shivering and muddy that night, he'd not shown it.

Annabelle dropped to her knees and leaned over the table until her fingers, pinned to her chest by the sling, could grasp a crayon. In her state, this clean-up effort would take twenty minutes. Her doctors assured her that if she let them, all of her fingers had an excellent chance of full recovery. Seeing them limp and crooked at the end of her arms in the emergency room, it had been hard to believe.

As Annabelle rolled the crayons into their bin, she upset the sheaf of Heath's drawings. They floated to the ground and slid under the table. As they floated, one caught her eye. Peering under the table, Annabelle saw a drawing in all black, six eye sockets in a skull with an open grin.

Annabelle pinched the drawing between her fingers. Knowing she would not be able to feed the paper into the shredder, she dropped it into the kitchen sink and turned on the faucet. With the long spoon Paul left on the counter to help her do things she pressed the sodden drawing down the drain and pushed on the disposal. She let it run and stared out her window at the suburban skyline.

# READERS GUIDE

1. In the first chapter, Annabelle hopes and fears her job will be replaced by a robot. In what ways do her conflicting views on technology guide her decisions?

2. What does it reveal about Annabelle that she paints her human subjects as "sloe-eyed and expressionless" (chapter 3)?

3. What criteria have you used to choose a new home? How were your criteria similar or different from Annabelle's? Would the Grangers have moved if it weren't for Heath's playground discovery?

4. Annabelle says, "It is easier to fix a robot than a child" (chapter 7). How does repairing a robot and healing a child represent similar and different processes?

5. What preconceptions about rural life were shattered for Annabelle?

6. The adage "As the old sing, so pipe the young" from which the title is derived refers to bad examples set by adults influencing children.

What are the bad examples in this story and how do they influence The Six?

7. What role does Maud, the deaf flea-bitten dog, play in the story?

8. Annabelle describes her hands as her best feature. How does she use her hands and what makes them her best feature?

9. How did Dan Quintana's narration change your perspective on Box Elder? How did Paul Granger's narration change your perspective on Annabelle?

10. How are Harley and Heath's experiences of death different?

11. There is a sheep and shepherd metaphor running through the story. Which characters are the sheep and which shepherds?

12. In what ways does Annabelle embrace the Stoic principle of *memento mori*—remember that you too shall die—and in what ways does she shun this practice of reflecting on one's own mortality?

13. How does Annabelle change throughout the story?

14. Is Annabelle a sympathetic character?

# ABOUT THE AUTHOR

**Jen Watkins**

Jen lives on a gentleman's farm in Santa Fe, NM among a plethora of backyard fowl and beasts. Tired of the nine-to-five hustle, she left on an adventure spent learning to sail on the *S/V Red Herring*. She traveled over 5,000 nautical miles up into the wilds of British Columbia and through Pacific Mexico. Her writing career began while living aboard. Learn more at www.jenwatkins.com.

**Etheridge Press**

We publish the books you want to read

Our newsletter celebrates indie authors and helps readers find new authors they love.

www.etheridgepress.com

# AUTHOR NOTE

Thank you for reading.

Some time ago, I received a rejection from a literary agent for a manuscript I had submitted to her one year and three days before. That same week, a literary magazine informed me I had won their writing contest. It was a strange mix of discouraging and encouraging news out of which I gleaned two things: one, when people read my stories, they like them and two, the traditional publishing route takes too long to get to the part where people read my stories and like them.

That is when my writing career zagged over to Etheridge Press. I went from submission to on sale in a flash. The benefit of working with a small publisher is huge: my work gets to my readers in a timely manner. What else could a writer want?

The downside is that this entrepreneurial route requires more marketing hustle than I am strictly comfortable with. But here it goes.

Please consider leaving a review or telling others about this book. I read my reviews and you can too. Pithy, catty, funny, quotable, I love them all.

Thank you reader,
Jen

Made in the USA
Middletown, DE
19 November 2021

52948683R00189